# Surface Tension

*Vega,*
*Enjoy diving into*
*this one!*

## S.R. Atkinson

*S.R. Atkinson*

First Edition

ISBN- 978-0-9964550-5-3

Printed in the U.S.A. by IngramSpark

# Surface Tension

For those struggling with difficult decisions,
may you choose adventure over comfort.

*S.R. Atkinson*

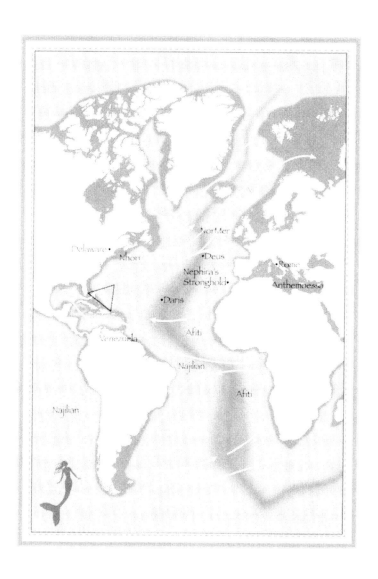

# Surface Tension

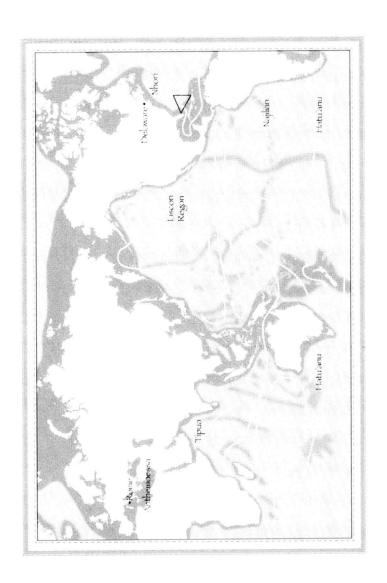

*S.R. Atkinson*

# *Prologue*

## Marisole
### *Off the coast of São Paulo, 1944*

Marisole arranged the otter-pelt blanket over her daughter's body before heaving rocks onto each of the corners and along the sides, pinning the child in place.

"Do not tell our kinsmates we do this," she said, placing a hand on her cheek, eyes wide in mock-horror as she observed her finished work, her tiny daughter trapped beneath the soft brown fur.

Rodrigo laughed and placed his hand on his Bondmate's shoulder.

"You would be surprised at what other Serras do to keep their night-swimming pups in place while they sleep."

Marisole shook her head. "She is two years old. I thought she would have grown out of it by now. We never had to do this with her brother. Even when Fernando went through that stage of thrashing wildly in his sleep, he never wandered farther than his nest."

"Come, my love, relax." Rodrigo moved to the corner of their daughter's room and picked up an extinguisher—a round, hollow rock—and placed it over the luminescent orb. The room was immediately cloaked in darkness.

The couple left the small room, arranging rocks along the bottom of a dividing curtain—another precaution to keep their daughter in their shelter at night—and made their way down the short hall to the main living space. Marisole's Ku was brimming with love and worry for her daughter at the same time. For a two-year-old, she already seemed to be more precocious and determined than anyone else her age. Marisole often wondered if the sleep-swimming could somehow be a deliberate expression of the little girl's determination to do what she wanted. In this way, her tiny stubborn daughter decided when she would be in bed and when she would not.

As they reached the big room in the front of their shelter, Rodrigo sighed and turned back to the hall.

"Fernando is up playing in his room again."

"No," Marisole responded softly, grabbing his arm. "I love the feel of his happy Ku when he is wrapped up in imaginative games. Give me ten more minutes to enjoy him like this."

"You know, usually it is the children who ask for longer to play, not their mothers." Rodrigo gave Marisole a teasing half-smile that made his deep dimples pop.

Marisole's eyes sparkled at her Bondmate as she placed her hand on his chest, absorbing the teasing adoration in his Ku. She knew such happiness existed and had always hoped for it for herself, yet sometimes she couldn't believe the absolute perfection of it all. Often, reality could not live up to dreams, but it truly did for Marisole. It was everything she had hoped it would be.

Eight years ago, Rodrigo was part of a group of Thaeds who had been badly injured in a scuffle with Crurals. The land-walkers had betrayed Rodrigo's crew and tried to trap them to bring onto land. In the fight that ensued, several Serras were critically injured. Marisole was one of the Healers called to treat them. She stayed by Rodrigo's side through his entire healing process—which she knew from his Ku he exaggerated towards the end of recovery—and by the time he was fully improved, they were Bound. He would still tell her that he had a false pain in an effort to have all of her attention to himself.

"I have cut myself very badly!" he'd say, making her drop whatever she was doing and rush into the room to help only so he could swoop her up in an embrace when she arrived. She knew he was lying—and he knew she knew he was lying—but it was his little way of getting her alone to smother her with kisses.

"Rodri..." But she forgot whatever she was going to say about the memory. An odd, unsettled feeling was creeping into her Ku. It was as if an extinguisher were being placed over her heart, and the light within her was struggling to hold onto the happiness she had felt only moments ago.

"What is that?" Rodrigo asked, concerned, as the same unsettling feeling came over him.

"I don't know." Marisole felt sadness and pain swirling in the water around her. "Someone is very, very sad. They are hurt."

S.R. Atkinson

Marisole scrunched up her eyes and focused on her children's Kus. Sometimes one of them would have a terrible dream, so real to them that she could feel the pain in her own heart. This was not one of those times. They were both peacefully in their rooms, as she had left them.

"It is our kinsmen," Rodrigo said with realization as he swam to the mouth of their shelter and pulled back the curtain. What he saw made him stop dead in his strokes.

Marisole felt a chilling grip of fear in his Ku. Her voice was shaky as she asked, "My love, what is it?" But she was sure she didn't want to know.

Rodrigo didn't answer. His eyes were wide, and the arm holding the curtain began to shake. Marisole rushed to his side but immediately wished she hadn't. She could have been very happy to live the rest of her life without witnessing the gruesome sight before her.

Two Sirens were nearly ripping a Serra dam in half as they tugged and tortured her. Rodrigo and Marisole looked down from their high-rise shelter. The sight was the same the whole way down. Serras were being dragged out of their homes, killed, and flung around as if they were toys in a bloody game; dead bodies sank to the ocean floor far below.

"We…" she stammered in her heart. "We have to get the children out of here."

"Where?" An edge of panic strained Rodrigo's voice. "Marisole, the Sirens are all around us."

He gingerly lowered the curtain as if they would be safe hiding behind it.

Marisole blinked rapidly, but the image of the Sirens—looking like death incarnate—were burned into her mind.

"How is this happening?" she asked incredulously, her voice wavering.

In her entire lifetime—nearly thirty years—there had never been a Siren attack on a kinship. The Siren problem had been so entirely under control that she often forgot their existence.

"How are they here? Attacking our kinship?" Her voice was becoming high pitched and frantic.

Rodrigo was talking, but Marisole barely noticed. Her mind was spinning. The reports were always that Siren's numbers were way down. Although no one could kill Zitja, the population of Sirens was supposedly near extinction.

"Rodrigo! How?" she kept repeating, flailing her hands in the air, gripped with hysteria. "How!"

"Marisole." He shook her shoulders. His voice was determined and frightened, but she could feel him trying to control his Ku as he spoke. "You need to calm your Ku."

She knew he was right. Strong emotions resonated more powerfully than docile ones. If the Sirens didn't know that they were hiding in their shelter before, they surely would now. She only hoped her emotions would be masked by all that was going on around them.

"The children! We have to get them! We have to escape!"

They lived in one of the largest kinships in the Najilian Clan. It was a bustling metropolis with nearly as many shelters and people as the city of Daris. Thousands of Serras lived in the city, and many more came in every day to preform their Opuses. Chaos would be all around. Luckily, their shelter was in a towering conglomerate of shelters, theirs being near the top. She wasn't sure how many Sirens were in the area, but she knew it was enough to make any escape dangerous.

"If we swim to the surface, we can hide amongst the waves and rocks," she said desperately.

It was risky for weaker swimmers to get caught up in the tide, as their kinship was nestled against a cliff that protruded high into the sky. Many a Serra had lost his or her life while playing the popular sport keda when they were dashed against the rocks. However, those same rocks could save their lives today.

"Go get Fernando," Rodrigo whispered as he simultaneously nodded his head in agreement to her plan. It was their only option besides staying inside and hoping to be left unnoticed. She could feel his inner turmoil raging as he tried to remain calm to hide their presence.

Marisole turned, but was only two strokes of her tail away when she felt Rodrigo's Ku tighten in anguish, and she knew it was too late for them all.

She turned just in time to see him—the literal other half of her Ku—frozen in place. A Siren dam had slipped into their shelter and was Singing to Marisole's Bondmate. Marisole had never seen the effect, but she had been warned about it enough times to know what she saw. The Siren would surely kill him--kill them all, if it had its way. Without thinking of the consequences, merely of her love for Rodrigo and their children, she rushed at the Siren. It was a small dam, barely older than a teenager. Surely Marisole could take her on.

But as Marisole got within arm's reach, the Siren flipped tail over head in a tight circle. As she came around, her tail whipped Marisole so fiercely in the chest that

# Surface Tension

Marisole soared through the water and slammed against the far wall of their shelter.

Marisole's back hit first, followed by her head. She hung limply in the water for just a moment as the pain in her head and spine rendered her immobile. Marisole closed her eyes to stop the room from spinning. Fighting was not something she had ever had the misfortune to get mixed up in, and with that first hit, she saw their simple way of life disappear. Rodrigo was springing back into action by the time she opened her eyes, and relief washed over her. He wasn't dead, and neither was she, and for now the children were out of reach from this Siren. Surely, the two of them could overpower the Siren and save their little family.

Rodrigo lunged at the Siren as he spoke to Marisole, his Ku so forlorn Marisole felt the despair as a weight in her own chest.

"Forget me. Get the children away!"

*Forget me.*

The words pierced her Ku, made it feel as if it were breaking. But she knew he was right. She rushed into her son's room but did not see him.

"Fernando," she said to his Ku, for she knew he was in the room.

Her eyes scanned his toys littered on the smooth stone floor. A doll she had made for him, stone blocks cut into cubes and carved with intricate designs stacked into a mighty tower, a seal bladder filled with sand, and dozens of other trinkets littering his floor. The disarray was a familiar sight but chaotic. She couldn't find Fernando. Her heart nearly stopped beating.

S.R. Atkinson

Piled in a heap in the corner was a woven rug that usually covered the floor. She rushed to it and untangled her son.

"It is ok, Fernando. It is ok."

She clutched her shaking child.

"We are going to leave. Ok? We are going to keda. Would you like that?"

Fernando had wanted to keda since he had watched from below as the Crurals rode the waves above him on their long wooden boards. Serras had been kedaing the waves long before the Crurals ever discovered the sport. Fernando always begged his mother to let him do as the bigger pups were doing, but she felt that at four years old he just wasn't strong enough of a swimmer should the surface waters turn hostile.

"Come, my dear." She grabbed his tiny hand and turned towards the opening of his room; but, suddenly, she felt Rodrigo and the Siren's grappling fight turn down the hallway.

Fernando's room had a passageway to the outside, but her daughter's did not; they would have to swim down the hall to reach her daughter's room, the same direction in which a Siren was quite possibly killing the father of her children. She whispered in her Ku, if only to herself, "Please keep the battle in the hallway. Please do not take the fighting into my daughter's room."

She and Fernando stood frozen, staring at the dividing curtain, waiting to make a decision. They clutched each other, paused in time, as if all that stood in their way was the blue fabric obstructing their access to the hall.

❖14❖

# Surface Tension

Suddenly, a rock came flying through the curtain, opening it for a fraction of a second--just enough time for her to see down the hall. Enough time to see that Rodrigo was being severely overpowered and the fighting had taken him into the one room she hoped the Siren would avoid. Marisole clutched Fernando tighter. There was no way she could bring him with her to fetch his sister.

If the Siren wasn't aware of Fernando's existence, Marisole didn't want to make it so. She could hide him in here, sneak in and grab her pup, then rush back and get both of them to safety through the exit in Fernando's room. Marisole thought quickly.

She seized Fernando and wrapped him back up in his floor rug.

"Son, stay here. Do not move. I must go get your sister before we keda."

She placed him on the floor and then, as a last minute thought, moved his nest and placed it on top of him. The tangle of seaweed was much lighter than her own moss-filled sleeping cushion. A scan around the room proved it to appear empty. She only hoped the Siren's Ku wasn't as astute as her own. She felt Fernando quaking in fear.

"Be strong, my son. Stay hidden and stay calm. I love you," she said and rushed out of the room.

Down the hall she saw the dividing curtain of her daughter's room lying on the floor. She rushed in, blind with rage. Not her little baby! Marisole's happy world of only moments ago was torn apart and crumbling around her. To take away the innocence of her still sleeping daughter was the last straw. She must protect that innocence.

Rodrigo was bloodied and writhing in the water when Marisole burst into their daughter's room. The Siren's mouth was agape and ferocious, teeth jagged and filthy, the back of her throat vibrating in Song. The dam turned and saw Marisole, and then, as if deciding her fun with Rodrigo was over, she Sang a sharp, piercing note.

As quickly as the note rang out, Marisole felt half of her Ku disappear in her chest. It felt as though she had been two people living inside one body and now she was only one. In these seven years with Rodrigo, she had forgotten what it was like before his Ku was Bound with hers Now that solitary feeling returned, only this time it reappeared as a gaping hole in her chest. Her Bondmate, her other half, was dead, and her heart felt like it died with him.

She cried out and reached for Rodrigo, but her daughter must have felt something dramatic, as well, for it was at this moment she awoke. Marisole stopped mid-stroke and turned to look at the nest where her daughter was perfectly concealed beneath her blanket imprisonment. As she did so, the Siren turned her attentions from Rodrigo.

Suddenly, Marisole's head was filled with a most horrendous screeching and piercing sound. The Song filled up her entire body and occupied it with an agony unlike anything she had ever felt before. A fire, white hot and engulfing, raged from the inside out. There wasn't a bit of her body that wasn't in agony.

Marisole reached up with her hands and tried to rip the pain from her chest. She scratched at her skin to release the pressure. Her blood began to seep into the water around her as she broke the skin with her nails. A loud, guttural scream reverberated around the room, and Marisole realized it was her own voice that filled her ears. Slowly, her mind began to fog with the pain, and she quickly looked towards her daughter's nest. She could see her daughter moving around underneath, trapped in safety by the weight of the stones along the blanket's corners and edges. Through all the wiggling underneath the blanket, however, Marisole saw a tiny face appear through the mess of seaweed, and she looked right into her baby's eyes.

She tried to touch her Ku, to tell her child to be still and hide, but was incapable of reaching out. At that moment, she arched her back as a wave of pain caused her muscles to spasm. Beyond her control, her muscles tensed and contracted. She rolled forward into a ball and screamed. Suddenly, another tremor seized her, and she was thrown violently backwards. Her back arched in a tight 'C' shape, and her muscles stiffened so suddenly she heard a loud crack within her. The pain subsided from the lower half of her body.

The temporary relief was liberating, but as she tried to swim away, she realized she had no feeling, no control whatsoever, from the waist down. The force of her spasming muscles had broken her own spine.

The pain raged on in her upper body, and Marisole began bleeding from her pores and clawing fiercely at her arms and face. Yet there was no relief from her pain. No relief but one. Marisole knew that she would end up just as Rodrigo had, and she only had but moments left in this world. Above her pain, her heart ached for her children. Would they face the same fate as their parents or would they be left unscathed—saved by their hiding places—only to be doomed to grow up without their parents? Her children. Marisole ached for them.

Suddenly, she screamed out again, the same animal noise as before—so wild she scared herself. One last look told her that her daughter was still fully hidden, save for her tiny brown eyes that peeked through the nest, watching her mother's every move. Her heart ached more for her children than from the pain of the Song. Their tiny family would cease to exist on this night.

And then it happened. Marisole reached out to touch her daughter's Ku. To tell her to stay hidden, that she loved her, but could not. A last note rang through her body, lighting her on fire and turning the whole room white.

# *Chapter 1*

## Santiago

"Journals!" Santi squealed. "Mommi, it's Abuela's journals."

She lifted the small black book into the dusty sunlight of the attic window.   Celia glanced up from the photo album she was looking through and sighed.

"Put them back."

She spoke in English, which startled Santi so much she almost dropped the book. Never in Santi's entire life had her mother spoken English in her Abuelo Santiago's house.

"So, Abuelo is truly gone now, I see," Santi replied in Spanish and with as much sass as she dared. Spanish was the language they spoke when they were in Venezuela, in Abuelo's house. Abuelo insisted on it.

Celia scowled for only a moment before the unexpected defiance left her. "I just don't think we should be reading her private thoughts," she replied in Spanish, much to Santi's relief.

The funeral had only been three days ago, and they were nearly done cleaning out Abuelo Santiago's house. Santi wanted to hold on to him as much as she could before they went to California.

"Nonsense," Santi replied. "That's what journals are for. So that after you've died, you can live on; so your family can get to know you better."

Celia still looked hesitant, but she nodded.

"I know you are right but..."

She took such a long pause Santi wasn't sure whether she was going to say whatever it was she wanted to say. Finally, Celia nodded, stood up, and walked over to the chest of journals.

"My mother told me to read these. She said I need to know what's in them."

"You knew they were up here this whole time? We could have read them years ago." Santi was incredulous. Her Abuela had always been a beautiful mystery. The dark haired, dark-eyed enigma that both Celia and Santi looked exactly like but of whom neither they nor Abuelo Santiago ever spoke.

Celia knelt down and lifted up one of the books with so much care the journal might have been made of sand on a windy day.

The two of them quickly searched through the leather-bound books until they found the journal with the earliest date. Unspoken, as if this was their entire plan upon entering the attic, the women made themselves comfortable and Celia began to read. Abuela Carmen's Spanish words filled up the musty air around them; the language belonged in the home in a way that brought her back to life.

> *March 1978*
> *I need to write this all down.*
> *My heart is so full of joy and so*
> *heavy with sadness at the same time.*
> *I need to work through it all, but no*
> *one will understand. I also need my*
> *daughter to know. I feel it is*
> *important that she understands*
> *everything but I can't possibly tell*
> *her. How could I tell her? What*
> *would I say?*
> *So this is for you Celia, my*
> *precious daughter, may you*
> *understand everything.*

Celia's voice caught. She gave a little cough to clear her throat and wiped her eyes before continuing.

> *I think it's best that I start at*
> *the beginning. However, that's not*
> *where my heart is at the moment. So*
> *I will come back to the beginning*
> *later because I do want to cover*
> *everything, but for now I want to*
> *write about this moment. In this*
> *moment, in Venezuela, speaking*
> *Spanish when I was raised speaking*
> *Portuguese, living in a place so*

*strange and so different from where I
come from, I want to go back home.*

Santi looked up at her mother in surprise. "Where was Abuela from?" She had always assumed it was Venezuela. But Celia didn't answer. She knew something of the mystery surrounding Carmen and she was keeping it to herself just as Santiago had done before her. Santi scowled but said nothing. She would just wait and find out from Carmen's own words.

Celia continued to read to Santi from the thick volumes, enraptured, until the sun began to rise and the two women could no longer keep their eyes open. Finally, mother and daughter fell asleep thinking of a woman they were getting to know through her memoirs.

In the morning, they took the third leather-bound book to the *panaderia* for breakfast, and Celia continued to read while they finished their coffee. Neither of them spoke aside from the reverent lullaby of Celia's voice and Abuela's words.

"Wait!" Santi almost shouted. "I didn't hear you. What did you say?"

"Santee, shhhhhhh." Celia put her finger to her lips and hissed, "You are yelling."

Santi lowered her voice. "I am?"

"Yes, I'm very worried about you."

"Speak up, please," Santi said while looking intently into Celia's eyes, hoping to understand the meaning of her mother's words without being able to hear them completely.

"Last night you kept yelling at me to speak up too. You aren't hearing me very well lately."

# Surface Tension

Santi looked at her hands. Since regaining her hearing in the fall, it had begun progressively getting worse again. Research online had informed her that with a minor tear full hearing should return—as it had for a time—but Santi had done significant damage. Not to mention whatever the Siren's Song had done to harm her ears further. Her hearing might never return to normal.

"I think it's time you saw a doctor," Celia chastised. "I'm going to take you when you are in California for Christmas." She said it with such resolve that Santi knew she couldn't argue.

"Let's finish Abuelo's house and we'll read these when we get home."

"That sounds like a nice Christmas." Santi smiled outwardly, but secretly she was worried. She had hoped to squeeze in a visit to Rogan before she had to return to school, but with Santiago's death, the doctor visit, and now Carmen's journals to read, Celia wouldn't likely let Santi mysteriously disappear again. Celia was still upset that Santi wouldn't explain where she had inexplicably vanished to for two weeks in July or why she was in Delaware for a month without any explanation. But Santi couldn't very well tell her that she had been kidnapped by evil sea monsters and then spent time reconnecting with her long lost mermaid friend.

She would think of something; but for now, they only had one day left to clean out Abuelo's belongings and turn the house over to the realtor.

The next morning as they prepared to leave for their flight to California, Santi said with a catch in her throat, "I think we're done here." The two women looked around. Santi breathed in the old wooden house and sea air one last time. They were done. It was time to leave and say goodbye to Santiago, his home, and Venezuela for good.

As soon as they stepped through the door of Celia's Palo Alto home, Santi flung her bags on the floor and said, "Pull out the journals, Mom. Let's get back to it."

"First I wan' to make joo an appointment."

Santi nodded agreement and smiled lovingly.

"I'm not sure what I like best: hearing you speak Spanish or your accent when you speak English," she said.

Celia rolled her eyes and began scrolling through her contacts to find the family doctor. She always thought Santi was teasing her about her accent, but Santi did love it. It was rich and comforting, and she hoped her mom would never try to lose it.

Santi found the luggage that contained the journals—they had to buy another suitcase and pay for the extra weight, but it was worth it to not leave any of the books behind. She began unpacking the volumes and arranging them chronologically. When she got to the bottom of the suitcase, she stopped, surprised. Santi pulled out a small photo in a gold frame, the glass front smudged with fingerprints and dusty with time.

Her abuelo stood tall and handsome—and quite youthful—with his young wife sitting next to him in her wheelchair. Santi knew her abuela used a chair but had never pictured it before; all of the other pictures were not of her full body. On her lap was a small child of about three or four years, and all of them had smiles bright enough to crack the frame. Santi stared at the picture for a long time and felt she could absorb the happiness from the photo and keep it with her endlessly.

# Surface Tension

At that moment, Celia returned and caught Santi looking at the photo.

"Mommi," Santi nearly whispered. "I'm glad you brought this home." Santi had never thought much about it—maybe it was because photos of her mother were too painful for her—but Celia had no pictures of her mother in the house. Celia gingerly reached out and took the framed photograph in her hands and looked at it silently. She regarded it so intensely, so lovingly, that Santi turned back to what she was doing to give her mom privacy with her emotions.

After a few moments Santi cleared her throat and cautiously asked, "Shall we read more?"

Celia was shaken from her reprieve and answered, "Not now, Santee, my doctor can get joo in right away."

Santi scrunched up her face but reluctantly set the journal down. She felt like she'd never find out the mystery surrounding Carmen. Why was everyone so secretive? And why didn't her mom seem as determined to find out the answers as she was?

"Well, Miss Morales," the balding but young doctor said, "if you are hearing well right now, and you won't tell me what happened that lead to these bizarre scars in your ears, then I can't really help you further."

"Santee, just tell us what happened to joo!" Celia nearly shouted. She had always been a passionate and emotional woman, and Santi's secret was driving her crazy. "We can' help unless joo tell us."

"I'm going to refer you to an ENT," the doctor said, and then quickly clarified. "An ear, nose, and throat doctor will be able to help you more than I can. This is very unique, and I've never seen anything like it."

"Thank you," Santi said, hopping off the table so quickly her jeans ripped the tissue paper. "I'm hearing just fine now."

She smiled weakly. She had never wanted to see a doctor about her hearing, but Celia would not be put off the idea. There was only one person from whom Santi could get real answers on the matter, and she would have to return to the ocean for that. Amed would be the only one who could help her. Her biggest obstacle was going to be getting away from Celia with time left in the break. Celia was already so angry with Santi being secretive, and she expected her to stay until the start of the semester.

That evening, while Celia decorated their Christmas tree, Santi finally got to dive back into the journals. As Celia lovingly filled the pine with the ornaments of her childhood, Santi read. She was in the middle of a passage when she stopped.

They were deep into the fourth volume, and Santi had begun putting clues together: Carmen missed her home and talked about how she could never return; she was in a wheelchair but no one ever talked about why; journal number one was dated in 1978, just after Celia was born; Carmen hadn't learned to read or write until she was an adult; and now Santi had just read a passage about the importance of making decisions with her heart. Santi wasn't sure what it all meant yet, but she felt she was on the cusp of something just out of reach.

# Surface Tension

Carmen would skip around in her writing, switching between making a record of her life with her husband and daughter to talking about her past when she was a child herself. The latter entries were fewer and farther between but they captivated Celia the most. Carmen hadn't talked much about her life before meeting Santi's abuelo, and after Carmen died, Abuelo Santiago had seemed determined to keep Carmen's secrets as well.

Santi reread the passage that made her pause. It was about how Carmen had been conflicted between leaving behind her family and everything she knew to be with Santiago in Venezuela. Carmen talked at length about the perils that she faced if she went back to where she came from. Santi reread the passage to herself several times.

*I miss my family and the Najilian.* She looked up at her mother and chewed her lip in concentration. She recognized that word. *Najilian.* Where had she heard it before? It must be a Spanish word.

"What does *Najilian* mean in English?" Santi asked her mom.

"I don't know this word," Celia responded. "It's no' Spanish."

Santi closed her eyes. Najilian. She knew the word. If her abuelo hadn't said it to her, then where…?

Then it hit her.

Her eyes flew open. Rogan had used the word before. The Najilian was a Clan. Santi didn't know where it was located, but she was certain she was correct.

Slowly, she lowered the book and set it on the coffee table before she said, "Mom… was Abuela Carmen a…"

She stopped. She couldn't very well ask her mother if her abuela was a mermaid. That was ludicrous.

Celia looked at her expectantly and Santi nearly whispered, "A Serra?" Santi used the word *Serra* instead of *mermaid* to see if her mother knew more than she had let on. Celia's response would tell her everything by knowing that word.

Santi waited anxiously as she watched her mother's reaction, but Celia gave away nothing. Her face was calm, though Santi could see her eyes go through a range of emotion. *Of course she wasn't a Serra*, Santi though, chiding herself for being too imaginative.

Finally, Celia's eyebrows furrowed for a moment before her face went calm again and she slowly and carefully replied, "Jes, jor abuela Carmen was a Serra."
Santi's mouth widened and her eyes flew open so that all three were making perfect circles.

"I did not remember that word *Serra* until joo said it just now. But jes, that is what she was."

Santi felt a confused lump in her throat. Anger and sadness swirled within her and queasiness overtook her stomach. She froze in that position, too shocked to say anything, her mind reeling. Questions raced to her lips, but none of them broke the seal. She was completely incredulous. This changed things for Santi, though she did not know exactly how just yet.

Mostly she had an uneasy feeling of deceit. How her mother had kept something so remarkable a secret her whole life? An anger towards her mother returned that she hadn't felt since she was a child, when Celia spent all her time working. It was uncomfortable yet familiar. Santi had spent a lot of time with these feelings, hating her mom and thinking she was unimportant to Celia. It wasn't logical, but it came back to her effortlessly. It seemed in that moment that everything had changed between the two of them and that so much had changed about who Santi was.

It took her a full three minutes to regain control of her voice. When she finally did, she spoke fast but with a clipped anger in her tone.

"Why didn't you ever say anything? That's why she was in a wheelchair! Didn't you ever see her tail? How did she meet Abuelo? Why don't you have a tail? This means I'm part Serra, too. Do we still have family down there? Do you remember me telling you about my friend Rogan when I was a child?"

Her line of questioning kept changing direction. She wanted to know everything. And anger boiled in her for having been in the dark about something so huge. So many more questions swam through her mind that she didn't even have a chance to speak them all out loud as she kept throwing questions at her mother.

"Did Abuelo know? Did she ever go back and visit the other Serras?"

Santi suddenly realized that she could tell her mom about being kidnapped, a secret that hurt Santi to keep.

That's when Santi realized that her mom would be just as angry with her about keeping the kidnapping a secret as Santi was about this. She relaxed a little in her aggressive questioning, and Celia seized the opportunity.

"Santee!" A hint of anger in her voice, too. "If joo want jor questions answered, joo have to be quiet for a minute!"

She nodded but frantically wanted to get the most important question answered. She burst out quickly, "Why didn't you tell me?" And then she held her breath and waited for the answers to her questions.

"I didn' tell joo because my mother didn' tell me much. She told me only one thing before she died and that was, 'Believe in magic, that mermaids are real, and that it's important to protect the world from bad guys.'"

Santi scrunched up her face, and Celia let out a tiny laugh, breaking the tension for a moment.

"Jes, it's cheesy, but she was speaking to a little girl. After that, I only got a little more information from her before she change the subject. It sounded so ridiculous. She told me one day to read her journals and to believe everything in them. I was joung and confused, but I believed her."

"That's it? She told you that and then changed the subject? Just 'believe in magic, and mermaids, and to protect the world from bad guys?' That's nonsense." Santi swore and Celia looked hurt.

"I'm just as mad as joo are. Tha's why I never read her journals. I was too confused and hurt."

Celia looked hurt, and Santi could tell it was as much because of Santi's anger as it was her mother's lack of communication on the matter. That calmed Santi down as she proceeded. "Remember when I was a little girl and I had that friend Rogan? You told me he was my imaginary friend. Remember? You told me that mermaids weren't real. It turned out for the best because I was told to keep the Serra's existence a secret. After that, I stopped trying to convince you. But you knew the whole time and you made me feel like a fool."

"When joo met your friend Rogan, I could have died from shock! I could not believe joo, of all people, would meet a Serra. I think I was envious." Celia took a deep breath before she went on.

"I was angry that my mother sprang such a big secret right before her death. As a child, I believed in mermaids like I was supposed to. And magic. And I always imagined that I was destined for something important. It was part of the reason I had the courage to move to the United States by myself when I was eighteen. But as I grew older, I became more confused and angry than I was optimistic for adventure. In the end, I grew hardened to anything... fantasty?" She stumbled to think of the right word in English. "Fantastical? ...Eventually I forgot about my mother's words."

Santi nodded. "And my friendship with Rogan brought back those sad, angry, and confused feelings all over again."

"Above all," Celia admitted, "I was envious that joo got to spend time with a Serra and learn about the world my mother had kept a secret. It was like I didn' get to learn about mysel' because she kept it from me. I missed my mother— what I remembered of her, anyway—and joo playing with that Serra boy reminded me of all she caused me to miss out on."

"I'm so sorry, Mommi. I didn't realize you ever believed me about Rogan."

"One day when joo were eight," Celia explained, "I snuck down to the little beach where joo two played. Joo were playing a game that for as long as I watched, I could never figure out."

Santi smiled, remembering back to those days.

"If I was eight, that means I hadn't yet gone underwater. We used to play so many silly games."

"I watched joo two play for hours while I crouched behind a tree. It took me a long time to get control of my conflicting feelings. The sight of that little Serra boy, with his amazing blue tail flicking in and out of the water, made me feel so many emotions: anger, jealousy, envy, regret, longing. And among them, I was happy for joo.

"But my anger with my mother returned. How dare her she keep this from me for my whole life and then simplify it all into one conversation before her death? After watching joo and Rogan, I put that wall up firmly around my heart again. It was too hard to accept the truth of my mother's past.

"Jears later, when joo said joo never wanted to go in the water again, I was relieved. I gave myself permission to forget about everything under water once more and took the job in California.

"I'm so sorry, Mommi," Santi said with sincerity.

"I don' wan' to be mad at my mother anymore. I wan' to read her journals and learn to love her like I never did."

This decided things for Santi. She had so much she needed to discuss with Amed.

"Mom," She said with conviction, "I have to go to Delaware."

She wanted to see Rogan during her break, but she *had* to see Amed.

# *Chapter 2*

## Santiago

"I'm ready!" Rogan shouted exuberantly, waving his arm above his head to call for the pass. Santi knew she couldn't throw the *dwattle*—a seal bladder full of sand—that far. It was one thing for Serras to be able to flick their tails and send it careening towards their teammate, but her wimpy arms just weren't sufficient. She and Rogan were probably going to lose because of her pathetic little throws.

Sully was charging at her quickly. He was going to steal the dwattle from her and score yet another point for his and Tizz's team. Santi couldn't let it happen. Sully pretended to be valiant by picking Tizz for his team and taking the disadvantage of having a small six-year-old, but they soon learned that Santi was a bigger handicap. Tizz might have been young, but she had grown up playing dwattle for many years, and she was surprisingly good. Santi was sure now that Sully had known Tizz's skill all along.

Looking back, he did seem a little smug when they were choosing teams.

Santiago pulled back her arm and was about to chuck the dwattle in Rogan's direction. *He'll have to dive for it before it hits the sand,* she told herself, frustrated. The game only had two big rules: the dwattle couldn't hit the ground, and every member had to be HaruKu the entire time. Haru was easy for Santi. Closing off her Ku during the game so that she and Rogan couldn't secretly communicate was how all Crurals played sports; letting the dwattle hit the ground, on the other hand, had already forfeited two points to Sully and Tizz. Rogan was carrying their team completely as it was, so if this pass didn't make it all the way, what was a little more work for him to do? Suddenly she was struck with an idea she had seen other Serras do a thousand times before.

Serras didn't have professional sports the way Crurals thought of them, but they did hold dwattle tournaments. Anyone who made a team could enter. Some teams took it casually, would enter for fun, and weren't too disappointed when they are eliminated in the first round. Other teams, however, stuck with the same players for years and trained together very seriously. They gave themselves team names with colors and emblems, and many of them didn't have other Opuses. Santi thought that seemed very much like professional sports, but she liked the idea that anyone could enter and play if they wanted to.

During the final matchup of a tournament a few years before, a well-known player on the defending champion team made an epic move. Santi forgot the name of the team but could never forget the name of the player: Landry. The maneuver was so remarkable they named it after her. The

# Surface Tension

Landry Tuck became the hottest move amongst pups playing dwattle in their free time, and every team that entered the tournament afterwards had practiced it. Santi thought the move looked almost like a bicycle kick in soccer but if both legs were pinned together and if the soccer player was extraordinarily graceful.

Santi tossed the ball in the water a few feet above her. Then she contorted her body quickly to get her feet and head horizontally in the water. When the dwattle fell back down, she pinned her legs together tightly and flung her upper body backwards towards the ocean floor, and just a second afterward, she pulled her legs toward her chest tightly in a quick sweeping arc, which connected with the dwattle. The weighted bag went soaring in Rogan's direction with enough speed that he didn't have to dive for it. He easily snatched the orb as it coasted by him, swam up to their hole in the rock, and stuffed the dwattle inside.

"WE SCORE!!" he roared. Then, just as excitedly, he shouted, "The Landry Tuck!" Rogan swam over and scooped her up with as much ease as he had the dwattle and then swung her around.

"I cannot believe you did that!"

Santi allowed herself a smile of satisfaction and laughed.

"We still lose, though," she responded, but she couldn't muster any feelings of disappointment. "We scored four points against their twenty."

"But look what you did with your kickers!" he said, giving her feet a shake. "You are a natural!"

Santi smiled from the memory and chuckled at the irony. A couple of times in their childhoods, Rogan had told her that she was a natural underwater. No wonder. Her own abuela was a Serra. She still couldn't believe it. Was it just chance that she happened to meet a Serra, or was it more? Maybe kismet. Maybe all along she was supposed to go back underwater to where her grandmother was from and experience the world she lived in. It was her destiny. Santi's chest swelled with the thought. Maybe she would live under the ocean for the rest of her life with Rogan. It was a wonderful idea.

Santi shivered as the frigid January air hit her skin when she removed her jacket. Her pants and shirt came off next to reveal a blue one-piece swimsuit underneath. A wave of shudders consumed her, and goose bumps covered her skin before she focused her mind to warm up her internal body temperature. She had never done this exercise on land before because she could put on coats and hats if she needed, but, standing on the edge of her old familiar pond, she just couldn't bring herself to step into the icy water with the wintery winds swirling around her. She would have to get warmer before taking the plunge.

While she worked on warming up her body, Santi folded her pants and shirt. She set them on a high rock and hoped they'd be dry when she returned.

As she set her socks neatly on top of the pile of clothing, Santi couldn't help wondering what a person would think if her clothes were found. Would someone stumble upon them and wonder what had happened to their owner? Might they think she had drowned? The spring semester was starting in a week, and she sure would be grateful if her clothes were still waiting for her. She didn't want another awkward bus ride like she had experienced after the kidnapping. Thankfully, someone let her have a shirt so that she didn't have to travel all the way back to Florida in just her swimsuit.

Santi pulled her long curly hair into a sloppy bun to keep it out of her face in the current and stepped off the smooth sand into the water.

She had butterflies in her stomach as she jumped in the cold shallow pool and swam down the familiar tunnel to Rogan's kinship. None of the fears that plagued her before were present this time. She had survived so much already; she couldn't muster up any distress for her old stomping grounds.

When she left Rogan six months ago, it was uncertain when she would return, though she thought it would have been sooner. At the time, she knew she had to finish up the summer with her mother, and then the fall semester was starting. But then her grandfather died, and her mother wouldn't let her leave California until Christmas was over. Now that the new year had arrived, she was much later in seeing him than she had hoped but wanted to make the most of her last week before school.

After her kidnapping, she and Rogan spent nearly a month together as they had when they were children. It was like old friends and new paramours testing out their boundaries with each other.

"Santi, reach your hand in that hole,." Rogan had teased her when they were out exploring. His mischievous grin lit up his tan face all the way to his dark brown eyes. He pointed to an ominous hole dug in the sand beneath a moss-covered rock.

Santi rolled her eyes at his joke and couldn't believe he remembered the incident with Tizz when they were children.

"You stick your hand in there and see what kind of sea demon you pull out."

Rogan knelt down to the opening and looked in.

"Looks empty."

He pretended to roll up his sleeves, which she found particularly endearing because he had never worn anything with sleeves in his life but was referencing another one of their jokes: a gesture she had told him long ago meant hard work.

She got on her hands and knees next to him. "Do not stick your arm in there. You might not pull it back out."

She peeked into the hole.

"Or worse."

They both looked in, heads side-by-side, when a crab sprang out of its burrow, pinchers clacking. Rogan and Santi fell over each other as they rolled away laughing, fumbling through the water, and shielding each other. Both made grand gestures to "protect" the other from the vicious five-inch crab.

"I'll protect you," Santi proclaimed.

"No, he'll take your nose off!" Rogan bellowed as he wrapped his arms around her waist and spun her away from danger.

When they righted themselves, they were laughing and tangled together, and then, without either of them taking the lead, they were kissing.

# Surface Tension

The memory made her face grow hot, but truthfully she was hoping to do more of it when she saw him this time. They had shared a couple small kisses and one quick talk about Santi living underwater, but mostly they explored and swam carefree and found new—and more daring, now that they were older—ways to explore the ocean.

After Santi's brush with the Sirens, she knew she needed to get her life in order on land before she could ever make a decision to live underwater. She couldn't leave things hanging with school and her friends. Besides, she and her mother had a lot to discuss so that Santi's choice to live with the Serras didn't prohibit Celia from being able to see her. Still, she had hoped to be back sooner and wasn't happy with how much longer everything took. Now her heart was in her throat in anxious anticipation. She kicked her legs fiercely but felt she couldn't get there fast enough.

The decision to live underwater would be fairly easily made if—and only if—things developed between her and Rogan in the course they were headed. The decision didn't revolve around him, but it certainly didn't proceed without him. To hear one of the elders in the kinship, Flora, talk about it, Santi and Rogan should have been Bound during the summer, and it was nonsense for Santi to go back on land. But whether she decided to live under water or not, she would make the decision wisely and not based on anyone else's opinions.

Santi's heart beat rapidly, and she was filled with endorphins as she swam over the familiar dwellings in the kinship. As she closed in on Rogan's home, she reached out her Ku to the inhabitants and found that Coral was the only one inside. By the time she reached the shelter, she was welcomed in warmly and enveloped in a loving hug.

"Santiago!" Coral cooed to her, not letting go of the long embrace. "We thought you would be back sooner. No one is even here anymore! Both Amed and Rogan are away at Daris."

Santi couldn't hide her disappointment. She couldn't expect him to be sitting around waiting for her, but school started in a week, and she would hate to miss him entirely.

"When will Rogan be back? Why is he there?"

He had promised to be here when she returned, and her Ku betrayed her disappointment to Coral.

Coral laughed knowingly at Santi's misery.

"Rogan went to advocate to be a Sentinel. Now that you are back amongst the swimming, he has no need to look for you—not that he does not think being a Guardian is a noble Opus, but he would like to work with his father. He has always felt it was his duty, having the bloodline that he does, to be a Sentinel."

This news made Santi stop and think. She had forgotten that Amed was half Crural. It warmed her heart to think that Rogan was just as much Crural as she was Serra, but she realized she was being rude.

"How are you Coral? I've missed you. What are you working on right now?"

Coral's Opus was Artisan, and she was very good at it. When Santi had left the Nhori four months ago, Coral was working on a stained glass window in the roof of a neighbor's shelter. She made the glass in lava streams above water and then painted it. When it was dry, she brought it underwater and fastened each piece to the larger pane. When the whole thing was finished, she would put it in place in a window or roof. It let light into the room in a colorful and beautiful way.

Coral laughed gently at Santi's good manners, her blond hair bobbing behind her and held back by a headband of woven hair and seaweed.

Coral retrieved a jellyfish that glowed blue.

"Here," she said, a laugh still dancing in her blue eyes. The way she handed it to Santi made it clear she should know what to do with it.

"Um, Coral? What… what is this for?"

"Oh, you've never used a *nuntium*?"

Santi cocked her head to the side. "The jellyfish?"

Coral smiled, though she tried to be polite about Santi's ignorance.

"Yes, the jellyfish. But when someone fills it with a message, it is a nuntium."

"There's a message inside?" Santi flipped it over and suspiciously looked at the underside.

Coral continued to laugh at Santiago's blunder. It wasn't a mocking laugh, but soothing and warm.

"Not literally inside," she said.

Santi squished the jellyfish around in her hand, surprised that it wasn't stinging her. Her puzzled look elicited further explanation from Coral.

"To send a message through the ocean, a Serra will catch a jellyfish and put a message in it. Then the nuntium finds the recipient. Quite speedily, I might add."

"It's magic!" Santi said excitedly.

"No, darling, it is not magic." But then Coral seemed to hesitate, and with an air of confusion, said. "What you call magic, we call *Vis*. It has been gone from the waters since the curse was placed on the Sirens."

"Well," Santi said, "everything Serras do with their Ku seems like magic—Vis—to me."

"That is an interesting thought from a Crural. There has been a debate for centuries about whether the KuVis is gone from our waters or we have just forgotten how to use it."

Santi watched Coral mull the thought around in her mind for a moment before snapping out of her reverie and saying, "Reach out and touch the jellyfish's Ku."

Santi had connected to animals' Kus on many occasions, so this did not seem like an odd instruction. Instantly, she was filled with Rogan's voice.

"Hello, mother, I hope you are well."

Hearing his voice warmed her body and sent her heart racing. She hadn't realized just how much she missed him since their separation.

"I saw Tizz," Rogan's message continued. "She is doing well in Daristor surrounded by a gaggle of excitable girls. Not surprising, she is extremely popular.

"I have been able to switch my Opus, so that is fortunate. Unfortunately, I will be detained here about six months. Luckily, I don't need to do all of the training. There is a lot of overlap in the Guardian training that I have already had. I imagine being the son of Amed helped."

Santi could hear a strain in his voice that told her he didn't like the special treatment but appreciated being moved through the process quickly.

"However, I will have to come back out here to do more once the new round of training starts.

# Surface Tension

"When Santiago gets back tell her to stay there."

Hearing her name in his voice made her break into a grin.

"I do not care how bored she gets. Maybe she can get an Opus in the kinship, but make her wait for me. I would die if I lost her again. I have a lot to discuss with her." He chuckled to make light of it, but Santi could hear the weightiness hidden in his voice. "I worry that she has been gone so long she may not come back down. Oh, I have to go. I love you, mother. Keep Santi there."

Rogan's voice was gone, but she replayed the words over and over in her head. *"I would die if I lost her again."* Santi felt her face grow hot, and she shook it off, not wanting to embarrass herself in front of Coral.

Santi handed the nuntium back.

"Chimba," she said, using the Serra word to show pleasure with something. Whenever she was under the surface, Santi tried to do their things and use their words, always trying to slide into her Serra skin.

Coral gave a knowing smile but spoke to Santi in a light tone so as not to embarrass her.

"I saved that for you so that you could hear it, but let's release this poor little guy, shall we? He's been waiting nearly three months for you."

Coral must have done something with her Ku because Santi didn't see anything happen, but suddenly the nuntium stopped glowing blue and began swimming around. Santi reached out to touch it and Coral grabbed her arm.

"Do not touch it. Jellyfish will sting your skin rather fiercely."

Coral turned her forearm so that her scales touched the jellyfish and gently pushed it out of the shelter.

Santi couldn't help but sound disappointed when she said, "I have to get back to school in a week. I can't wait another three months for Rogan to get back."

Coral pondered what Santi said for a moment before she replied, "I hope you will stay this week anyway? We can have a good time, you and I. And Amed will be home this evening."

"Oh, of course!" Santi said immediately. In her desire to see Rogan, she was being inconsiderate of Coral's feelings once again. "Of course I'll stay."

"Come on, we will catch that poor jellyfish again and you can send Rogan a message."

Santi liked that idea very much, and her face lit up as she followed Coral out of the shelter.

A few hours later, Amed return to the Nhori. It was a mini reunion of sorts between the lovers. He had blinders for all but Coral as he came into the shelter. They placed their hands on each others' hearts and gave one another a look so full of love that Santi turned away, feeling like an intruder on an intimate moment.

After releasing Coral, Amed turned to greet Santiago and was full of fatherly love for her. He wrapped her up in an enthusiastic hug that made Santi laugh out loud. Hugging was not a Serra custom, and to a Crural observing the greetings, it would look like Amed cared more for Santiago than his Bondmate. But Santi knew that his greeting with Coral was far more intimate and meaningful than any amount of hugging—no matter how enthusiastic.

# Surface Tension

When he finally released Santi from his mighty embrace, Amed informed her, "I have just left Rogan a couple days ago. He is very anxious that you might not be here. He will be extremely pleased to see you."

Then Amed reached up and touched his right hand to his right eye. She had never seen the gesture, but its meaning was irrefutable. He had given her the Serra equivalent of a wink. He was teasing her. She tried not to blush.

Santiago, Coral, and Amed spent the evening catching each other up on all that had happened since they last saw one another, and Santi was bursting to tell them all she had learned in her abuela's journals, but the conversation kept eluding her. They asked so many questions and had fascinating things to update her about, so she let the conversation take a natural course and decided to bring up the information in the journals when the time was right.

"Sully seems to be in troubled waters with the Sirens after his failure at bringing about my death," Amed said in answer to Santiago's inquiries about what had happened with the Sirens since the kidnapping.

"We are not certain, but he has been causing more and more trouble for the Sentinels, and it is my assumption that he is doing it to try to win their favor."

"Oh, no. I'm sorry you have more to deal with now," Santi offered. "That is horrible for you." She mused to herself for a moment before saying, "And for Sully."

"I find it surprising that you would have compassion for Sully after all you have been through with him," Coral said without actually sounding surprised. Of all Serras, Coral had more empathy for others than anyone Santi knew.

"I don't know that it's compassion, per se. But..." Santi thought about it. She had thought about Sully a lot while she was on land and was still uncertain about her feelings. "Well, he was a very good friend, wasn't he? Of course I'm very angry."

She paused again as she remembered all he had put her through. Sometimes, she would still cry angrily at the frustration she felt.

"I mean... how could he have done that to me!" she nearly shouted. "We were such good friends as children. I just feel so betrayed! And... and I would really like to punch him in the face." She unconsciously balled up her hands. "But I also think it's just a shame the way things have turned out."

"Rogan feels the same way," Amed said with a touch of sorrow in his voice. "He is very sad for the loss of his friend."

"Amed?" Santi started, unsure if she wanted to know the answer to the question she was burning to ask. "What happened to Sully? I know his mother was killed by Crurals, but that doesn't seem like enough to make him so hateful... to make him hate me." Throughout her kidnapping, she had often wondered how her friend could be so different from who he once was.

"Did I do something to him? Is he... is he mad at me for something?"

Amed and Coral filled the room with their empathy for Santi's heartache, but it was Coral, not Amed, who answered her question.

"Sully's mother was taken by Curals. That you know. But the things that happened afterwards caused the greatest change in Sully. He searched for her. Up and down the shore where she was taken, he searched for months. He befriended a couple of Crural women to help him search where he could not go.It surprised us all when the women found her."

"They found her!" Santi sat up straight in surprise. "Was she alive?"

"Barely."

At this, Amed interjected, "I often think things might have turned out better had they not found her."

"Why?" Santi asked.

Coral resumed her explanation.

"The women dragged her to the beach where Sully was waiting. His mother was battered, bloody, but her emotional wounds were worse." Coral grimaced. "As she lay there dying, rather than comforting her, Sully badgered her for information. He made her recount the details of her capture and every aspect of the brutality she went though."

"That is horrible." Santi's chin quivered. She felt appalled.

"After she died, he took out his anger on the women who returned her, and then he continued to find women…"

Coral cringed and faltered, so Amed took over.

"He would seduce them and do horrendous things to them and any other Crural he came across. He was convinced that every Crural was trying to harm the Serra world. I had to take action as Commander. It pained me to be harsh with him during his grief, but he was breaking Serra law and becoming a threat to everyone."

"And this was while he was still in Daristor?"

Amed nodded and added, "Rogan did not know how to help him, and I think he still has guilt for not doing more to change the trajectory Sully was headed on. Though, now, Rogan is very angry and not willing to soon forgive Sully. He may be much angrier than you, even. My son is very protective of you."

Suddenly, Santi felt very uncomfortable talking to Amed about Rogan's protectiveness of her, and her eyes began darting around the room. The heaviness of the conversation and unpleasant feelings in everyone's Kus were becoming unbearable.

Luckily, Coral sensed Santi's discomfort and graciously changed the subject to Rogan's Sentinel training. She and Amed talked about what their son would have to do to change his Opus, but Santi couldn't listen or follow the conversation. She found she couldn't stop thinking about Sully.

What would happen to him now? Surely he would have a punishment for his actions. And how could he work with the Sirens without being one? The thought of him was making her skin grow hot and her fists ball up again. She was distracted from the conversation in front of her until Amed said something about Rogan needing proper training so that he could take over for Amed one day.

This shocked Santi. She did not think the position was inherited.

"Amed, how did you became the Commander? Was it passed to you from your father?"

"No, Sentinel Commander is not a hereditary position. It is usually the process of an individual working up the ranks and proving themself. For me, however, it was more like my destiny. I was raised knowing that I would train to be a Sentinel, and it was only logical that one day I would command. Just as Rogan will most likely after my time is over because of our bloodlines. But aside from the specific knowledge that my mother was the heir that could defeat Zitja, most *Demis* are conscripted for the Sentinel Opus because of their Crural relationship."

"What is a Demis?"

Amed chuckled.

"A Demi is someone with both Serra and Crural blood in them."

"Oh! A Demi. Like a demi-god. But doesn't Demi mean 'half?'"

"The term originated with Zitja, the original Demi-Serra. After that, it sort of stuck and incorporated anyone with some portion of Crural blood in them. For thousands and thousands of years, that is what we have been called. You think our terminology would be updated." He gave a small "hmm" to himself.

Santi was eager to tell him that she was also a Demi, but he continued with his story, and her ever-present fascination with anything Amed had to say kept her silent.

"It was always clear that I would be Commander, but I did not allow anyone to cut corners in my training. Just as my aunts made sure my childhood was as normal as possible with the looming responsibility of being the Heir. They were big proponents of doing things the right way. If I was going to lead, then I wanted to know everything and be ready for it.

"When Rogan was born, it was time for a new Commander when the previous one, Terret, became too old to continue. I refused the position at that time. I was still young and wanted to learn more about leadership. I was made second in command instead, and I studied avidly under the tutelage of my Commander, Kylr. Eight years later," Amed cast his eyes downward at his hands, "he was killed in battle, and my turn was up again."

The sorrow in Amed's Ku filled Santi with sadness at his lost mentor. He looked back up at Santi as he finished.

"This time, I readily accepted."

At this Coral interrupted. "Amed has changed the ocean in such a short time. When we were young, under the leadership of Terret, it was not a safe place. Somehow, that buck managed to undo all of the good works the previous Commander had put in place. No one would ever travel alone, and hardly anyone dared leave their kinships. The entire world underwater was nearly ruled by the Sirens. Things have been much different these last twelve years, since Amed took over."

"Why is it that Tullus's heir has to be the one to kill her? Why is she invincible and clearly immortal while other Sirens can be killed? They can, right? I've seen them die. Do they come back to life?" Santi shuddered at the thought of the corpses coming back to life like some sort of zombie-Sirens.

Amed raised a hand to slow Santi's train of thought.

"When Nephira died," Amed answered, "she placed an enchantment on Zitja, cursing her so that her father would be the one to kill her. Zitja had her father killed immediately after that, but he had many children, and it was discovered that one of them—or one of their descendants—would also be able to kill her. He was a man who…" Amed paused, not knowing how to say the last part. "Shall we say, he had a lot of descendants. Both legitimate and illegitimate."

# Surface Tension

Santi got his meaning, and said, "So you are a descendant of him, but probably millions of other people are, as well."

"This is true, of course, but my children and I are the only known ones."

Santi nodded subtly to herself. There was so much to think about, and she was fascinated by the history of the ocean. Finally, she had run out of questions after having her curiosity piqued for more than an hour, and she was bursting to tell him her news. Santi decided this was as good of a time as any to tell them what she had learned.

"While I was with my mother in Venezuela, we found my abuela's—that's my grandmother's—journals. You'll never believe this: she was a Serra."

Santi said it quietly, as if she couldn't believe it herself. In truth, she was still having a hard time wrapping her mind around this new reality.

"My mother and I tried to look her up on the Internet and, sure enough, we couldn't find a record of her existence anywhere. No birth certificate, college degree, driver's license. Nothing!"

When neither of them said anything—probably from her mention of the Internet—Santi added, "I'm a Demi, too."

They were both very silent, and it began to fill the water around them, weighted with the implications. Santi felt Coral and Amed's Kus touch, as if they had stolen a glance at each other the way Crurals communicate only through a glance.

"Are you sure?" Coral asked.

"Yes. I mean, as sure as I can be. She wrote it all down in her journals."

Suddenly, Amed's Ku was very lively.

"Your grandmother was a Serra?" His tone was casual, but his interest was intense. "And she chose to live on land? I have never heard of this happening before! That's not to say no one does, but surely it is rare. What happened to her? And she had children. Clearly," he said, almost chastising himself. "Your mother is the daughter of a Serra dam, and she wasn't born with a tail?"

Santi had never seen him so curious and fascinated before. He was reeling with the novelty and the science of a Serra living on land. She laughed to herself.

He began swimming the room slowly, back and forth, pacing as he thought and rambled questions, not necessarily *to* Santi, but *at* her.

"Did your abuela struggle with the thin air? How did she get around?"

On an on he chattered, talking about the possibilities, and asking all sorts of absurd questions about Celia.

"Was she accepted as an equal among the Crurals? How many people did she tell she was a Serra?"

Santi waited until he appeared to expect answers more than merely pondering aloud.

"My abuela was always in a wheelchair. I know that," Santi started. "I don't know how she died, though, and I don't know if my mom was born with a tail—she wouldn't remember either way, but I doubt it. A tail doesn't just disappear, right?"

She continued telling Amed what she knew, but he still wanted more information. He was nearly interrogating her in his quest to learn all he could about this novel situation.

# Surface Tension

After a few hours of back and forth, Santi let out a giant yawn. "Amed, I'm so tired."

"Let her go to sleep," Coral said gently. She put a hand on Amed's shoulder as if to bring him to the present.

"Amed, I wasn't able to finish the journals before leaving California," Santi said with disappointment for not learning how they ended and also for not being able to tell Amed more. "But I will be able to finish them before I come back down again." She nodded encouragingly, hoping Amed would be satisfied and let her sleep.

But Amed's mind was full, and his Ku was still racing.

"Tell me about this Internet business. What did you mean you 'looked her up' with it?"

"Amed, let the poor girl sleep!" Coral said forcefully as Santi's eyelids blinked slowly.

"Right, of course. Goodnight, Santiago. I will think about this."

Lying in Tizz's old room in a bed of soft otter pelt stuffed with down gathered from seafaring birds, Santi only had a moment to be grateful that she felt so accepted by Amed before drifting off to sleep. She almost thought she wouldn't go back to school at the end of the week.

As Santi slipped into unconsciousness, she felt sure that staying underwater was the direction her heart and her abuela's history was guiding her to take.

# Chapter 3

Carmen
1972

Carmen waited anxiously on the shore, flicking her golden tail in the water and fidgeting with her bag of treasure. *Treasure* wasn't her word for it, but upon giving her Crural assistant, Jolene, her first payment—a sack of pearls—the description stuck. Jolene had oohed and aahed so delightedly at the "bag of treasure" that Carmen laughed more heartily then she had since she was a child. Carmen enjoyed Jolene very much, and the latter seemed to like doing top-secret work on land for the Serra world below. Jolene said she felt like a spy and relished every meeting she had with Carmen.

Today, Carmen hoped for the news that would finally allow her to do her job and not just wait while Jolene did all the legwork. Once Carmen got the information she was waiting for, it would allow her to prove to her leaders that this whole endeavor wasn't pointless; that the single-minded purpose of her whole life wasn't pointless. Then she could change the fate of the ocean forever. And she was hoping for a little recognition along with the peace. Maybe one day she would be Sentinel Commander. The prospect made her shake with anticipation. Failure was not an option.

Finally, Jolene emerged from the trees and began sprinting along the shore, waving her arms and yelling excitedly. Carmen had worried when she chose this girl to work for her—Jolene was hardly more than a child at twenty-two—that she was not right for the job. She had a couple assistants before Jolene, but they were just stepping stones in the process of finding the right assistant who could investigate and find what Carmen sought. To those first two Crurals, she hadn't even revealed her identity as a Serra—hiding her tail under blankets—but there was no point hiding from Jolene, who was hired to uncover the truth for the Serras. When the girl ran about and shouted as she was now, these were the times that Carmen second-guessed her choice. However, the work was unique, and Carmen knew she needed someone young, creative, and up-to-date on the latest the Crural world had to offer by way of resources. Thankfully, along the way, she had never been disappointed by the information that Jolene provided. Jolene was smart, diligent, and willing to travel wherever needed, so Carmen put up with the follies of Jolene's youth because of the merits of her work.

Jolene plopped down in her long, flowing dress with big bell sleeves. Her straight, waist-length hair was parted in the middle, and a leather strap was bound around her forehead. Carmen noted that she was a pretty girl and was glad that her looks didn't inhibit her from being a smart girl, as well.

"Carmen!" Jolene gasped, out of breath but still rushing as she pulled open her large floppy bag. "I found him! I did it! Can you believe it?"

Carmen could not, in fact, believe it.

"Jolene," she said with caution, "are you sure?"

"Relax, mama, I'm sure! Look for yourself."

She handed Carmen a yellow folder that was stuffed full of papers and photos bursting from every side. When Carmen opened it, the inside was chaos. A large stack of paper in the center was surrounded by small scraps of paper with names and numbers clipped and stapled to the cover. Other loose notes with contact names and several small notes slid into her lap. It was messy, but Carmen could see that Jolene had put a lot of work into researching this project.

"Groovy, isn't it?"

Carmen let Jolene's odd Crural jargon hang in the air between them while she perused the documents. The collection of papers stapled together on the top of the stack was the document she had been waiting her entire life to see—the entire ocean had been waiting centuries for this very information—and she held it in her hands.

This was the Heir. The one she was sent to find.

Seeing it before her was almost more than she could take. She closed her eyes and took in a deep breath. This was the person that could change their world, their awful, ugly world, forever.

Carmen wanted to know everything with an earnestness that made her heart pound. Her eyes flew open from their grateful reprieve and scanned through the documents swiftly but meticulously. She had seen most of this information before during their past meetings, but she studied it again thoroughly. She wanted to follow the trail the entire way. Carmen read aloud, though it was more to herself than to Jolene.

"Tullus Hostilius, third king of Rome, died in 642 BC."

Carmen read on. She was captivated by the report Jolene had prepared. Her eyes and nose scrunched in disgust. This man was truly evil: conquering lands, pillaging and murdering, stealing property and women. No wonder it was easy for him to take Nephira and make off with her as if she belonged to him. He felt that she did. It made her stomach turn. He seemed to have thought that he should own and rule everything.

Carmen and Jolene had hit a lot of dead ends in the past following trails from his wives where the line ended with a war or tragic impotence and many *almosts* and disappointments as they followed leads and lineage. The two of them had spent a lot of time tracking down ancestry that ended without progeny. That all changed when they found a line from one of Tullus's mistresses that lead them to a woman named Valentina Canius.

Valentina went to Venezuela from Rome in 1672—almost 300 years from this bright sunny day that Carmen sat reading about her. She was the one who brought the family line to the Americas and the one whose line continued up to this very day.

Carmen devoured every word. As she read through the lineage, she found more of the same: names, birth and

S.R. Atkinson

death dates, addresses, men and women. It was all there. The last few pages contained information about the Heir's grandmother and father, who had both passed away.

Then she found the page she was anticipating, the one that brought them to the Heir. The Heir that was still alive and whom she would use to rain down destruction on Zitja.

Carmen's heart began to race as her eyes scrolled down the page. Jolene's handwriting was very neat and tidy, but as Carmen turned to the last page in the stack, she noticed Jolene had taken the time to diligently type it up. Even the young Crural girl knew how important this page was for the ocean.

Carmen took note that the Heir lived here in Venezuela. They had suspected as much when they learned about Valentina and decided to move their operation from the shores of Massachusetts—where she met Jolene—to here. Luckily, Jolene was young and adventurous and jumped at the opportunity for a paid trip to South America because Carmen couldn't have done it without her.

Carmen continued looking through the papers and had been completely wrapped up in the information for over twenty minutes before she realized that Jolene was sitting patiently waiting for her.

After she had finished, Carmen straightened up. She took in a deep, cleansing breath of the salty air and said, "Yes, it is groovy."

Jolene laughed. "So this is what you've been looking for?"

"Jolene, this is what I have been looking for—what everyone has been looking for—for over two thousand years. You have done well. Very well."

# Surface Tension

She had a smirk on her face and wanted to celebrate in a Crural fashion, but couldn't bring herself to do the strange high five thing Jolene had taught her. She settled on reaching out and giving the girl a pat on the arm.

It had taken Carmen years to track down this anthropology student in the United States and make sure she was worthy of the task. Jolene was top of her class and tenacious when tracking down information. Carmen needed someone with Jolene's cunning and charisma to work for her. After finding the energetic, confident brunette, Carmen and Jolene had worked for years to find information about Tullus and to follow his genealogy. When they came to Venezuela just a few months ago to track down the Heir, there were so many barriers and blockades in their search that Carmen didn't think they would ever arrive at this day.

"There is just one problem," Jolene said apprehensively. "The Heir," (she said the title as though it were odd to be calling someone such a thing) "… speaks Spanish."

At this information, Carmen burst out laughing. Of all the setbacks they'd had, this absolutely was not one of them.

"No es una problema. Yo hablo Español."

"You speak Spanish?" Jolene said, surprised by her shift in language.

"Jolene, have you never questioned that I speak English? That I read? That I write or know so much about humans?"

Carmen decided to use the human word instead of saying "Crurals" just to prove her point.

When the girl still seemed bewildered, Carmen pressed on.

"I am from the Najilian Clan. It is located here, off the waters of South America. A version of Portuguese is my first language. I have learned English for you. Well, that is not entirely true. My journey to find someone who could help has given me reason to learn English. I speak four languages, actually, one of them being Spanish. And I read. You also speak English and Spanish, so is it so absurd that I would as well? This has been my entire life's work."

At this, Jolene scoffed. "I don't mean to laugh, but, *entire life's work*? You take yourself too seriously. You are so young. It cannot be your entire life's work."

"It is true, I am young. I am only thirty, but I have been working towards this goal since I was seven."

This answer seemed to satisfy Jolene, so Carmen pressed forward.

"Of course, Jolene, this information does nothing if I cannot meet this person. Can you arrange it?"

"I knew you were going to say that, Carmen, and I've taken the liberty of contacting your *Heir* already."

Carmen was stunned. She knew long ago she had chosen the right girl, despite all her drawbacks, yet she was always pleased when the girl could still surprise her.

Jolene twirled her hair up into a knot behind her head and held it in place with a pencil before she pulled out another folder and scooted closer to Carmen so they could both look at it.

"All we need is a ruse to lure the Heir to the beach to talk to a mermaid. Then it's up to you to do the convincing that saving a race of mermaids is the right thing to do."

Carmen pursed her lips together, not sure where this was headed.

# Surface Tension

"Luckily, I have a plan for that as well." Jolene gave a self-satisfied smile.

Carmen made her way back to her headquarters at Daris as quickly as she could, which didn't feel fast enough. She had so much to tell her Commander that she thought she would burst from excitement before she arrived. When Carmen originally presented the idea of employing a Crural to find Tullus's heir ten years earlier, she was laughed at. No one thought it was possible, and she had to practically plead with them to let her try. They were reluctant to let her, and the Commander all but told her she would fail, but he had finally acquiesced. She didn't receive much support from the Sentinels, but it had been just enough to keep her work going. Her support had grown when she reported that the operation was moving to the Americas and that they had traced Tullus's line to this century.

Now she would finally be able to tell them that she had succeeded. Pride swelled through her as she pictured introducing the Heir to the Sentinel Commander, presenting Ocean Mother Yazi with the fruits of her labor, and grand ceremonies in Carmen's honor.

It wasn't Carmen's idea that finding the one that could kill Zitja would break the curse of the Sirens; that had been the working theory for thousands of years. Even if Zitja's death didn't dissolve the curse and rid the ocean of the Sirens, taking out their leader—one who was supposedly invincible—would definitely put a damper on the damage they could do. However, it had been Carmen's idea to finally seek out the Heir. After all these thousands of years, Carmen couldn't believe no one had tried. She was determined to follow through to the end. She had wanted this since she was a small pup.

The sun was just rising in the sky and piercing the depth when she swam up to Daris. The city shone brightly, giving her a boost of adrenaline. She had barely slept during the three day journey, but as she entered the city through the gold archway, intricately carved and gleaming brightly and standing nearly sixty feet tall, any fatigue she might have felt was pushed from her mind.

Carmen wasn't a stranger to Daris as her work brought her here often, but every time she entered, her breath caught in her throat. The whole city permanently felt aglow from the stunning white and gold buildings. This time was no exception, though her excitement didn't allow her to stop and enjoy the sight of it. Carmen rushed through the streets and over buildings, avoiding other Serras in her focus to reach her destination.

She was familiar with the Sentinel command building. It was the largest in the city and elaborately adorned from by the ancient Crural civilization that had built it. She swam through the pearl white corridors and up several floors, bypassing the staircase around her. Any Serra that found himself in this building had speculated on the zigzag contraptions that connected the levels. There were many theories as to their function, but everyone agreed that walking up them had to be an extremely tiresome way to travel.

When she arrived outside the chamber where the Commander was meeting with his officers, the young buck who stood guarding the door ushered her in without pause.

# Surface Tension

"Carmen, we await your news anxiously," Captain Terret said, inviting her to speak. The discussion was halted when she arrived, and all attention turned to her.

It had taken a long time to be taken seriously by this group of Serras, but with every report she brought to them, she was greeted more and more enthusiastically and with what she interpreted as anticipation. Now, as they sat around a large oval surface, tails perched comfortably on carved rocks, she held the attention of these powerful bucks and dams and her confidence faltered, if only slightly.

Carmen jumped right in.

"The Heir has been found. My contact on land has given me a full, detailed report of Tullus's lineage, and it all appears to be in order without any holes."

Carmen had wanted to bring down the paper documents, but there was no way to preserve them from water damage. Besides, this group couldn't read the contents anyway. Carmen hoped her confidence would be impressive enough.

"The Heir lives on the South American continent, the landmass off of the Najilian Clan's. My contact has arranged a meeting for two weeks from now."

Carmen paused for what she expected would be cheering or praise, but as she stared around the room at the bucks and dams seated on their high-backed, stone-carved chairs, their faces were impassive, and their Kus gave off an essence of disenchantment.

"How can we be sure this is truly the Heir?" asked a stern-faced dam.

"Can you guarantee this *Crural*--" the buck said the word as if it tasted terrible in his mouth, "will come and help us?"

Carmen was disheartened by their lack of enthusiasm, but she could feel more questions about to come at her, so she stopped them right away.

"This is who we've been looking for," she said authoritatively. "I do not care if the Heir helps us willingly or not. We can kidnap if we must, coerce and threaten if we have to. If necessary, we will use the Heir and sacrifice this Crural, but we will be rid of Zitja for good."

It was callous, sure. Carmen had been told that she was more logical than emotional, but it didn't bother her. She had grown comfortable with the dam she had become, and it suited her goals.

Carmen could pinpoint the events that caused her to lose her sensitivity and empathy towards others. It happened when she was seven. Their grandfather raised Carmen and her brother, Fernando, after their parents were killed when she was two. He was as good of a substitute for parents as anyone could have hoped for—patient and loving—and he made sure they were well taken care of. That was why, for second time in her short life, when she watched her caretaker killed in front of her, she never quite recovered. This time, she saw Zitja brutally kill first-hand, watching over her brother's shoulder as Fernando swam her to safety. In that moment, her desire to find the one that could kill the Sirens began. She put up a wall around her heart so that she never cared enough to be saddened by death or loss again. After that time, she cared less about living for herself and more about retribution. She did not care whom she had to use to get the job done.

"Good" Terret finally responded after a pause. "You have done good work, Carmen. If you can pull this off, every Serra will praise you for saving them."

Terret's words, although stiff, made her heart swell. She did not care what happened to the Heir—a horrible descendant of a devious man that ruined the Serra way of life. Carmen would bind this Crural with rope herself. She would manipulate the Heir's arm to stab Zitja through her heart and use the Heir's body as a shield. Whatever she had to do, she would see this through to the very end. Whether the Heir survived or not was none of her concern. She would avenge her parents' deaths.

Not many could recall things that happened to them when they were two, but Carmen could still clearly remember. Her brown eyes had peeked through her nest as her mother screamed, blood filling the water before her limp body drifting to the cold stone floor. Carmen had worked so hard for this when no one thought she could.

"I will not disappoint you." Conviction pulsed through her Ku. She gestured towards the ocean full of her people. "I will not disappoint them."

# Chapter 4

## Carmen

Carmen hovered directly in front of her shelter—a large black rock that stood out in stark contrast to the moss covered homes of her neighbors—feeling ambivalent about being back home. Going inside felt wrong to her, like she didn't belong. She had rarely been home since going to Daristor. She only kept the dwelling because this was her home as a pup. She and Fernando moved into this small home with their grandfather when their parents died. Later, when her grandfather had also died, a caring kinsman moved in to take care of them until Carmen was old enough to go to Daristor. Since then, she had only been home when her Opus brought her to the Najilian. Her memories in the shelter weren't necessarily bad, but the solitude she felt in it made the remnants of her past feel hollow. She felt uncomfortable every time she had to enter, like she needed to reclaim the home again. It belonged to the water and fish, not to her.

# Surface Tension

Carmen picked a barnacle off the outer wall and looked up at the surface to see the sun shining into her home. Her shoulders raised and lowered with the effort of an unnecessary sigh. She entered her home and coasted around the room, lazily picking off barnacles and escorting them outside.

This was what she did every time she came home. It felt ritualistic to reacquaint herself with her shelter in this way. The water seemed stale, though there were plenty of openings in the shelter for water to flow through. It was as if the heart of her home was stale—or gone. By the time she was finished removing the crustaceans, she no longer felt like an intruder, although she still couldn't allow herself to completely relax. There was always a touch of haunted emptiness in the home. The sun lit up the room in a would-be cheery way that never seemed to penetrate Carmen until after being home for a few hours.

Suddenly, her Ku was touched in a familiar way that made the sunshine find its way to her heart.

"Finally!" she called to him.

A large, bronze-skinned Serra buck with a broad chest and dark blue scales plunged into her shelter and placed his hand over her heart.

She returned the gesture, and they sat in silence for several minutes, absorbed in each other's presence.

"Samir! Where have you been? I've been here for over an hour now!" she teased him, as if it were his responsibility to seek her out.

He gave her a wry smile. "I could say the same thing to you! It is not as if I knew you were back."

"Well," she teased, "you need to make a better effort to find me when you are home!" She drank him up with her eyes. It had been a terribly long time.

"And how do I know when *you* are home?" he teased her back, though his tone held a hint of seriousness.

His eyes were nearly charcoal colored, but they usually looked lighter because of his carefree spirit. As he spoke to her now, they looked as black as their true color.

"When you are not working in Daris, you are in the Nhori, or sometimes even on land! How am I supposed to know where to find you? I don't even know where to send a nuntium."

Now she knew he was being dramatic. Nuntiums found their recipient on their own.

"All right, I get it. How about if we both try harder. We cannot let so much time pass without seeing each other. How long has it been?"

"Over a year!" Samir responded with false exasperation.

Carmen knew he couldn't be too angry with her for being hard to reach. His work as an Artisan took him all over the ocean wherever inspiration guided.

"Oh! I am so sorry!" She was shocked. She knew it had been a long time, but she hadn't realized they hadn't seen each other in over a year. "I have been so wrapped up in this project. But I have found the Heir, Samir! I must tell you about it. I have finally done it."

They spent the rest of the evening nestled amongst her cushions, once they shook off the debris that had settled over time, and talking languidly about Tullus's heir, Samir's art, and the goings on in their lives. All the while, Carmen was wracked with guilt about letting their friendship once again drift to the side because of her Opus. How long had it been since she had even seen her brother, Fernando? He lived in the Nhori—where she would stay for months at a time—but his kinship wasn't close to the shore where she met with Jolene, so Carmen never made the effort to stop by. Not even on her way to or from Daris could she be bothered to make time. Was his kinship so far out of her way? She had to admit to herself that it wasn't. She resolved to make her family and Samir a priority.

Just as soon as she finished the business with the Heir.

"I am headed back to the Tipua tonight," Samir said, breaking her out of her reverie. "You should come with me. You know Fernando and his Bondmate live just a few kinships away from me now?"

She hadn't known that. She fidgeted, feeling ashamed at her lack of knowledge about her own family. Fernando had moved and she didn't even know? Guilt raked through her again. How long had it been since she had done anything that didn't center around the Heir? She had let her Opus run her life for so long. Yet she was so close now and there was so much to do. Carmen couldn't run off to the Tipua just yet.

"I can't. You know what is coming up! I have so much to do. I am going to be bringing the Heir down! Do you not know what this means? It is such a bad time. After this is finished, then I will come and spend every day with you."

"Carmen." Samir looked at her with a grave expression, his heart expressing serious concern. "I worry about you. Since your grandfather's death, you have been determined. Determined to a point it has become detrimental.

I know that you want to avenge your family's deaths, but at what cost?" His countenance was completely void of its usually carefree spirit. His dark eyes penetrated her to her core.

She tried to brush off his intensity. "What do you mean? It has been at no cost."

"Carmen!" He seemed to laugh her name more than say it. "I am your only friend. Does that not seem strange? You hardly make contact with your family. I know because I see them more than you. You have been driven by your Opus and desire to vanquish Zitja at the cost of your Serraty."

"I have not lost my Serraty." She was highly offended by his implication. "I am still Serra. I am still driven by my Ku. I am…"

But she didn't know what she was.

If Carmen were honest with herself, she couldn't remember the last time anything but revenge and thoughts of her parents' death propelled her motives.

"Carmen," he said calmly, his words and Ku oozing with compassion. "I am just saying not to let anything overshadow the Serra in you. Do not lose who you are because of your pain. Put yourself first. For once."

Carmen couldn't even argue. She knew for certain she never put a single one of her desires above her Opus. Even eating had often taken a back seat. If Jolene didn't bring Crural food to eat while they talked on many occasions, she would likely starve.

"Hava is due to have a pup in the next few months."

He let the statement hang like an accusation. Carmen accepted it as such.

"I did not know Hava was pregnant."

## Surface Tension

She was truly ashamed of herself now. Luckily, she had pulled her head out of her Opus long enough to make it to Fernando and Hava's Bonding celebration two years ago. She quickly sent up a thankful prayer to Nephira that she had also seen them since the celebration. However, Carmen had not known Hava was pregnant. It was hardly a victory for her that she had seen them more recently than two years ago if she didn't know important information about them. A big move, a pup, and Carmen chasing a Crural around the world without knowing any of it. And Samir knew more about her own family than she did. Carmen was sufficiently ashamed.

"Promise me," Samir stated forcefully. "Promise me that you will not lose the good inside of you. I often fear that you may have already when you talk ceaselessly of revenge. What do you do that makes you happy? Who do you surround yourself with that makes you laugh? Who do you love?"

"I love you." Carmen answered in a tone meant to be a joke, but the look on his face wiped the smile from her. They did not have that kind of love. He had been a brother to her since he moved to the Najilian when they were pups. The truth was, she could not remember the last time she laughed, and, aside from receiving good news about the Heir, she didn't know what made her happy.

"I promise… to try."

Carmen sighed at the look her friend gave her. Samir's easy lifestyle and search for beauty made him such a gentle soul. Such an artistic life made it easy to think there wasn't anything more wonderful than the way the sun broke through the surface and made the sand sparkle on the ocean floor.

"Carmen," he said sternly, but not without concern, "find happiness and follow it anywhere."

Carmen bit the inside of her lip. He always had a way of making her feel like there were no troubles to be found in life.

"I promise."

"Good," Samir said with a nod. "But you will not come with me tomorrow?"

"I just cannot. Not now."

"Fine. I will not go, either. I will stay here with you and make sure that you have some fun in your life."

"Really, Samir? I would love for you to stay!"

After an evening spent fulfilling his promise to make her have fun—finding and playing with seal babies, racing dolphins, and eating oysters—Carmen lay down on her bed of seaweed, relishing the new memories she had made with her oldest friend and contemplating all that he had said. Could she put her own desires above seeking a way to annihilate Zitja?

But wasn't that her ultimate desire anyway? Carmen was struck with an unsettling thought: twenty-three years she had spent obsessed with the Siren problem, and what was she without it? When Zitja was no more—if her death eradicated all Sirens—what would she do then? Who was she? Carmen, on her own, without a driving vengeance?

The thought made her feel ill. Samir was right. Carmen wasn't sure where the line between her personal happiness and vengeance for her people was. Had she gotten so lost in revenge and misery that there was nothing else left of her? Samir's words haunted her: *"Find happiness and follow it anywhere."*

# Surface Tension

"Here, put this on," Jolene said as she handed Carmen some red fabric.

Carmen held up the strings of an object that didn't look like there was anything to "put on."

"What is this?" she asked, pulling at the little triangles of fabric and trying to guess where they went.

"It's a bikini," Jolene said as if it were clearly obvious. "They are very popular here in South America. I'm going to bring one home with me. We have them in America, but they are nothing like these."

She drew out the word "these" in a way that let Carmen know that the little red string was very exciting.

"But what do I do with it?"

"Oh!" Jolene laughed. "You wear it. I thought it would be easier for the Heir to meet you if you looked a little more like a human girl. Don't get me wrong, I love the pearls and seaweed you have wrapped around you. It's beautiful, but it could be startling. I'll take your hair out too. It's also very lovely, but-"

Carmen waved her hand back and forth. She could tell Jolene was going to keep rambling, so Carmen cut her off.

"Jolene, can you please just show me how to put this on?"

Jolene was a very intelligent university student with an excellent education, but she could chatter on for hours, and Carmen didn't care about why she should wear the bikini, just how to do it.

Jolene stopped unfolding the blanket she was about to lay out and looked at Carmen a little bewilderedly.

"I'm sorry. I forget sometimes."

Jolene scooted over on her knees and picked up one of the pieces and slipped it around Carmen's head, then tied it behind her neck. Then she pulled the other strings around her middle and tied them behind her back.

"There! Now you can take off the stuff you have under it."

Carmen unwound her coverings from under the bikini top and took in the new garment. She liked the look of the red cloth and found it to be very supportive and comfortable. She gave a smile of approval at yet another one of Jolene's successful ideas.

"This part, however," Jolene said, lifting up the other bit of fabric, "you're going to have to put on by yourself. I got the kind that ties on the side, so it should work. Just slip the entire thing through your leg gap between where your tail ends and the, um, rest of you begins."

Jolene paused as she pondered Carmen's anatomy. A Serra dam was built just like a Crural woman if that woman's legs were bound together at the top of her thigh.

Jolene pressed on quickly to escape embarrassment. "Then cover up your important bits and tie the side."

Jolene showed Carmen on herself how it should work, and then handed over the bikini bottom before standing up to work on Carmen's hair.

Carmen picked up the bikini bottom and held it at arm's length. This was almost identical to the item she was now wearing, except this was a beautiful red and very soft, whereas hers was made from animal pelt. Hers was effective but not nearly so lovely.

# Surface Tension

She wasn't as afraid of nudity as Jolene seemed to think, so Carmen ripped off her loincloth and threw it to the side. As she did so, Jolene released her long black hair. It had been tied in a knot on the back of her head with a skinny, long braid, and several woven strands of seaweed had held it in place. Carmen preferred not to have to fuss with her hair in the current and was often too preoccupied to do anything elaborate. Today, it had dried in the twisted bun, and as Jolene pulled it free, it fell in waves around her shoulders.

Carmen slipped the back of the swimsuit through the gap in her thighs at the point where her scales and her skin met and pulled it up to cover her front and back. Once it was in place, she tied the strings on the sides of her hips. The little red bikini bow sat neatly on top of her golden hip scales that shimmered up her waist. The whole effect was rather stunning.

"There. How do I look?"

Jolene was quiet for half a beat before she said, "Fantastic! If you weren't here for business, you could easily get any of these men to fall in love with you." She made a sweeping gesture around the beach that made Carmen laugh.

Everyone on the beach was so far away from them that they all looked like tiny guppies. In all their meetings they had never been close enough to another soul to even see their faces. There were no men in the vicinity to fall in love with her or otherwise.

Suddenly, Jolene let out a laugh and said, "If you told me two years ago that I would not only meet a mermaid but that I'd work for her and help her put on a bikini, I would have asked you what you were smoking."

"What does that mean? Smoking?" Carmen asked, always curious to learn new things.

"Oh, never mind." Jolene quickly changed the subject. "Your Heir should be here really soon. I came up with an elaborate story about a secret underwater society. That merpeople are in need of an ambassador on land to help them keep their secret."

"What?" Carmen was incredulous. "Jolene, that sounds so… ludicrous. It is not a good ruse. No one would fall for that!"

"Yeah, I was worried about that. After I said it, I knew it was lame, but then I brought out that picture I took of you and explained that mermaids are real and needed help. That did the trick."

"That is all it took?" Carmen was suspicious and skeptical.

"Carmen," Jolene said with a look of admonition, "chill, mama. He clearly saw your beautiful face and had to meet you."

"Hmmmm," Carmen grumbled.

She had thought the contraption Jolene brought to take a picture of her was suspicious, but after a tiny white piece of paper popped out the bottom, and Jolene showed it to her, it seemed like a safe enough device. However, Carmen made her destroy the picture as soon as Jolene returned from showing him.

"But are you sure we will not be sitting here all day, waiting for someone who is not even coming? There were a lot of different stories we had agreed on that were much better than this. Or!" Carmen suddenly exclaimed with worry, "what if he brings others with him? How can you guarantee our secret's safety?"

"Carmen." Jolene was calm, unaffected by the panicking Serra. "If he brings others with him, you jump into the ocean, and I'll tell him I lied. Now relax and wait. I did what I could. Stop worrying so much."

The women didn't have to wait long to find out. Less than an hour later, Jolene jumped to her feet and almost yelled, "There's your heir now!" And the girl took off running up the beach.

Carmen pulled another blanket up around her tail to hide it from first sight just in case it was too startling.

And that's when realization sunk in hard.

This was a critical moment. During this conversation, she would have to convince the only person alive that could save them that he wanted to save them.

Carmen began to panic. She should have prepared more! What if she messed the whole thing up? Her chest felt tighter and her breathing became shallow. This was such a big moment. What if she couldn't make her case for help? What if she couldn't get the Heir to come down with her today? Their world would be in ruin. And she would be a laughing stock. She began wringing her hands and looking up the beach to where Jolene was walking back.

The Heir was coming.

Carmen pulled herself up to look poised and collected. She could fret all she wanted, but she had to present a confident, superior exterior. She was here to do a job, and no amount of uncertainty would intimidate her from that duty.

Suddenly, there was a splashing in the water behind her. When she turned around, her anxiety heightened. This was a terrible time for such nonsense.

"Samir! What are you doing here?" she said with her mouth and words, as was habit for her to do on land, though she had never before talked to Samir with anything than her Ku.

He could sense the anxiety in her voice and feel the worry in her Ku. "Carmen, you didn't think I was going to let you have all the fun today, did you?"

He also spoke with his mouth, something she did not know he knew how to do.

"I need to meet this Heir. I want to talk to Crurals and have adventures, too."

"Samir, this is not an adventure! This is our lives. The thing I do today is so important and it must be taken seriously. Samir…" She didn't know any other way to say it but to just be honest. "We can't afford your jokes and nonsense. You never take anything seriously."

She felt she had offended him, but his face and Ku gave nothing away.

"This is where you are wrong, Carmen. This is the perfect time for my jokes and nonsense. You will surely scare our rescuer away with your serious demeanor and factual way of speaking. Do you need this person to help us? Truly, truly need their help?"

"Of course! That is what I'm try—"

"Then do it my way. Relax, Carmen. The state you are in now will scare away any chance of obtaining help! You are all scrunched up with worry."

# Surface Tension

At his words, Carmen noticed for the first time that she had been wringing her hands, and her shoulders were so hunched they were nearly touching her ears. She took a breath and released the tension from her body.

"There. You look almost pretty now."

He laughed. It had always been his favorite joke to tell her that she wasn't pretty even though she knew he meant the opposite.

"When the Heir comes you will not—let me be clear—you will NOT jump right into your speech about Sirens and a world at war. If you do, surely no one would want to come rushing into the water to face a foe that is causing Crurals no harm. You will spend today getting to know this person for the *person*"—he emphasized the word—"that he is. Do you understand?"

Her eyes widened at her own mistake. He was right. She needed to talk and laugh and enjoy this person. She needed the Heir to feel comfortable with the concept of Serras and learn about how wonderful the water could be before any mention of a destiny and fighting. She would have surely ruined everything without Samir. Carmen reached out and gave his hand a gentle squeeze.

"Thank you," she whispered.

With that resolve, her chest lightened, and she breathed a sigh. She had practiced several versions of different speeches, but she had never been able to come up with anything she thought would be convincing enough to work to bring the Heir down straightaway. This way, there was no pressure today. The four of them could spend a lovely day on the beach together, and then, maybe, when she brought up the true reason for their visit, no trickery would be necessary to lure the Heir into the water.

"Besides," Samir's words broke her train of thought, "I could not risk the chance that this Heir is the one I'm destined to fall madly in love with. I picture her to be the most beautiful woman on land. We will fall in love and, after she has defeated the Sirens for us, we shall make beautiful babies together."

Carmen laughed out loud. "Oh Samir! How have I not mentioned it before? The Heir is a man."

Samir's expression fell from hopeful beaming to complete despair so abruptly it looked as though weights pulled his face downward.

"You have always just said 'the Heir.' The romantic in me just assumed it was the love I have been waiting for."

Carmen laughed a truly free and happy laugh at this.

"I'm so sorry for crushing your dreams."

As if to prove her point, just then Jolene arrived with a tall, tanned, and very attractive man who knelt down to greet Carmen at her level.

Her breath caught in her throat as she extended her hand, just as Jolene had taught her to do. She was barely able to exhale a faint, "Hola, me llamo Carmen."

This was supposed to be the man she was going to lash a knife to and sacrifice for the greater good? This man with a warm smile that filled up his entire Ku and burst through his dark brown eyes to looked at her sincerely? This man who made her heart hammer in her ears and nearly forget why she had come?

He extended his hand eagerly and looked at her with stunning earnestness. His wide, beautiful smile made Carmen suck in a shaky breath. He grabbed her hand in both of his, losing her tiny hand in his massive grip.

"Hello," he responded in Spanish. His heart was full of an honesty and sincerity that Carmen didn't often feel, even amongst most Serras. "My name is Santiago."

# *Chapter 5*

## Santiago

The morning after telling Amed about her Abuela Carmen—and him grilling her for information—Santi was prepared for more questions. They went about their business that morning, but all seemed to have been forgotten. However, while they were hunting for their breakfast, Amed turned to Santi and casually said, "You know, Santiago, you could become a Crural Guardian, a Thaed, or even a Sentinel if you wanted. Those are typically Opuses for Demis. You would do particularly well as a Thaed or even a Magister of Crural Studies at Daris. If you chose to live down here, of course."

This line of conversation took Santi aback. She was still mulling over the decision of whether to live in the ocean or not, but she had never thought about what she would *do* if she chose life underwater. She grabbed a fish from the water and distracted herself by connecting to it and feeling its Ku.

"A Thaed, that's like an anthropologist. They study Crurals and… what?"

"*Anthropologist* is a good word for it," Amed answered thoughtfully. "They learn about Crurals and help the Serra world stay on track with them. That is how our language has adapted with yours and how we know so much about you. We realized centuries ago it was too dangerous for us when we were unaware of what was happening on the surface."

Santi nodded. "That makes sense. And you need your language the same as ours so that you can communicate when necessary."

Amed smiled proudly at Santi for understanding.

"Being a Thaed seems… silly. I already know about Crurals." Santi laughed. "I am actually an anthropology major because I am fascinated with learning about different cultures. But living down here, well, I don't know… It seems like it would almost be a waste to continue researching my own species. I'd rather learn about all of the different clans of Serras."

This idea excited her. She had only ever been in the Nhori and wanted to visit the other clans.

"Magister at Daris teaching Crural Studies, though." She mulled the thought around in her mind. "That would be quite easy, I imagine. And maybe I could still work with the Thaeds to help Serras know more about my kind."

"There are many possibilities," Amed said with a smug smile.

Santi could see he was rooting for her to choose a life under water, and it warmed her heart.

The fish in her hand was full of life and not in the slightest bit through with its time on Earth. Santi let it go and turned to Amed.

"I could be a Sentinel? That doesn't seem logical."

"True, it would be unorthodox. Usually, Demis are recruited as Sentinels just in case they possess Tullus's blood in their lineage. But most often, those Demis are Serras. We have never had a Crural Sentinel, and you would be at a disadvantage for sure."

His eyes drifted ever so slightly to her legs and Santi felt self-conscious about her Crural-ness for the first time.

"But you proved yourself to be brave in the face of the Sirens, and you did some training with Grendor on how to fight. I do not want to discourage you if you would like to be a Sentinel."

Santi felt uneasy. She didn't think her "training" had been very successful. Grendor easily bested her when they sparred. However, he was very encouraging and said she picked up on new techniques quickly.

"Maybe that year of karate I took when I was fourteen really paid off," Santi joked, but quickly changed the subject. She didn't want to have to explain karate, and she had never even taken it very seriously.

"I'll think about all of it. I still haven't decided what I'm going to do. I have two-and-a-half more years of college to get through first."

In what remained of her week in the Nhori, Santi kept busy. Coral quickly put her to work around the kinship in service of other Serras and tending to the community garden.

# *Surface Tension*

Santiago also sat in on a lot of lessons amongst the children. Amed was adamant that she learn all she could about being a Serra and know everything that Serras knew. If she were going to live down with the Serras, he felt she should be educated as one, and Santi was more than happy to oblige.

The constant swimming was exhausting, so when she could, she found activities where she could be sedentary until she built up her muscles to this way of living. She had to wonder if she could ever be a strong enough swimmer to live under water. Maybe after a full year of Serra life no one would notice that she was a Crural by her inabilities. Santi wondered if an Olympic swimmer could come down and adapt seamlessly. When she returned to school, she would take a swimming class or join the swim team and make sure to swim every day to keep up her skills.

"Besides the mobility aspect," Santi said by way of answering Amed's questions about her Opus, "I feel like I belong here, much like I did as a child. Everyone has been very accepting of me, and it's only magnified with my age and eagerness to help."

What she didn't mention was that everyone she talked with brought up Rogan without fail, as if they had all conspired to convince her to love him. She had to roll her eyes at the obviousness of it all. She was definitely interested in this life underwater, and she was sure she could love it, but it would be a decision she would make on her own, not because of what the Serras in the kinship wanted; and it especially wasn't a decision to make based on a boy—as much as she liked the direction they were headed.

"I'll just take it one day at a time, Amed, but I will think about the options you've suggested."

"I accept your answer and appreciate your thoughtfulness on the matter, Santiago. It's very clearheaded of you." Amed raised his right index finger to his right eye again.

Santi laughed and gave him a punch in the shoulder. "Stop teasing me Amed. You never did when I was little."

"On the contrary, I teased you all the time. You were just too afraid of me to realize."

Santi's mouth dropped open in surprise. She definitely remembered being intimidated by him as a child. He was so impressive a figure and always busy with important work. She never thought of him as being silly. Santi closed her mouth and scowled at him in mock scorn.

"We'd better hurry and find breakfast or you'll be in trouble with Coral," she said.

On the day before she had to go back to school, Santi was puttering around the community garden, though not really tending to any of the plants or making progress in removing the parasites. She was distracted with thoughts of underwater verses land life and—if she were honest with herself—she missed Rogan and wanted to discuss it with him. She wished for the hundredth time that he could text her. She really missed her phone when she was down here and thought maybe she was going through some sort of withdrawal. Endlessly being updated on her friends' every movements with social media had become so normal. It grew overwhelming at times, but now she wished for a status update to say *Rogan checked in at Daris for Sentinel training*. Just something to let her know what he was doing.

# Surface Tension

Santi laughed at the absurdity of it and was thankful this world would never be tainted with status updates and sepia-filtered pictures of food.

While she was pondering what Fishbook might be like, her Ku was touched and she heard Rogan's voice like a warm bath soak through her.

"Santiagooooo." He drew out the 'o' in a tease.

Her eyes flew open wide, and she forgot all about the sea slug she was removing from some kelp. Santi opened her heart wide and touched him right away. She enveloped his Ku in hers. He was close. So close!

Before she could ask what he was doing home, he swooped down into the garden and wrapped his arms so far around her waist he clasped his own biceps. She yelped and squeezed him around the neck. She was filled with a childlike glee at seeing her best friend again. They hadn't seen each other since August, when Celia had bought her a ticket and demanded she come home. Now having been in the Nhori nearly a week without him left her feeling surreal that he was actually here.

Without preamble, without warning, Rogan pulled away from her and planted a soft but not delicate kiss on her surprised lips. The touch, so tender, so full of feeling, was quickly received by her. The intimacy they shared between the connection of their Kus combined with the physical touch to light a fire in her that started just above her diaphragm and spread through her wildly. She had kissed Crural boys before, but obviously never while her Ku was engaged. And she and Rogan had kissed before but those were friendlier kisses, more chaste. This was not one of those kisses. She was lost in the kiss and absorbed by him so thoroughly that when they pulled away, she felt lightheaded.

This was the first time they had kissed like this, and Santi felt overwhelmed and a little cheated. It was too quick and unexpected. She wanted to be ready for it, to fully enjoy every bit of it. It felt foreign, and yet nothing had ever felt so right at the same time. How did Serras do anything besides kiss all day long? It was so personal, intimate, and knowledgeable. She had never felt closer to him. When she looked up at him, she nearly had to uncross her eyes to focus, her head felt so fuzzy.

She ran a hand through his dark shaggy hair—something she had always wanted to do but refrained for reasons she didn't understand—and breathed out a sigh.

"Rogan, I'm so glad you are here."

"From here on, you do not leave my side," he said, squeezing her in a tight embrace. "You were gone so long, I was afraid you would never get those kickers back down here." He laughed and squeezed her tighter.

She pushed back from him to see his face; he had a sharp jaw and friendly cheeks, and always a look of mischief in his eyes.

"What are you doing here? I thought you had to be in training for three more months."

He had a little twinkle in his eye as he said, "I can take a couple days off. My father needed me in the Nhori. Urgent business." He touched the side of his eye with his finger and Santi laughed.

"But how did you get here so fast? It's like a five day swim here, and I sent you the nuntium that long ago. You must have left as soon as you got it!"

## Surface Tension

"I took a cryptid. It only took half a day. In fact, if I said I could take you back to Florida for school in just a few hours so that you did not have to take a 'bus'... how much longer could you stay down here?"

"What's a cryptid?" Santi asked with wide eyes.

"You'll find out when I take you to Florida. Now answer my question."

Santi was glad he didn't try to guilt trip her about going back to school. When she left him in August to go to her mother's and back to school—with the plan to visit after the semester—he had put up such a fight. He had assumed she was under the water to stay with him for good, but she had only intended to visit. It was their first heated discussion, which unraveled into an awkward conversation about their future together. Neither of them were ready to have that conversation, so things were left uncomfortable and unsettled. Finally, he conceded that giving up her life on land was a big ordeal, and she would need to make the choice thoughtfully. She was glad to see he was respecting her decision still.

"I guess I could stay two extra days."

"Great!" he said enthusiastically. "I think that is just about how long I have urgent business in the Nhori. Now..." he said, as if there was more to discuss; but instead he gathered her back into his arms and resumed their previous activities.

When they finally pulled themselves away from their love bubble, Santi got back to the work of weeding the garden. She was a responsible member of the community and was still expected to do her job. Rogan dove right in and helped her while he told her all about advocating to be a Sentinel and how the process was almost too easy.

"My dad had a hand in that, no doubt." Serras didn't roll their eyes, but Santi strongly felt that Rogan would have if he knew the gesture.

He told her about his training and the interesting secrets he had learned about Sirens that weren't common knowledge. He updated her on the few people she knew, all about Tizz's adventures in Daristor, and told her that Torrin asked about her constantly and was concerned about what Sully had done to her.

Santi waited anxiously through all Rogan had to tell her. She ate up every word, but in the back of her mind, she was impatient to tell him her news. When he finally asked her what happened with her during their separation, Santi somberly began, "While I was gone, my abuelo died."

"Oh no! Santi, I am so sorry."

"Thank you," she replied, touched.

Often, when Crurals said they were sorry for a friend's loss, it was apparent they were saying it only because that was customary in such an occasion. But Rogan's Ku was so earnest and sincere. He truly was sorry for her loss.

"It was very hard to say goodbye to him after his passing." Santi was quiet for a moment while she thought about her abuelo. This was not where she was trying to go with the conversation, and now she was feeling sad where her news was actually positive. She shook her head and tried to clear the mood.

"Anyway, we found my abuela's journals. It was so wonderful. My mom and I were grateful to have found them.

# Surface Tension

We learned so much because of them. You'll never believe this, but my abuela was a Scrra. She chose to live on land when she met my abuelo when she was thirty."

She could tell by Rogan's Ku that there was nothing she could have said that would have shocked him more. He took a moment to let it sink in before his face broke into a giant grin and he laughed out, "That is so… it is just so… unexpected. Crazy! Don't tell my father or he will have you training to be a Sentinel before you can finish your sentence."

Santi gave a small chuckle as well. "I have told him. And he suggested it, but only as one of a few options."

"No!" Rogan said almost dismissively, then kicked himself up from a sitting position. His countenance quickly changed from the joyful amusement she loved to a serious and angry Rogan that she was not familiar with. "You absolutely cannot do it."

"Calm down. I told him that was crazy too."

Rogan sat back down, but she was feeling a little defensive now. She always rose to opposition, a trait that infuriated her mother when Santi was a child.

"Why can't I be a Sentinel? Because I'm a Crural? Because I'm weak? Because I'm a girl?"

"Well, yes!" he said with a smile. "But you are only weak compared to Sirens because you are a Crural. And I want to protect you because you are my Santiago. I would not want a single harmful thing to happen to those little kickers you have."

Santi tried to rein in the conversation. She did not want to get into an argument when they only had a couple days together.

"Rogan, be serious. Of course I can't be a Sentinel."

"Listen, I do not mean to doubt you. I apologize for my immediate reaction. It is just too scary for me to comprehend. Besides, I am surprised you would even consider it after all you have been through at the hands of the Sirens. I do not think it is a good idea. It is very dangerous, not because you are a Crural or because you are weak or a girl, but because I do not want anything to happen to you again. Ever! When Caliapi told me that Sully had kidnapped you and was taking you to the Sirens, I could have killed him with my bare hands right there. I would never forgive myself if you were deliberately put in harm's way every single day. It is such a dangerous Opus. I cannot believe my father suggested it."

"It was merely one of many suggestions," Santi said, pursing her lips tightly in annoyance. Still feeling defiant she added, "But he said he'd support me if I wanted to do it." She shook her shoulders a little haughtily. "I do not want to be gardening forever. I want to do something important with the rest of my life."

This seemed to both catch Rogan off guard and please him very much at the same time. He smiled wide and the tease came back to his voice.

"You want to live down here for the rest of your life?"

Now it was Santi's turn to be caught off guard. She hadn't really been paying close attention to the words she had said. As if, unconsciously, she knew what she wanted more than she admitted outright. While she had been underwater this week, she had grown accustomed to the thought of life with Rogan. It felt comforting.

# Surface Tension

She consciously kept her thoughts away from her disappointment, but she had thought maybe they would be Bound today upon first connection. For a couple to be Bound, there couldn't be a trace of doubt in either person's mind or heart. For a Bond to take place, both parties had to know Binding was what they wanted for what remained of their lives. The fact that they still remained unbound let Santi know someone still had reservations. She was sure that hesitation must be within herself.

"Oh." She tried to nonchalantly answer his question. "I'm thinking about it."

The mischief returned to Rogan's countenance and he said, "This is the best news I have heard yet."

"I'm glad you're excited about it." She gave him a wry smile. "My hearing might make the decision for me in the end. It's been difficult on land to deal with."

"What do you mean?"

Santi shared the news of her difficult hearing, but Rogan stopped her halfway through. "I think we should find my father for this. He'll know more than I do on the matter."

Santi nodded. "I can't believe I haven't brought it up with him. That's part of the reason I'm here. But I've been communicating with my Ku, obviously, and it completely slipped my mind."

When they didn't find Amed or Coral at home, they asked a few Serras around the kinship if they had seen him and were directed to the *mercatura* cart.

"What is that?" Santi asked, with a little hop in her swim as she clasped her hands together. "I've never heard of it before."

Rogan laughed. "It is not that exciting."

"Doesn't matter. I love learning new things about… well… this." She spread her arms wide and gestured around her.

"The mercatura," Rogan explained, "is the Serra who travels between kinships and trades with the locals. He often takes requests to find specific items along his way, if you need anything. He is where we get all of our bioluminescent bacteria from to make luminescents because he most often visits the Dumkes, who gather it."

Santi was so fascinated she almost stopped swimming.

"I never even questioned where you got supplies from." Santi laughed at herself. There weren't any stores in the kinships to shop. "How have I never even wondered about this before? I guess I have a lot more to learn than I thought."

"I'll gladly teach you everything."

Santi ignored his comment, not interested in getting into a discussion about her future right now; she had too many questions.

"So…" She scrunched up her face to figure it out. "You have money?"

"No, we use a barter system."

"Oh!" This excited Santi. "What do you use to trade?"

"Anything, really. It does not have to be a direct trade, so long as he gathers enough things at each kinship. Some people can take without giving. And some people give services instead of goods."

"That sounds very magnanimous." Santi was a little incredulous that Serras could basically "go shopping" for free.

"I think Wilfie is much more strict at the bigger kinships." Rogan bit his lip as he thought about it. "I know that at Daris he is very particular about everyone trading for the items they need. He would surely go out of business if he worked everywhere like he did here."

"What makes it different here?"

Rogan pointed to a large table made out of driftwood set upon two rocks to make the base.

"I will show you."

They arrived at the mercatera's cart to find Amed and Coral talking with him, Coral's arms bursting with glass orbs and small stained glass charms on strings. Santi connected to Amed, Coral, the mercatera, and the crowd of four other Serras around the cart, and they stopped their conversation to introduce Santi.

"Wilfie, this is our other daughter, Santiago."

Wilfie laughed good-naturedly. His balding head was covered in gray hair around his ears and sprouting from his nose to blend in with his mustache.

"I can see the family resemblance." He nodded to her legs.

"Hello, Wilfie. Amicus," Santi said in the typical Serra greeting. She had to consciously remind herself not to stick out her hand to shake.

"Amicus," he replied, and then turned his squinty eyes back to Coral. "I just don't think I can accept all this Coral, my flower. Because of your glass-blowing, I am the most popular mercatera in Nephira's ocean."

"Just put it towards my future claim," Coral responded. She flicked her turquoise tail nonchalantly as she began putting her items on his table with the authority of someone who had done so a hundred times before. She nestled her orbs between a stack of balls of twine and a giant jar of green glowing bioluminescent bacteria.

This looked to be the more business-centered end of the table. It was full of products Serras needed, like braids of seaweed, fishing nets, and starfish for the Healers. At the other end of the table, the items looked more for fun. Coral set her stained glass decorations among several brightly colored fabrics, what looked like homemade dolls, and a few Crural items. Santi was so interested in everything on the table, she had forgotten why she'd come.

Wilfie was still arguing as Coral put out her wares. "You have so much claim, I fear your whole kinship could rob me blind twice over and I'd still owe you."

Coral only waved a pale delicate hand as a response and began browsing his merchandise.

"Oh," she gave a little sigh. "What is this item?" She picked up a computer mouse and Santi put her hand to her mouth to suppress a giggle.

"Father, Santi wanted to talk to you," Rogan said when it became apparent Coral would take a while with Wilfie.

"Of course, Santiago. What is it?"

Santi was disappointed to be distracted from the cart. She wanted to know how Wilfie would explain the mouse's purpose. She smiled because it reminded her of their old friend Wayne and his love of Crural items. She would be sure to bring down a gift for him next time she returned.

# Surface Tension

They swam a few yards away from the crowd at the mercatera so it didn't appear rude when they disconnected their Kus from the group.

"My hearing is coming and going. Sometimes I've been completely deaf for up to three days. But then it always seems to come back. Obviously, the doctors are perplexed, but I can't very well tell them what happened."

Amed shook his head. "No, that is true. But I can tell you that it is normal. Sometimes the deafening ceremony is not thorough enough, and a Serra will get their hearing back. However, those that have experienced the Siren's Song have had the same coming and going with their hearing. Are you experiencing any pain in your ears or head?"

"No!" Santi was surprised by the question. "Thankfully, no. Others experience that?"

"Yes, some people struggle with their Song-induced afflictions for years. Our poor friend Wayne is often wracked with pain, and he says it feels like he is experiencing the Song all over again. It is truly a mystery to us how the Song works and its lasting effects."

"So I could possibly be permanently deaf?"

"Almost certainly."

Santi contemplated this quietly. She didn't say anything for so long that Amed shrugged and lightened his tone.

"Who needs hearing? I have not had mine most of my adult life."

Santi nodded. He was, of course, focusing on the option that her life was going to be spent under water. Neither of them wanted to mention the possibility that she would remain a part of the Crural world.

Coral joined the group holding several balls of new twine, a large white sail folded into a bundle, and more bioluminescent bacteria. She and Amed made their goodbyes, leaving Santi alone with Rogan. Santi was glad no one chose to dwell on her hearing problems. Through her doctor visits, she had decided that if she were to remain on land the rest of her life, she would take up sign language and carry on. However, she knew most people would see her as someone to be pitied now. She could not bear that.

She and Rogan began swimming aimlessly, casually talking about Wilfie, and Coral's contributions to his stock, but her head wasn't as curious as it had been. She had too many serious matters weighing on her mind.

Now was the time to lay it all out. They were leaving for Florida soon, and she couldn't bear to leave things unsettled as they had last time. This was Rogan. He was her best friend, and she could tell him everything. Besides, he already knew the feelings in her Ku. No reason to hold back now.

Without much warning, she turned the conversation somber.

"I have been considering staying down here more seriously than ever. And... and I just want to talk about it."

He stopped swimming and turned to her. "I do, too."

"The thing is... I... I sort of thought you would want me to stay down here with you?" She was beginning to feel awkward discussing her future—their future. "'From here on, you don't leave my side,' remember? I thought that, maybe... you know... Well, you know! I thought we might be together."

## Surface Tension

When it came right down to it, she couldn't ask his feelings about being Bound. It tasted too much like rejection.

"Yes! Of course I know," Rogan responded enthusiastically. "It is just that… well, I did not know that you were leaning towards living down here. You would be away from your mother and the life you have now. I mean, I have never really been up there, so I do not know what you would be giving up, but I know it is a lot. Cell phones and…T…V?" He hesitated over the abbreviation. "And cars and stuff. Not to mention your friends."

"Please," she swiped her hand through the water dismissively. "I have more friends down here, and you know it. I feel like I've been pretty honest with my thoughts and decisions on the matter, but I don't feel like you've done the same."

She paused with eager eyes. Rogan would have to pick up on her Ku to understand the words she couldn't bring herself to say. Did he or did he not want Bonding and children and a future, or should she figure out her future without him?

He hesitated for a long time, and she could feel his Ku rolling in turmoil. Finally, he whispered, sounding almost ashamed, "It's true, I have been using your hesitations to work through my own. I have… complications."

Rogan paused for so long Santi feared she would never find out what these "complications" were.

She waited. Finally he began to speak again.

"I have to tell you everything. Eventually, I knew we would have to discuss this, but it is so difficult. And it is quite weird for me. You had not been underwater for six years. I began to plan my life. Santiago, I never thought I would see you again."

Santi had to restrain herself from fidgeting. Her stomach began clenching uncomfortably. She didn't know what he was implying, but she suspected it had to do with Caliapi because of a conversation Rogan had started but never finished. She had wanted to know the details ever since, but she was sure she wasn't going to like hearing about it.

Suddenly, Amed's very unwelcome connection to their Kus interrupted Rogan's explanation.

"Rogan, Sully has returned. He is about an hour away, and it looks like he has brought Sirens. Come, we are going to meet them before they get here. We have to keep them away from the kinship, if possible."

Rogan's Ku filled with anger. "Not again," he growled.

Rogan grabbed Santi's wrist and swam her quickly to his shelter. He pushed her inside to wait and hastened a short explanation.

"He keeps returning to look for you. We will be back soon."

"Wait!" Santi yelled to Rogan. "Take me with you. I can help, I know it."

He continued swimming away, making it obvious how little he thought she could help as he said, "Absolutely not."

Instead of arguing, she jumped out of their shelter to follow, but as she propelled herself over the shelter and stood on the roof, she saw the wake Amed, Rogan, and Coral left behind. Santiago knew she could never keep up. They were already so far away she almost couldn't see them anymore.

Santi rolled her eyes and then closed them tightly. She scolded herself for even thinking she could fit in with them. All this time tending the garden and helping her neighbors was child's play in the realm of real Serra life. She opened her eyes and swam back into the shelter in frustration. Maybe underwater was not the place for her after all. She would always have to be left behind and protected from tasks that were hard or dangerous.

# Chapter 6

## Santiago

When Amed, Coral, and Rogan returned a few hours later, Santi met them at the entrance to the shelter, defiance radiating from her. She'd had time to think while they were gone, and now Santi knew what she wanted.

"Amed, I want you to teach me how to fight."

She could tell by Rogan's Ku that he would laugh or tell her no or make a joke of it, but her intensity kept him silent.

"Sure, Santiago, I can teach you to fight," Amed answered with a degree of seriousness that Santi found respectful, "though I still think we would leave you behind in situations like these."

To explain further, Coral expounded, "Sully was here looking for you, starfish. I do not think it would help to have you present yourself to him. I, myself, did not go to fight but merely to help make our numbers look larger."

"And it worked," Rogan interjected, though Santi felt a bit of defiance from him. "We did not even need to fight. Sully only brought a couple Sirens with him, and when we told him you were not here—and he saw how many of us there were—he left without further trouble."

"It's true," Amed conceded. "None of my kinsmen I brought with us are fighters, but the Sirens did not know that. However, having you with us would have caused a real conflict to erupt."

Santi had assumed they'd present this line of argument, and she was ready.

"I understand that, and I can agree with you, of course. But what if one day in the future I'm out on my own and I run into Sully? I'll need to be able to defend myself."

"Then we will never leave you alone," Rogan answered.

"That's no way to live," Santi responded, shocked and angry.

Everyone was silent.

Finally, Amed spoke. "I think that old sai you found is around here somewhere. Tomorrow I will teach you how to use it."

"Thank you," Santi said softly.

Amed nodded, then he and Coral headed towards the back of the shelter to their room, leaving Rogan and Santi staring at each other.

Santi felt a small victory at having convinced Amed, but still felt challenged by Rogan in a way she did not like.

"Rogan I—"

But he cut her off.

"I know. I am sorry." He grabbed her hands. "I felt too overprotective. I was unreasonable. I know you cannot live your entire life never being alone. I apologize."

Santi, deflated of her previous anger, only nodded.

"Obviously, you can keep using the sai," Amed said the next afternoon. He flipped Santi's scavenged sai over in his hand.

"I can train you or I can see if Grendor has the time. He is the best buck I know with a sai. I use a *khert* more than anything else."

"It's remarkable," Santi said, eyeing the weapon at Amed's side. "I've never seen anything like it."

Amed unhooked the brass knuckle-like device from the belt on his blue-scaled hip and slid it onto his fingers. The blade, almost like a large, wide arrowhead, ran across his fingers.

"It is the only one of its kind. It was forged for me from my own design when I started my Sentinel training."

Santi gave him a look of admiration for designing his own weapon. It looked extraordinarily menacing, but maybe that was because she had seen Amed wield it and knew how brutal a weapon it could be.

"Would you like to try it?" Amed offered.

"Oh, no. No, thank you," Santi said, and he slid it off his fingers and refastened it to his belt.

The thought of using his weapon made her uncomfortable. Maybe the whole fighting thing in general made her uncomfortable, but she was determined to push through. She wanted to be able to defend herself but not necessarily hurt or kill anything. Amed's weapon looked so ominous, she'd rather avoid the thing.

"If you would like to use a short sword like Rogan does," Amed said, pulling her out of her thoughts, " I can also teach you this. He uses two at once, but that might be a bit much for you right now."

Amed handed her a short sword he had brought along.

Santi weighed it in her hand and held it extended in front of her.

"Why doesn't anyone use a regular long sword?" she asked while making slashing movements in the empty water.

"There is too much resistance through the water," Amed answered. "Whenever long ones make their way down here, we cut them down to a more efficient size. Well, when they used to sink." He mused, "People on land do not use swords anymore, do they?"

It was not a question.

"So, how do you get them now that Crurals don't fight with swords?"

"We make them, of course. Serras are not as reliant on Crural items as we once were. Sure, there was a time when all of our weapons—and most of our other items—were Crural-made, but we have cleverly devised ways of making things ourselves."

"How do you find the heat when you can't start a fire?"

"Santi, if you have learned nothing else from me, I hope you would at least learn to expand your mind to possibilities. The hottest places in the world happen naturally under or near water. And you know we are not held captive to the water like the fish."

Santi thought about all of the naturally hot things her mind could come up with. Hot springs and volcanoes—thinking back to what she knew about Coral blowing glass—were just a couple of things she knew would create extreme heat in the water or close to the shore. She let her mind wander about how they might actually forge a sword when the item in her hand brought her back to the present.

"No," she said, handing the short sword back to Amed. "I like the sai I found. I think I feel more comfortable with it than I would a sword. I only wish I hadn't lost the other one." She examined the lonely sai with a frown.

"We can get you another one. That will be easy. Now, show me what Grendor taught you. Do you remember his lessons?"

It had been many months since they had battled with the Sirens and escaped—months that felt like years with all that had transpired between then and now. Since the trip to the Nhori, when she had trained with Grendor in their downtime, she hadn't even picked up this sai.

Santi made a couple of pitiable swipes like Grendor had taught her—how she *thought* he had taught her—before it was clear that she wouldn't be a foe for even an already-dying Siren.

Amed used the short sword because that was the weapon she was most likely to face from an opponent. Sirens had once relied on their Song or brute strength alone, but they faced so many deafened opponents that they, too, now learned to use weapons just as the Serras had.

While sparring, Amed brought his skill down to Santiago's level so that she didn't get too discouraged by her inability to fight effectively. It frustrated Santi, but his consideration was ultimately appreciated. She slashed and jabbed with fury, but he parried every blow effortlessly.

After training in this manner for about twenty minutes, Santi was exhausted from the effort and discouraged with her ability.

"Amed, I think this is not going well. I'm no match for you."

"Santiago! Of course you are not a match for me." Her look of complete dejection made him hurry on. "But I have been training since I was a boy younger than you. I have had a sword in my hands for many decades, and, before that, it was a stick. Keep working on your craft. You will get there, I have no doubt."

Santi nodded but still looked dejected. "You're right. I just can't imagine I'll ever be an adequate swimmer."

"Then you are right," Amed challenged her. "But you can't give up."

Santi pursed her lips in concentration. She gave him a short, quick nod, and he continued.

"Remember the tips Alanna taught you about swimming more effectively. And, if you cannot make it to your opponent, make your opponent come to you. You will reserve your energy that way." Amed said the last statement with a small shrug, as if that truly would give her the upper hand.

Santi scrunched up her eyebrows and thought about the dozens of movies she'd seen where the weaker, more agile fighter was given the same advice about facing a stronger but more lumbering opponent. Letting their opponents wear themselves out seemed to work in the movies. Santi gave Amed another quick nod of her head, feeling more confident than she had a moment ago, and they got back to practicing.

They practiced for hours, and as she lay on Tizz's bedding that evening, waiting for Rogan to return with their mode of transportation, she felt battered and broken. Amed was hard on her, which was good, but she didn't seem to be improving. Her legs weren't helping the situation, either. Amed could attack and retreat so much faster than she was capable of keeping up with.

By the time Rogan swam into her room to check on her, she had made up her mind.

"I don't know if Warrior Woman is the Opus for me."

Rogan laughed, sat down at the end of the cushion, and picked up her legs to massage her calves.

"You have not been swimming much. You will get stronger once you live down here every day." Rogan raised his eyebrows and smiled mischievously.

Santi appreciated his hints, but she was too focused at the moment.

"I don't know if I've ever told you that my abuela was in a wheelchair. I had always known that, but now I see it in a different light. She gave up everything, even her mobility, to be with my abuelo. She knew she wouldn't be able to walk on land, and yet she did it anyway. This semester I have to finish her journals. I have to know how she had the courage to do it and how she knew it was the right thing to do."

"That is an excellent idea, Warrior Woman."

Santi finally roused herself out of her thoughts and sat up sharply.

# Surface Tension

"It must be time to go. I'm dying to know how we will get to Florida this evening. I have to check in to school by morning. How are we going to get there in time?"

"We will fly."

"Fly?"

Rogan said seriously, "We will fly underwater."

Within the hour, they had made their goodbyes to Amed and Coral and, of course, they stopped by Wayne's shelter before heading on their way. They swam out of the kinship towards the open ocean, far from the Delaware coast. Twenty minutes passed, then another ten. They traveled for such a long time that Santi could feel herself slowing. It had been months since she had covered such a distance, and she was becoming tired. They had been swimming so long, she thought they might swim the entire distance to Florida—had they not been going the wrong direction.

The whole time, they talked casually, as if nothing were out of the ordinary, and finally Santi couldn't take it any longer.

"We are just swimming! Where is this flying contraption?"

Rogan chuckled at her palpable eagerness.

"Just wait. They are not allowed in the limits of any Clan save for the NorMer, where they are native inhabitants. We have to meet them where I have left them on the outskirts of the Nhori."

Santi knew from experience that the perimeter of the Nhori clan could take a couple hours to swim even when she was on Rogan or Amed's arm. Swimming there on her own was entirely too daunting. Santi thought it very unlikely that she would be able to cover the distance, but she refused to ask to be carried. Wasn't she trying to see if she could hack it down here? It would not help her in her effort to be treated like she was capable if she asked him to carry her so soon.

To help pass the time, Santi decided to bring their conversation back where they had been interrupted the other day. She surely couldn't make it the entire semester without knowing what Rogan had to say about his complications.

Living in his kinship this past week and feeling a part of his world had her mind wandering to thoughts of a future with him. She would make the decision to live underwater logically, of course, but it did seem... romantic? Adventurous? Most of all it was feeling natural for her old friend to one day be her Bondmate.

She blushed and hoped Rogan didn't notice.

She took a brief moment to be real with herself. They had never seriously discussed their future together, and before she came back down, she had planned a future for herself on land. She was finishing those plans before making any sort of decision, yet she was feeling jealous that he had made plans for himself, as well. Suddenly she felt selfish for not realizing that he probably had an entire life planned without her, and now she thought she could implant herself into his life after college?. And above all, she still expected him to sit by and wait to see what she decided?

"So..." Santi tried to sound nonchalant, but she knew her heart was hammering in her chest, and Rogan could feel the self-conscious air that consumed her. "What was it you were going to tell me before Sully came? You were saying that you didn't think I'd be back down and that you had to plan your life..."

# Surface Tension

Her sentence trailed off. She had never discussed such serious and personal things before. She'd never had a boyfriend that she really cared about in high school, and had never broached such a topic. Santi felt his eyes on her as her face grew red with embarrassment.

"Just be honest," Santi said, uncoiling herself from her angst and addressing him with the maturity the situation needed.

"Tell me straight. That's how we've always been, haven't we?"

With great effort, Santiago swam in front of him so she could look him in the eye, knowing he could feel the mortification in her Ku.

He hesitated only a second before rearranging his demeanor. The look of a silly, joking boy she was used to changed to the confidence of a man and a friend who respected her.

"Yes, Santiago. I think that is a good idea."

He reached out and squeezed her shoulder. It was a very Crural gesture for him to make, and the sentiment brought her comfort. The two of them continued swimming side-by-side.

"While I was in Daristor, I met Caliapi, whom you remembered from Sariahdiem when we were children. I did not realize that we had met her there. She and I became good friends during our training to be Crural Guardians. We became really close. Things are different down here, but you might call what we did *dating*. We spent all our time together, and everyone assumed one day we would be Bound."

This broke Santi's heart to hear, but what had she expected? That he would just put his life on hold to wait for her? *She* had not done so. She felt a little queasy, and her heart was pounding. The sweat along her arms and legs broke through her warm skin and gave her a chill as it met the cold water. Remaining stoic, she encouraged him along with her Ku while he continued.

"When we finished Guardian training, Caliapi began to talk about what we would do and where we would go. She talked about us being together and once even mentioned in an off-hand way that she was surprised we hadn't been Bound yet. I knew her heart, and, although we never discussed it directly, we had conversations that hinted at the direction our future would take.

"During this time I was thoroughly conflicted. Caliapi and I could never bind Kus as long as I was always thinking of you. And I could never seem to clear my mind and heart of you, Santiago."

Heartbeat pounding in her ears, Santi knew her emotions couldn't be disguised. She found it hard to make eye contact and wished she could disconnect Kus through this conversation to maintain some sort of dignity. Her feelings were displaying themselves clearly into his Ku, and she cringed at the nakedness she felt.

Luckily, he carried on, allowing her to try to regain her composure.

"It was not fair to Caliapi. I was disjointed in my thoughts and actions. Everyone knew I had become a Guardian to find you. Yet I carried on with Caliapi as if we would, one day, be together. So…"

He paused, and Santi waited anxiously, not sure if she was even still swimming.

"This was only a couple of months before you were kidnapped…"

He paused again, and Santi's impatience to hear what he had to say made her head ring. When Rogan spoke, his voice was quiet in her head and sounded ashamed.

"I finally decided to give you up for good."

Santi's heart sank, but Rogan carried on.

"I was not being fair to her, and honestly, I was not being fair to myself. By this point, I had just finished Crural Guardian training, and I was feeling foolish for dedicating my entire future to finding you. It was—sorry, Santiago—it was foolish of me to do."

Santi nodded. She couldn't disagree with him, though she wanted to very much.

"I was going to go to Daris to advocate to change Opuses, but I decided I would first work as a Guardian for a little while. I also wanted to clear my head. Be on my own for a while and decide what I truly want. Not make my decisions based on what anyone else wanted."

Santi nodded. "I can't argue with that line of thinking."

"When you were kidnapped, I was actually down in that area making my way around to the Liscon Region. It is on the other side of the Americas land mass. It is off of California."

"California?" Santiago said in surprise. She did not know Serras lived there. She had never heard of the Liscon Region. Was that a Clan? "Why would going there help?"

S.R. Atkinson

"No one actually settles in the Liscon," he said resuming his explanation. "No kinships or families take up home there. It is inhabited solely by Guardians in a yearly rotation to protect the Crurals on that side of the Americas. We station there because of the Crurals' need for our help. There are many shipwrecks from the amount of large passenger ships and fishing boats. Since it is not a long-term settlement, I thought it would be a reprieve for me. I could escape Caliapi and thoughts of you for a short time and… think… Just think."

He paused for so long that Santi was tempted to speak, but she could feel him mulling over a thought and she waited it out.

"The truth is, Santiago, I worried about what I would do even if we did find each other again. Six years is a long time for things to change, and you were only twelve when we lost touch. I loved you with the immaturity of a fourteen year old, but there is so much that changes in that time."

He shrugged a shoulder and picked up his pace a little in his agitation. Santi tried to swim faster, but at this point she was too exhausted and actually slowed down. Finally, Rogan came up to her and silently scooped her up in his arms. No words were necessary between the two old friends. She couldn't bring herself to admit that she wasn't capable of spanning the distance, and he would never make her do so. They carried on as usual, though Santi felt awkward at their close proximity during such an intimate conversation.

"I worried that you would not be able to make it as a Serra."

# Surface Tension

"Rogan, I..." she swept a hand across her useless body, frustration burning in her Ku, to indicate that she was indeed not making it right now.

He gave her a little squeeze.

"Not necessarily your ability to swim long distances. There are other things. I do worry that you might not adapt, and that our life could never be full because I would have to take care of you—which I am happy to do—but I did not think either of us would want a life like that. I had to be real about my choices."

Santi felt rejection burning her from the inside. He was saying everything she had worried about herself, driving a needle into her insecurities with impressive precision. When she spoke, her insecurity displayed as anger.

"Rogan, I worry about that every day! How could I not when everything I do is a challenge because of my lack of knowledge or ability? I try to fit in and do for myself, but it's a very real possibility that I can't do it!"

She felt insanely vulnerable in his arms, letting him carry her as he spoke about her not being able to cut it amongst the Serras. Suddenly, she wanted to be sitting in class amongst the walking and put the ocean far behind her.

"But if you always see me as nothing but a pair of 'kickers,' then that's all I'll be to you."

"I call them kickers lovingly," he said, and his smirk was back for a moment before he became serious again.

"You are right," he said, mulling her words silently while Santi calmed her racing heart. She was up and down in her emotions and was beginning to feel a bit like her mother, who was always the more passionate one of the two of them.

"I cannot think of you as helpless or you will be. I want you to know that I have seen so much in you since your return and kidnapping that makes me ashamed for thinking you would not be able to adapt."

"Thank you," was all Santi could muster to say.

She was truly touched by his newfound faith in her abilities, but her thoughts were still reeling with annoyance and jealousy. She wanted Rogan to finish his explanation about Caliapi, but she did not want to bring it up. What had happened? And where did the two of them stand now?

As if reading her thoughts, he looked her straight in the eye and said, "While you are in school, I plan to figure it out. I will be honest with you: Caliapi and I have not had any sort of relationship since I planned to go to the Liscon, but that does not mean things are finished. She had expectations that we would reconnect. I owe her, at the very least, a conversation. When you come back down in the summer, I'll have talked to Caliapi and be halfway through Sentinel training. Can we resume *this* conversation then? After we have both had some time to think?"

Santiago gave herself a minute to calm down. It wasn't fair for her to harbor any jealousy. Hadn't she also had a few boyfriends over the years? Hadn't her reasons for having them been exactly the same as his? And she absolutely had to decide if she could live underwater, constantly being at a disadvantage and, possibly, a burden. Coral was always telling her that in small kinship life, she wouldn't notice her inabilities because things were simpler.

Santi didn't have grand plans of joining the Sentinels or Guardians, so maybe she could work in the community garden for the rest of her life. The thought actually depressed her more than comforted her. Santi would never be happy with such an easy existence. She had always wanted more for herself—travel and learning and challenging adventures. Santiago smiled up at Rogan, lightened her Ku, and nodded once.

"I think revisiting the topic after we've had time to think is a good idea. We'll talk in June?"

Santi felt Rogan's Ku lighten along with hers—almost in a collective sigh to wash away the tension. He leaned over and gave her a kiss on her forehead. It was comfortable and warming, and she relaxed in his arms.

A few minutes later, he finally stopped and let go of her.

*This is it!*

Santi was suddenly filled with excitement. She would finally get to see what this "flying" device was. They had done so much as children, and she had experienced a lot of Serra life, yet she knew there was still so much she didn't know. Her lessons with Coral, Alanna, Amed, and Grendor told her as much, yet she was still surprised that there could possibly be more to find out about their world.

Santiago felt Rogan reach his Ku out and summon their rides. She scanned the area vigorously, trying to get a glimpse of what it could be.

Santi only had to wait a moment before she saw, charging straight towards her, two massive gray beasts. They were unfamiliar to her, larger than an elephant but smaller than a whale. They had giraffe-like necks and four fins the shape of Amphitrite's, but no less than five times as large. Massive tails protruded from their backsides, and their eyes were as large as her head. They swam promptly towards

Rogan's beckoning, these large aquatic… dinosaurs? The beasts seemed so familiar, but what were they? She felt she should cringe and hide as they charged at her, but she trusted that Rogan would not put her in harm's way.

Once the mythical beasts were about six feet in front of them, the animals reined in and waited patiently, looking monstrous and harmless at the same time.

Santi was about to ask what these strange creatures were when it hit her and she shouted out with her Ku as her mouth fell into a gaping "O" shape. "Loch Ness Monsters?!"

Rogan burst out a quick, loud laugh like a gunshot before becoming consumed by a fit of hysteria, rolling through the water and clutching his sides. When he finally regained his composure enough to speak, he laughingly teased her, "Loch Ness Monsters!"

Santi seethed at his response and once again hated that she was embarrassed by her Crural-ness.

Rogan sensed her annoyance and quickly pulled himself together.

"These are cryptids!" he said, and then hastily added, "I do love Crural-lore. I think you should be a Thaed. You could really help Serras to learn about Crurals." He spoke in a tone that was informative and encouraging without a hint of condescension. "They are going to take us on our trip so speedily you will never desire an airplane again. Come here and meet them. They are quite gentle."

Rogan placed his hand on the small of her back and ushered her over to the nearest of the two creatures.

Her resolve to be upset with him faded the instant she touched the animal. The back of its neck was firm and rough without being coarse—just like Amphitrite's—but the underside of its neck and belly was as smooth and soft as a dolphin's skin.

"Oh Rogan! They are beautiful!"

"Hop on."

He ushered her to an almost comically small leather saddle fastened at the nape of the animal's neck.

"There you go. Scoot up as close as you can. Keep your head directly behind its neck and the speed will not bother you."

He began fastening cords around her waist and her legs until she was veritably tied onto the animal and entirely at its mercy.

"And make sure you stay strapped in. This is going to be very fast."

She was so excited to be riding this beast and to see another factual manifestation of mythology, that she couldn't help but ask.

"Rogan," she said his name in a scolding manner, daring him to tease her next questions. But her tone quickly changed to childlike wonder. "I cannot believe these are real! But I thought these were lake monsters?"

"They come from a lake in the NorMer clan. They are bred and hatched there, and if it were not for Serra meddling, they would probably stay. But cryptids enjoy the open ocean. You'll see why in just a minute."

"What else is real? What else exists that we silly humans only think are legend and lore? What about krakens? Or kappas? And is the Lady of the Lake a real thing? How about the Bermuda Triangle; what's the deal with that?"

She had never even thought to ask about these things as a child—even if she had known the folklore then—and now she wanted all of her curiosity answered.

Before she could ask about more, he laughed again.

"Santi, the Bermuda Triangle? But how can you even ask! You know where the Sirens moved once Anthemoessa was reclaimed by the Sentinels."

Before she had a chance to process what his answer meant, her cryptid took off at such a breakneck speed it was all she could do to hold on.

# *Chapter 7*

## Carmen

Late into the afternoon, Carmen and Santiago continued to sit on the beach and talk. It had been hours since their initial meeting that morning, and he enchanted her. His voice calmed her like the waves, his smile was beautiful and freely given, and his mind was so sharp and open to learning everything. She taught him about being a Serra, and he listened, enthralled, and asked questions sincerely. He was reassuringly amiable, a soothing companion. Carmen felt things were going so well that surely she could bring up her purpose in finding him—disregarding Samir's advice. She knew he was the sort of person who would rise to the challenge. She assured herself that at the next lull in their conversation, she would promptly tell him how important he was to her world. She would tell him how desperately they needed his help.

But a lull never came.

"And you Crurals actually go to see this giant talking mouse?" Carmen asked, laughing incredulously when he told her the concept of amusement parks. Their conversation had trailed so far away from her purpose that they were talking about cartoons and anamorphic animals. She didn't even care.

"It seems as though we do." He laughed at the absurdity of it. "I've never been, but maybe some day."

There was hardly a moment's respite from their easy conversation and uninhibited laughter. When there was a break in the merriment, it was only for profound stillness. At these times, their words held so much meaning, their stares intense, as if nothing could be more important than the feelings they were relaying in that very moment. Through it all, his Ku was never devious or disguised. Carmen knew he wouldn't know how to conceal an ulterior motive in his Ku even if he wanted to, but he never had a moment of insincerity. Carmen had never met another being with as much depth of spirit or conviction of truth. This was a man to be prized.

She would tell him of the plan soon. Soon. But not yet.

"You know, for two people who come from completely different worlds, we have more in common than any two people I have ever known," Santiago said to her that evening as the sun began to sink below the horizon.

"I would never have believed it," she nearly sighed. She had worried that speaking Spanish all day would be difficult, as it was the language she was least familiar with;

but with Santiago, she felt she could easily talk to him with no language at all.

It was true they were very similar: both from families of two children—though Santiago was the only living one now—both raised by other family members after their parents' death, both working for the protection of their people—he being in the military for his country. He was dedicated to the things he set his sights on.

He told her about one of his passions that truly confused her.

"You volunteer with Crurals who do not have homes?" she asked.

"Yes, it is difficult to see them struggling, but I try to help in any way I can by providing meals and clothes and job interviews. Just anything that is needed from me."

"But what I am struggling to understand is why they do not have a shelter? The community does not make them one? Or give them one that is not being used?"

Santiago looked at her and sighed. "That would be ideal. If only we selfish humans were as gracious as Serras."

From anyone else, his words might have sounded condescending or sarcastic, but he genuinely wanted his people to be better than what they were.

Carmen scrunched up her face as she thought. "You genuinely care about your fellow man." She smiled at him, but inside she felt a pang of guilt. She could feel his heart was free of any secrets or ulterior motives, whereas she was sitting before him under false pretenses.

"Of course we cannot walk around thinking only of ourselves," he said.

Carmen nodded. She never thought of herself, only of the ocean full of Serras who counted on her and the job she was doing. She couldn't let fondness for him distract her from her purpose. He was a nobody among Crurals, just an average soldier; but to the Serras, he was everything. Carmen had gone so far as to promise her commander to sacrifice him in an effort to get what they wanted. She had to realign her thinking with that goal.

"So you do not have any family left alive," Carmen said, consolingly. "I am truly sorry to hear that."

Secretly, she saw this as a good sign. Hopefully, it would make him more inclined to leave the Crural world behind and help her cause.

"I do not have any blood relatives, it's true. But I don't feel like that means I don't have family," he said with a good-natured smile and true happiness in his Ku. "I have a very significant network of friends. They are important to me, and we are really like family. For many of us, we only have each other. We support one another just as any family would."

Carmen was a little disheartened to hear that he would have to give up so many he cared for, but it made her fondness for him grow. He had so many more people that loved and cared for him than she did. She was reminded again just how single-minded she had been her whole life.

Suddenly, Jolene was standing above them, dripping wet, smiling broadly. Carmen hadn't seen her since this morning when she arrived with Santiago. Upon seeing her youthful face and carefree spirit, Samir had quickly whisked her away.

# Surface Tension

"And who are you?" Samir had proclaimed, charming her with his sincere interest.

"I'm Jolene, Carmen's assistant," she answered, kneeling down next to him, full of interest and spunk. "She didn't tell me about you."

"That was very rude of her," he said in mock anger. "I could use an assistant, too."

Samir took Jolene's hand in his as he scooted towards the surf.

"Come with me. I will teach you how to breathe water."

"Far out," she said with wide eyes.

Carmen hadn't seen a hair of her since. Now, as she saw Jolene standing there, soaked to the bone, her eyes dancing, Carmen knew she had spent the day under the influence of Samir's ardent charm.

"I'll see you tomorrow, Carmen," Jolene said without really looking at anything in particular, and then she made her way absentmindedly up the beach and out of sight.

"I had better go," Carmen said, breaking out of the delusion she had allowed to consume her all day.

Seeing Jolene's dreamy state had made her realize how foolish she had been, and it snapped her back to reality. What was she doing? More importantly, what had her conversations with Samir done to her? She knew Samir's ways of drifting freely through the ocean and couldn't let his influence cause problems for her plan. She was doing much more important things here.

"I would really like to see you again," Santiago said to her with genuine interest. "And you still haven't told me the purpose for meeting with me. Don't get me wrong, I am so happy to have been chosen but your assistant said you needed an... ambassador. How can I help?"

*Oh great Nephira!* Carmen cursed to herself. She had forgotten all about Jolene's ruse. "Oh, well... You see, throughout time Serras have always relied on a worthy Crural to keep the secret of our existence so that if we ever have need of help from above, we have someone to rely on."

Her answer caught her by surprise. She wasn't used to lying, but spending so much time above water had slowly made her accustomed to the deed.

"We hope we can count on you to help our cause..." She was just rambling on in Jolene-type fashion. It sounded asinine, "...should we ever need you to act on our behalf. Or to... help us in any way..."

*Oh just stop talking*, she scolded herself.

He fervently responded, "Of course I will!"

She wasn't sure if he believed her explanation or was merely captivated by her, willing to do whatever she asked, but she wanted to move on.

"Why do you need me?" he asked, dashing her hopes of changing the subject. "Surely your assistant could do that for you."

"She is capable, yes. Well, tradition dictates that it be a man. And one in a position of authority."

She knew the last part was a mistake, and saying that somehow a man was more capable than a woman did not sit well with her. It was something that a small sect of Serras believed, but they were rare and generally regarded with revulsion. Sure enough, Santiago challenged her.

"I am hardly in a position of authority. And I cannot say that in matters of your world I would be any more capable than a woman."

"You qualify, being in the military for your country. But more than that, your heart is pure and you have good intentions."

She was becoming irritated with herself for not having better answers and irritated with him for challenging her. The haze of the brilliant day was shattering all around her.

He seemed to accept her answer and was silent for a moment.

"Will I be able to see you again? Before you have need of my... services?"

Carmen was brought back under his spell. "I would like that very much," she answered honestly.

But she was instantly filled with conflicting emotions. She wanted to see him again for selfish reasons but knew the next time they met she would have to bring him down to do the Serras' dirty work. She truly wished to see him again to have another evening just like tonight.

"I will be away for a while but we can meet again in two weeks. Here on this very beach. Will that be possible for you?" she asked him.

"Yes, I can be back. I don't live far," he said. "I can come as often as you'd like."

He was too eager. He liked her, she knew. That would make things easier for her, but her conscience was nagging at the back of her mind. It was not like Serras to be so devious and misleading. She had not been raised like this. Her stomach churned wildly. She had to remove herself. This meeting should have taken an hour instead of an entire evening. The stars were bright in the sky now. When did that happen?

"Ok, I must go. I have a long distance to travel, but I will see you in two weeks."

She began scooting herself towards the water, but the tide had lowered so much that she had much further to go than when Jolene had set up their rendezvous spot.

"Please allow me to help you," Santiago said as he leaned down and effortlessly scooped her up. He smelled like sun and ocean air. Carmen closed her eyes as she breathed him in before snapping herself to attention.

"Gracias," Carmen muttered weakly as he set her in the surf.

"It is my pleasure."

They sat silently for a moment, neither knowing what to say next. Over six hours of endless conversation, and now they were precipitously incapable of speech.

He rose slowly to his feet and gingerly took a step backwards, but then he came back and took her hand in his earnestly.

"Adios, Carmen." He looked deep into her eyes and said genuinely, "It was a pleasure to meet you."

Abruptly, Carmen forgot how to speak Spanish. Portuguese came to her, then English, but she was tongue-tied and flustered. All she could muster was a brief, "Adios, Santiago."

She did not sleep that night. She needed rest for the next day's journey, but sleep eluded her. She ran her fingers through the seaweed—a habit she had started as a pup when she couldn't sleep—and tried to focus on her goals. Tomorrow she would make her way to Daris, and three days after that she would be reporting good news about a brilliant man whom they could sacrifice for their cause. And then the ocean would be safe. And she would be happy. Samir would be very proud of her for finding happiness.

But somehow she didn't feel right. Her plan was brilliant when they assumed the Heir would be a terrible man. She had imagined Tullus's vile genes magnified by thousands of years of evil breeding, coupled with the notion that most Crurals were devious to begin with. But Santiago was the farthest thing from it.

She had to think of a new plan. Maybe she could convince Santiago to come down for the greater good. Maybe he would be allowed to train with the Sentinels and fight against Zitja. Maybe he didn't need to die for this cause. Maybe it was possible that he didn't need to be a sacrifice. He was strong and capable. It was possible...

No Crural had ever been a Sentinel before, but that didn't mean it couldn't happen. He was already a soldier.

Carmen finally drifted to sleep that night determined to have her kelp and eat it too.

"Carmen, how did it go with the Crural? Will we be able to entice him to the water's edge and entrap him? Have you gained his confidence?"

*Now is the time.*

"Terret, I think we will be able to do better than that. He appears to be a duty-bound man. He is a Sentinel, of sorts, for his people. I think that if we were to tell him what he can do for us, he would be eager to help. Just think how much more effective it would be if, instead of capturing him, he came on his own free will and was trained to fight. He could be a useful part of our army against Zitja."

She felt Terret's Ku practically assault her with anger at being challenged.

"That is not the plan, and it is not your responsibility to create a plan. Your job was to find him and get him to a place where we can trap him. From there we will take over."

"Why can it not be the plan? We can make a new one," Carmen suggested with authority, though she was feeling her resolve weakening the more Terret opposed her.

"I cannot change the entire Sentinel strategy at a whim. These things take a long time to put into place. Besides, what do we care for this Crural? He is nothing."

Carmen felt her frustration mounting. Surely, he was being adamant because he felt he knew best but she also thought she knew best.

"As a Sentinel, I feel that we are better suited-"

"You forget yourself. You are not a Sentinel."

She was speechless. How could he throw that in her face after all these years? It was true that after Daristor she had gone through Sentinel training, but when she decided she wanted to find Tullus's heir, she was told that was not the job of a Sentinel. She was made to train for the Opus of Thaed and work as a liaison between the Serras and the Crurals. She never dreamed they would take away her position as a Sentinel.

"I was under the impression that I acted as both! All I did as a Thaed I did for the Sentinels."

"And the Sentinels thank you for your work. Once you have brought him to the water, however, your job is done. Now, have you gained his trust? Will you be able to get him to the water so that we can bring him down?"

"Yes, I believe he will do whatever I ask of him."

"Excellent."

"But I think that-"

"What you think does not matter," said another Sentinel in the room that Carmen didn't know. "You have done your work, Thaed."

"I'm just-"

"Thank you, Carmen," Terret said in a tone of finality. "We will be leaving in two days' time. I trust you will be ready to leave with us?"

She hung her head in defeat. "Yes, of course."

"Excellent."

Carmen turned to leave the room, and as she did, Terret stopped her.

"I hope you know that we value all of the work you have done for us. When this is over, we welcome you to train as a Sentinel again. We can use someone with your determination and tenacity. You will be a valuable member of the team."

"Thank you,"she responded, as though the statement had a question mark at the end of it.

Carmen closed the thick marble door behind her and leaned heavily on the knob. She never imagined that they would not allow her to follow through after all the work she had done.

Carmen was boiling with rage as she floated down the hallway, but by the time she left the building and swam through the golden streets, her anger had turned to confusion and frustration.

When she arrived at the small dwelling where she stayed when she was in Daris, Carmen had finally resigned herself to the facts. It was Serra law, put in place for the safety of the people, that non-Sentinels could not perform duties of a Sentinel. Nor could they purposefully put themselves into harm's way where the Sirens were concerned. Ocean Mother Pilou had put that law in place at the beginning of her rule fifty years ago when many vigilante Serras tried to seek vengeance after the death of loved ones. They were untrained, susceptible to the Song, and ultimately perished in their attempts at revenge.

Carmen sighed again.

She was the key to all of this unfolding. The Serras were still relying on her. And Terret had said that they were not ungrateful. It was just duty. Right? She would not let them down because her feelings had been hurt. The moment Santiago was in the hands of the Sentinels, she would begin training again. Surely they wouldn't make her redo the entire Sentinel training. She could probably be ready in enough time to help them defeat Zitja. She was sure of it. They wouldn't make her sit idly by after all she had done for them. This had been her ultimate goal. The thing she had wanted her entire life. She couldn't let soft feelings stop her from saving her people. No, she would bring Santiago down to the water and she could still be a hero for that, if nothing else.

Carmen was sitting in the big room of her family home in the Najilian a week later. Samir was languidly sprawled on a cushion in the main room while Jolene kneeled next to him anxiously.

# Surface Tension

"I do not understand!" Carmen exclaimed in utter disbelief. "When did this happen? How?"

Jolene jumped to her feet at Carmen's response.

"Are you mad, Carmen?" Jolene implored. "Please tell me you aren't mad. I couldn't stand it if you were!"

Jolene's concern softened Carmen's response.

"Of course I'm not mad. I know the nature of Bonding."

If it weren't right, it wouldn't happen. A Bonding only occurred when both Kus knew they belonged with the other without any doubt or hesitation. Carmen's smile was reluctant at first, but slowly she allowed it to become genuine pleasure for her friends.

"I am just surprised, that's all. It seems so sudden."

Serra and Crural Bonding was not unheard of. True, it wasn't very common, since there were strict laws prohibiting Crural contact, but it wasn't forbidden. Carmen was sure that amongst Crural Guardians the practice was more common than Ocean Mother Pilou would prefer, but even still, it was a blessed union.

Samir pulled Jolene back down to share the cushion with him and wrapped his hands around hers.

"It was sudden," he responded, as if it had surprised him, too. "When you left to report back to Daris, I met Jolene on the beach that very same day. We were Bound the instant we connected. We've been waiting for you to get back to tell you the news."

Carmen thought back to the morning she had left and considered the timeline.

"You were Bound after knowing each other for one day? That rarely happens."

"It rarely happens," Samir agreed, "but it does happen. You know what is said."

"'The quicker the Bond,'" Carmen and Samir repeated together, "the truer the Ku.'"

Carmen made a face of disgust. She always thought it was a stupid saying. A way for youth to boast the legitimacy of their love to parents who worried about their age. But Samir was older than Carmen—if but only by a year or two—and Jolene... Jolene had only just learned how to use her Ku the day before her Bonding.

"I am truly happy for you both!" Carmen said, and she meant it. She had often harassed her friend about his free-spirited ways, telling him to meet a nice Serra and enjoy what Binding had to offer, as hypocritical as it was for her to say.

"We just wanted to say goodbye before we leave to see Samir's family in the Tipua." Jolene said as she wrapped her arms around Carmen, a gesture that was unfamiliar to the Serra, but after a moment of uncomfortable rigidity, she relaxed and found it rather pleasant.

"I feel like we have turned into old friends, and I will miss you!"

"I will miss you too, Jolene," Carmen said.

She had grown used to this odd, energetic girl and would truly miss conversing with her.

"If you will be taking up permanent residence in the ocean, then we shall see each other often. But how did you make such a decision? What about your family in Massachusetts? What about Wellsy?"

Carmen tried hard to remember the names of all of the things Jolene talked about—but the truth was the girl said a lot. Most of it was foreign words and proper names, which made it extremely hard to follow.

"You finally remembered the word Massachusetts!" Jolene said, as if she was proud of a child. "But I graduated from Wellesley last spring," she added with a laugh. "I think my family will do fine without me," Jolene said as a shadow crossed her Ku.

Carmen decided to let the issue go. Even amongst Serras, whose Kus were open and honest and who held the best intentions for each other, sometimes relationships between parents and their pups went astray. It was best for Carmen to focus on the positive. It wasn't her place to lecture about decorum.

"I am so glad it will all work out for you. It is truly wonderful that you two found happiness."

Samir and Jolene got up to leave, and as they did so, Samir placed his hand on Carmen's heart. She returned the gesture.

"Carmen, my oldest friend, please allow your heart to fill with warmth and find happiness for yourself."

Carmen wanted to be offended, but she knew that she had allowed her heart to grow cold over the years, and she couldn't remember the last time she had felt the kind of happiness he spoke of.

"Amicus," he said with the typical Serra word of greeting and departure.

"Amicus," she replied, filled with love and good wishes for their future.

She waved to them from the opening of her shelter, and as they faded from view, she held them in her Ku for as far as she could reach. When, finally, they had swum too far away, she lost the connection and sat quietly in her own reverie, absorbed in all that had just transpired. Their departure left her feeling lonelier in her small shelter than when she had first arrived.

Carmen continued thinking about Samir's urging to warm her heart as she sat alone in her home throughout the next week. Finally, Carmen was jolted from her reverie and swore to herself.

*Nephira almighty!*

She would have to warm up her heart later. It had reached the time to follow through with the plot, and she would need a cold, cold heart to do her job.

Carmen flicked her tail, and in only a few strokes, she reached the surface still yards away from the beach. Santiago was already there, waiting for her. He smiled brightly when he saw her and gave a giant wave of his arm over his head as if she might miss him sitting there, the only person on the whole beach.

Unexpectedly, Carmen's stomach tightened up and fluttered as if it were full of guppies. She attributed her reaction to the task set before her. She convinced herself she was nervous about pulling off the plan flawlessly and worried about Terret's wrath if she didn't; in the back of her mind, however, she knew her heart fluttered for a different reason.

She took the time to watch Santiago as she made her way to the shore. The beach was completely void of people—as it always was, which is why Jolene had chosen this beach in the first place—but even if it had been brimming with people, she only had eyes for him.

# *Surface Tension*

He was a striking tan figure against the clear blue sky. He wore a simple white button-up shirt left open at the collar, and tan shorts, and stood barefooted with his sandals in his hand. She connected to his Ku and felt his heart racing with excitement to see her. He had an aura of pleasure surrounding his Ku and a sincere interest in her. She felt guilty for knowing so much about his private feelings when he knew nothing of hers. Serras did not often have to discuss feelings in-depth with one another because their Kus were exposed before each other. She felt one-sided. She had an advantage over him, and he didn't even know he was vulnerable.

But she was here on business, she reminded herself. Her Ku was more devious than congenial, and she was very happy that he couldn't connect to her. If he had known how to use his Ku, she would be exposed and everything would be ruined.

Finally, she was close enough and she raised her arm high in the air and shouted, "Hola, Santiago."

He responded the same way and ran over to greet her in the surf. He was there by the time she hoisted herself onto the sand, and he knelt down, wrapping his arms around her in a firm embrace. Carmen stiffened for just a moment, but instantly liked it better even than when Jolene had done the same thing. If this was a Crural custom, she could quickly get used to it.

"I'm sorry," he said. "I shouldn't have hugged you. I was just so pleased to see you, and it's been so long since the last time we were together. It seemed natural."

"It's ok. It was nice. The hugged."

He laughed, and she could tell she had said something foolish, but he didn't correct her.

"I had an idea," he offered with a glimmer of mischief in his eye. "I thought we could do something today."

"Do something?"

This threw her off guard. The thing they were to *do* was to turn him over to the Sentinels. At this very moment, the Sentinels were getting in place so that they could ensnare Santiago as soon as Carmen brought him to the meeting point.

Her curiosity—and the warmth she felt in his Ku—overpowered her better judgment, however.

"What shall we do?" she asked.

Santiago's already smiling face broke into a larger grin, "Well, I thought I would show you around. I bet you have never come far on land. We are having a carnival in my neighborhood I think you would enjoy. Come, I've got it all arranged."

"Oh, um." What was she supposed to say? *I'm sorry, but you are due to be taken prisoner in less than an hour.*

"Is it far?" she asked instead.

"It's not far. You will have a wonderful time, and if you don't we can do whatever you want tomorrow."

Tomorrow? Tomorrow they would be on their way to Daris.

"I have to remain hidden. I cannot show myself to other Crurals."

"I have an idea for that, too," he said with a twinkle in his eyes.

# Surface Tension

She was torn. She had always wanted to know what life was like on land. A carnival, what was that? Instantly, she wanted to know what it was, and she wanted to see everything she had ever heard about. Streets, cars, dogs, and the food. Carmen loved everything Jolene had brought to eat at their meetings—so much so that the girl had taken to bringing food specifically for Carmen to try.

Carmen wanted to see and do it all. She could easily spend a few hours with Santiago on land and then bring him under water without causing much trouble. She would just tell Terret it was harder to lure the Heir to the location than she thought. It would all work out perfectly. She could see this carnival and be a hero to her people all in one day.

Carmen was about to tell him that she would go to the carnival with him, but he had already picked her up and was walking up the beach with her in his arms.

# Chapter 8

## Carmen

Carmen peeked her tiny eight-year-old head above the water but stayed behind a boulder. She was still ten feet from the shore—plenty of distance to be safe, but close enough to get a glimpse of the Crurals. She could get in serious trouble for even being above the surface. Ocean Mother Pilou was very strict about Serras making contact with Crurals. Especially pups. Any Serra who had not finished Daris was absolutely forbidden from coming anywhere close to the shore. But Carmen didn't care; she had an idea and wanted to see it through.

Carmen shimmied herself around the rock, hugging herself to it as closely as possible. The Crural pups were all delightedly distracted in their games, so she ventured a little closer. After a short pause to make sure no one noticed her, Carmen kicked herself under water and spanned the remaining distance swiftly. She stayed in the water but brought her head and shoulders up to the level of the other children. The water was murky enough today that she was sure she looked just like the rest of them, and she watched on in awe. The Crurals were running around and shouting, carefree in their youth. Envy washed over her as she watched their nonsense games take place. She had always felt older than children her age. She had witnessed so much at such a young age. Since her grandfather had been killed last year, she hadn't felt much like playing, and her heart felt burdened.

That's why she had the idea to find the Heir. Grown Serras were always talking about the Heir of Tullus and how that was the only person who could kill Zitja and finish the Sirens. Carmen thought it absurd that no one ever came to find this Crural. It seemed so simple: go on land, pretend to be a Crural, ask one of them to go get the Heir of Tullus, and bring him or her down to kill Zitja. Carmen didn't understand why no one would do it. Was it because of Ocean Mother Pilou's strict law? Carmen didn't care about laws when killing Zitja was so much more important.

Carmen looked around and found a girl about her size who wasn't consumed in a game at the moment. That was the girl Carmen would ask about Tullus. She had a smart enough look to her and didn't have her finger in her nose or anything, like Carmen had seen some of the filthier kids doing. She kicked her tail once in the girl's direction when a large rainbow colored ball landed in the water next to her shoulder.

"Hey! Throw it here."

Carmen looked at the ball bobbing in the water innocently. It was beautiful and bright and very enticing. Carmen picked it up and threw it to the boy, who caught it deftly. After passing the ball on to another child, he yelled to Carmen, "Want to play with us?"

Before she could answer, the friend threw the ball to Carmen, and she caught it with a small jump. Eyes wide, she looked around to see if the boys had noticed her scales. Her hegira was only now approaching her bellybutton, but she still had plenty of golden scales scattered along her lower ribs. It would be many more years before she would have an adolescent body with smooth skin down her stomach and back. The boys didn't seem to notice or care. She threw the ball back to them, getting lost in the game and forgetting all about her purpose for going to the surface.

Carmen rolled her eyes at the memory—an action she had picked up from Jolene. She had a habit of being distracted by the goings on of Crurals. They had always fascinated her. Maybe it was the idea of a world free of Sirens and the heartache she had ceaselessly experienced as a Serra. Land seemed so free of trouble to her. It was a utopia in her mind, and this day with Santiago had only proved this point further.

The carnival was a bit chaotic—as to be expected—but when a large Crural man bumped into her and jostled her in the wheelchair Santiago used to usher her around, he apologized profusely and tried to make amends to the point of excess. She had also felt Santiago's Ku burst with protection for her over the incident. By all accounts, the incident was harmless and inconsequential, yet everyone involved was so concerned for her. The memory made her smile. So far, she hadn't met any Crurals who were horrible like the stories suggested they would be.

# Surface Tension

Santiago lowered Carmen to the water, kneeling in the surf, his pants getting soaked by the waves.

"I had a wonderful time with you, Carmen."

"So did I," she responded honestly.

Santiago had been so attentive all day, interested in the things she had to say, and determined to show her what being a Crural was like. She had felt safe with him. Safe and accepted and fascinating and beautiful. It was a wonderful change from working nonstop and ignoring herself as she had always done.

As the day of fun was winding down, Santiago had looked at her with an idea brightening his eyes.

"I want to show you something," he said, clasping her hand in his.

This wasn't the first time today he'd proclaimed this. As if on a mission, Santiago tried to show her all things Crural during her one day ashore. She nodded, and he wheeled her up to a giant white circle shooting into the sky. They were ushered right on. Santiago was very careful to keep her tail hidden, choosing to pick her up himself and place her carefully in the seat. As he tucked in her blanket and rearranged her fin he whispered, "Did that hurt your tail?"

"No," she smiled at him, "not at all."

Santiago hopped into the seat beside her. She had a moment's panic when a bar covered their laps and they were ostensibly locked in a cage, but Santiago didn't seem worried, and she had seen people coming and going from the contraptions with pleasure in their Kus.

As she was recovering from her alarm, the wheel began to creak, and their seat swung slightly, startling her again at the odd sensation. It took a while to understand Santiago's excitement for this giant white wheel, but as more people boarded and they rose higher and higher, Carmen's chest and head felt light.

"We can see…" She didn't know distances on land exactly; they felt different than underwater. "Forever."

Santiago pointed ahead of them.

"That way is the Caribbean, and past that the United States. Back that way," he shifted in his seat to look over his left shoulder, "is Brazil and the end of South America."

"Oh!" Carmen exclaimed, "I am from the coast of Brazil."

"You are?" he asked in Portuguese. "That is so lovely."

Carmen's heart felt like it stopped. She didn't often get to speak her native language, and it sounded wonderful to her.

"You speak Portuguese?"

"Only a little." Then he laughed and continued in Spanish. "I'm not very good. It makes me self-conscious."

"It was perfect."

At that moment, their cart reached the top of the wheel, and Carmen exclaimed in awe.

"We can see everything!"

She leaned forward to soak it all in, and Santiago grabbed her shoulders as the cart began to swing.

"Be careful."

He wasn't upset, but he didn't move his arms from her shoulders either.

# Surface Tension

Santiago said goodbye to her as she scooted into the water.

"Meet me here tomorrow?" he asked.

Before she could respond, he leaned over and kissed her gently on the lips. It was soft and warm but over so quickly that when he pulled away, she leaned into him and kissed him again. This time, the kiss was longer and fuller, and she was so overcome by the feeling of his pounding Ku that when they finished she was shaky.

"Yes, I'll be here first thing in the morning," she answered without thinking.

"Good night, Carmen," Santiago said, but didn't make a move to leave.

"Good night, Santiago."

She knew she had to get away and think straight, but couldn't make herself reenter the water just yet.

Finally, Santiago stood and slowly walked away backwards, not breaking eye contact, until eventually he turned away. Carmen let out her breath slowly. She was going to have to answer for her actions and as Santiago walked further away, her head began to clear.

She had been gone with Santiago all day and couldn't even imagine what the repercussions were going to be for her. Terret did not accept excuses for failure. She thought about yelling after Santiago, urging him to follow her home this instant, but she was hours late for the rendezvous time, and knew she would have to face Terret's wrath alone and try again tomorrow.

She sighed and kicked herself swiftly towards the temporary Sentinel encampment. As she swam to meet

Terret, a million plausible excuses ran through her mind, but she knew there was no way for her to lie. Her Ku would give her away. She had never trained herself to be dishonest; nor did she want to. She would have to tell him the truth, or some version of it. But what would that be?

She couldn't very well say that the man destined to save their whole population had put her in a wheeled chair, wrapped her tail up in a blanket, pulled a shirt over her head, and pushed her into town looking like a Crural woman. She definitely couldn't tell them about all of his Crural friends she had met and how Santiago had paid her so much attention amongst the other women that she was sure she felt jealousy in their Kus.

The Crural emotions were the most conflicting and bewildering part of the day. Crurals harbored so many unspoken resentments and harsh feelings that Carmen could have become lost in the rolling tide of hidden human emotions if she had allowed her Ku to remain open to it all. She felt envy and anger from a woman who was giving Carmen a compliment; she felt desire from a man while he pointedly avoided eye contact as he took their money for a game. How did Crurals not go mad from all of the insincerity?

Carmen kicked herself further and further away from the beach. She had much bigger problems to deal with than the duplicitous moods of Crurals. She was going to have to answer for her actions. What was she going to say?

What *could* she say?

Would she tell the commander of the Sentinels that this morning their would-be savior had picked her up and put her on something called a *ride,* where she spun and spun in circles until she thought she would revisit the thing called an *empanada*, which she hadn't originally understood was food but now wished she could have another one of?

She swam up to their designated meeting point to find one lone Sentinel waiting for her, a grim and determined look on his face.

"Carmen, Terret is waiting for you. I will bring you to him."

His greeting was so cold that she knew she was going to be made to regret her day spent on land. But how could she regret such a wonderful day?

As they swam to where Terret had made camp while in the Najilian, Carmen thought about the last twelve hours. Never before had she felt more life flowing through her veins. Until today, she hadn't realized that she had been sad. She had thought she was happy—at least, happy enough. She had been angry and miserable about her parents' death, but she had never known that she wasn't happy. Spending the day—just one day—with Santiago had awoken so many emotions in her that she hadn't known she was missing. Her heart felt frantic and overwhelmed. She started sweating as her heart raced unexpectedly. It was terrifying to experience so many new emotions all at once, but, now that she knew them, she never wanted to be without them.

As they made their way around a giant boulder, Carmen saw the Sentinel camp sprawling along the ocean floor. Her heart dropped into her stomach, and for the first time, she felt true fear at seeing Terret. He had always caused her to feel anxious and intimidated, but this was the first time she was overcome by actual panic.

"I don't have to tell you that you are twelve hours late in returning, and that you appear to be empty handed," Terret said condescendingly to her when she arrived. "Unless you have him tucked away in your loincloth somewhere?"

She knew the question was rhetorical, but she couldn't help responding.

"No, I did not bring him down."

"And why not?"

"I…"

She faltered. There was no way to lie without him knowing. She hadn't trained with the Sentinels long enough to know how to communicate HaruKu, not that it mattered. The second she closed her connection and spoke to him, he'd know she was being deceitful.

"I was not able to bring him down."

It wasn't a lie.

"There was not an opportunity."

Again, not a lie.

"Carmen! You cannot wait around for an opportunity. You make one."

"I-"

She didn't know how to explain herself, but she didn't have to as he interrupted her.

"I need to know if I can count on you. Carmen, be honest with me. Are your emotions compromised?" He paused for only a half a second before he began again. "Because if so, you will face consequences."

He might have been vague about what the "consequences" were, but the Serra, Yron, who had escorted Carmen to Terret, felt it his duty to tell her the details of her consequences.

"If you are protecting this Crural, you will take full responsibility for delivering our people to Zitja."

Carmen was stunned; had her Ku betrayed her to these bucks? Could they feel that her Ku was starting to—as Terret said—become compromised?

"You are as good as choosing him over the safety of your fellow Serras. Is that what you are doing? Are you that selfish?" Yron continued.

The things he said were so wildly inaccurate that Carmen was furious. Zitja had been alive for thousands of years; Carmen had only found the Heir a little over two weeks ago. She would not be blamed for delivering her people to Zitja! Fury consumed her.

"No!"

"It sure seems like it. Your weak female heart cannot resist a handsome face and would rather sentence your people to death. You are pathetic."

"That is enough, Yron," Terret said before turning to Carmen.

Carmen shook her head as if to clear away her feelings for Santiago and Yron's hostility.

"No! I can do it."

She did not appreciate Yron's accusations, and her anger pushed the memory of the day on land from her mind. *My life's work*, she reminded herself. Carmen focused on the reason she had arranged this all in the first place.

"Give me another chance. I will bring him here tomorrow first thing." She took in a breath that puffed her chest slightly. " I can do it. I will not let our people down."

Terret seemed skeptical, but Carmen's heart was raging with anger and pride. Maybe Yron was right about her being a girl full of folly today, but it would not happen again.

"I will bring him down here and we will use him for Zitja's undoing."

She believed everything she had said, and she knew Terret knew it.

"Ok, go. We will follow through tomorrow. If you fail, you will not get another chance. If it is discovered that you are protecting him at the risk of the lives of all the Serras in the ocean..." He trailed off, leaving Carmen to imagine her consequences.

Carmen left his presence as hastily as she could without looking like she was already a fugitive on the run. Why did Terret have to make her so nervous? More importantly, why was she standing in her own way from bringing Santiago down? This is what she had been seeking her whole life, and now she was at great risk of ruining everything she had worked for.

Carmen scolded herself and tried to calm her racing heart.

She returned to her shelter with her heart hammering in her ears. Carmen knew what it meant for a Serra to collude with anyone who put the Serra way of life at risk: trial. If she were found guilty: imprisonment. While it was most common for a Serra to stand trial and be imprisoned for assisting Sirens, Carmen was sure they could easily make a case against her for withholding the man who could defeat Zitja.

Carmen sat on the beach early the next morning as the sun was just making its first shimmering marks on the water.

# Surface Tension

She squinted out into the sunlight, practicing her speech. She knew exactly what she would say to bring him under the surface, and she was sure it would be simple.

Barely a few moments passed before she saw him jogging along the sand towards her. And when he knelt in front of her, he wrapped his arms around her and planted a passionate kiss on her lips. Her stomach took flight with a confusing combination of pleasure and angst. When he pulled away, she put on an over-the-top smile that couldn't quite make its way to her eyes.

For the hundredth time, she was glad that he couldn't feel her Ku as she said, "Santiago! Yesterday we spent a wonderful day on land, and I learned so much about your culture."

She rushed on before she lost her nerve.

"Today I want to take you under water and show you all about my culture." She beamed at him like a woman in love, hoping to convince him that she was.

"Oh, no. No, I can't," he responded calmly.

Carmen's smile fell instantly, as if the corners of her mouth were too heavy to hold up anymore.

"What?"

"I cannot go under the water with you. I won't. I am so sorry. We can spend the day on the beach, though." He said the last sentence with hope.

"Santiago… I do not understand."

Carmen was a little hurt by his rejection, but mostly she was feeling angry. This was her only job. "I want to show you my world."

"I'm sorry, Carmen."

She was frustrated by his lack of answers. He was giving her nothing to go on. Why wouldn't he come under water with her?

Suddenly it dawned on her.

"You will be able to breathe! I'll show you. If you are worried about drowning, you will not. I promise."

"No, it's not that. I just can't." He looked truly sorry.

Carmen began to panic. She could *not* return empty handed today. Not again. "Santiago. I do not understand. Why?"

"I just can't. I'm sorry. I just can't."

"SANTIAGO!" Carmen yelled, her desperation rising. "Do you not care about me at all? Do you not want to learn about me and my world? Are you so selfish?"

She was the one being selfish, she knew, but this was her whole life's work. He was ruining everything for her.

"Carmen," his voice was gentle but she could tell he was losing patience with her. "You are also being selfish. I cannot go into the water."

And that's when she felt it. He was doing a great job of hiding it deep in his Ku—even though he was unaware of his Ku. It was hidden even from himself.

"You are scared," Carmen accused. "Tell me the truth."

Santiago did not answer, but his silence told her all she needed to know.

"I cannot believe this! You are a grown man. Afraid of the water? Pathetic."

He made to respond, but she overrode him with her words. She had to use what tools she had, and their would-be relationship was her only weapon.

# Surface Tension

"Yesterday you made grand statements about me spending many more days with you on land and how wonderful it would be to see me again and again, yet you will not even set foot in *my* home?"

"Carmen, I'm sorry. If you only knew."

"So tell me," she said in a manner that would not have allowed anyone to feel safe sharing his feelings. "Tell me what it is that prohibits you from going in the water."

He paused and looked like he might say something before he changed his mind and said, "I can't."

"So you will not come down with me then? Not today or ever?"

"No, I'm sorry. But we could—"

But Carmen never found out what they could do. She turned and pushed herself into the ocean and swam away. She was furious, both with him and with herself. Two days in a row, she had failed to bring Santiago to Terret, and she knew she was going to pay for it. What could Santiago possibly be so scared of that he would not get in the water? Carmen was suddenly full of her own fear. Terret would punish her severely for her failure and for wasting the Sentinel's time.

Santiago was putting her in a terrible position—one that left her people in danger and her own freedom at stake. Without Santiago, there was nothing. She couldn't start over in her search for another Heir; she had to use him. She swam towards the camp, a ball of dread filling her stomach at the thought of facing Terret empty-handed.

"This is quite unnecessary," Carmen said to the Sentinel who was her guard for the journey back to Daris.

After returning empty-handed for the second time in a row, Terret had ordered her to stand trial. It would take the group three days to make their way back to Daris, and this clownfish had been made her guard for the journey.

He took his job very seriously. Even when she needed to relieve herself, he stood right by her side, and at one point even threatened to tie her up and drag her behind him. *Overzealous is what he is.*

"Am I not coming?" Carmen snapped. "I will continue to go back to Daris. You can relax."

"I never relax."

"Fun."

Since her guard was serious about his duty and would not provide her any companionship, she was left with only her thoughts to keep her company. Carmen allowed herself to drift back to the day before. She was so furious with Santiago because she had felt certain he would do anything for her. As soon as she had jumped into the water, she had regretted her actions. She knew that returning without him would be suspicious, and she would have to stand trial for conspiring against the Serra greater good. She was just as much hurt by Santiago's unwieldiness as she was afraid of Terret's reaction. But what else could she have done? There was no way to get him into the water. She couldn't very well drag him. There was no way she had enough strength for that.

She and Santiago had sat right on the brink of the water as it washed up on shore, yet she couldn't get him to get in it any further. The meeting point they had set up for him was less than a tenth of a mile away. Once they submerged themselves, she would be able to get him there. If she could just get him to go under the surface…

# Surface Tension

Carmen felt her frustration mounting. She flicked her tail aggressively as anger started to roll through her. Her gallant guard felt the shift in her mood and grabbed her around the arm. Carmen left him alone. *Let him feel like he's doing his duty,* she told herself. Her mind was preoccupied elsewhere.

How many times had Santiago gotten the bottom of his pants wet while putting her in the water, or knelt down with her as the surf washed over his legs? It was clear the water didn't burn him, yet she couldn't get him to go in further. And now she would stand trial because of his childish fears of... of what?

And then it hit her.

The answer was so obvious, she felt quite foolish for letting their trip to Daris get a day underway before thinking of it. She picked up speed with her guard holding on tightly; hopefully Terret would listen to her idea. It would be the only thing that could save her.

# Chapter 9

## Carmen

The cell was all white, just like the rest of the building—and most of the buildings in Daris. Swirls of gray in the marble walls gave Carmen something to do. Her eyes followed a strand until it disappeared. Round and round the tiny square room her eyes coasted. When that got boring, she counted the bars that ran along one wall. Twelve. As many as there had been last time she counted. And the time before that.

In the six months she had spent in her cell, she'd followed every streak of gray and counted every bar hundreds of times. Terret was putting her off on purpose. These cells were hardly ever used, and only two remained of the dozens the building had originally contained. Rarely was a Serra imprisoned for life; it just wasn't their way. Reform and penance were nearly always the punishment. She was sure the council wouldn't imprison her for life, and this was

# Surface Tension

Terret's way of punishing her anyway. She hadn't been able to speak to him before being imprisoned, so her brilliant idea was still merely an idea, and she would have to stand trial.

If she was ever allowed to finally have the trial.

During her imprisonment, Carmen had a lot of time to think. Six months was enough time for her emotions to run the gamut and finally reach clarity. In the beginning, she was angry at Santiago. His unwillingness to go in the water was ultimately what put her in prison, and she held a grudge against him for several months. Then, once her anger faded, she remembered the desire she had for him and his gentle Ku and the curiosity she felt towards his ways. She only spent a couple days thinking of a life with him on land before she was snapped back to her senses. Santiago was the one that could save them. That needed to be her focus. Finally, she was left feeling numb and ready to be done with the whole mission.

It had now been so long that she had forgotten the intensity of the feelings she had for him. It was only one day, and she had been swept up in the moment. Now she regarded Santiago as nothing more than her duty, and she was anxious to be free of the whole ordeal.

Carmen pushed herself up from her seaweed nest.

"Samir! Fernando?"

Her breath caught in her chest, and she sent waves of gratitude and love at them. She reached her hands through the bars and placed them on each of their chests in turn as they exchanged greetings of amicus.

"Fernando," Carmen's regret and sorrow filled the water around them. "I am so sorry I have not given you more of my time."

His tone was casual, as if he'd brush off her apology. "Carmen it—"

"No, Fernando. You have had a child, and I was not there. Hava does not even know me. I have made terrible choices."

Fernando was quiet, but his Ku was forgiving. *He is a better Serra than I will ever be,* Carmen knew without a doubt.

"It is ok, my sister. You will do better."

Carmen nodded and knew that she would. She had to. She could not be so singularly focused. This she had also realized during her imprisonment.

"What are you doing here?" she asked earnestly. "How did you even know I was here?"

Samir looked at her with confusion.

"We are here to speak on your behalf."

"My… my behalf?" she asked.

No one had told her anything about the proceedings, and she had never witnessed a trial herself. She didn't know what to expect, but she was flooded with gratitude that she wouldn't have to go through it alone.

"We are here to speak for your character," Fernando answered. "Your trial is tomorrow morning."

"Tomorrow!"

Elation and panic consumed her. She was ready to learn her fate and stop waiting, but it was also a daunting prospect.

The two bucks' Kus grew darkened by shadow.

"Ocean Mother Pilou was outraged when she learned that your trial had been put off so long," Fernando answered. "The only time there was such a delay in swift judgment was when a defendant had to wait for their witnesses to arrive. And then the trial was only put off a few weeks. There are retransformed Sirens living in Daris who have not been treated as cruelly as you," Fernando concluded.

At this, both Samir and Carmen looked at Fernando in shock.

"Retransformed Sirens?" Carmen said, bewildered. "Sirens can… change back to Serras?"

"It does not happen often," he said conversationally. As a Sentinel, Fernando was privy to information that the average Serra did not know, and it was commonplace for him to know such shocking information.

"When it does happen, the Serra in question has to live the rest of their life in the city of Daris. They are not free to travel the ocean and are closely monitored, but even they do not have to live their entire lives in prison."

"How do they change back?" Carmen asked, completely distracted from her own plight by this remarkable revelation.

Maybe they could change Zitja back if they could not kill her. Carmen knew that the KuVis was long gone from the ocean, but the curse was still in place, and obviously Vis was still in the ocean if Sirens could retransform back to Serras. Maybe this was Carmen's answer. She was thinking of everything she could to remedy her situation. And if she were honest, she hoped to still be able to find a solution that did not include sacrificing Santiago. During her time in the cell, she had thought of him frequently and fondly, torn in two with her inner conflict.

"The same way Serras turn into Sirens," Fernando answered her question. "When their Ku turns against the

Serra way of life, they are caught in the old curse. When their Ku shifts back toward a Serra attitude, they change back. Though the latter does not happen as much as the former."

Carmen bit the inside of her cheek. That idea was out. She couldn't force Zitja to accept the Serra way of life again. She would have to resort to her original idea and hope Terret accepted it and let her go.

"So what I am saying," Fernando concluded, "is that no other Serra—or retransformed Serra—has ever been treated so poorly in our legal system. Pilou was angry and ordered your trial to commence immediately."

"That is good. She is on my side."

"I do not know about that," Samir said. "You know how she feels about Crural contact. She was against you seeking the Heir on land. You revealed our secrets to at least two Crurals."

"Yes, but one of them is your Bondmate!" Carmen couldn't believe her bad luck. Was anyone of authority on her side?

"Jolene lives underwater now. She is not a threat to us." Samir merely shrugged. He was on her side; it was no use arguing with him.

"We need to talk about our strategy," Samir said. "We should all agree on presenting evidence in the same way. A united front. I fear it is only the three of us against the Cor, Ocean Mother, and Terret."

The mood amongst the three of them grew somber and they nodded.

They discussed their strategy until late into the night, and even after her two champions left, Carmen sat up, thinking and fretting. Why were they all against her? She was trying to help. Had she really done so wrong by wanting to protect a Crural's life? For falling for him? She would have to put those feelings aside. She had to get herself out of this and prove she could save the underwater world.

Pilou's chamber seemed bare. It was large and cavernous and looked even bigger because of the brightness of the room, lit with luminescents and sunlight gleaming off the whiteness of the walls.

At the front, Ocean Mother Pilou sat on a white marble chair on a dais, against the left wall her Cor of seven, but against the right wall—where all Serras were welcome to sit to see the proceedings—sat only three. Her brother, Fernando, and Samir were the only ones there for her. Against the same wall but separating himself from where the general assembly would congregate sat Terret. No one was interested enough in her plight to join the hearing. She did not know if this was a good sign or bad. She didn't know what a normal trial should look like or if Serras didn't often come to see judgment rained down upon their peers.

Terret began.

"Ocean Mother," he nodded in her direction, "Balams of the Clans." He looked towards the Cor. "We are here today because Carmen has been consorting with Crurals and conspiring to allow Sirens free reign of our waters."

Carmen was shocked by his accusations. Not only were these things not true, but also she was sure even he knew they were false. He was actively lying. Could Pilou and the Cor not tell his Ku was dishonest? Carmen focused on the feelings he was projecting. Honesty. He either adamantly believed what he was saying, or he was so well trained in deceit that he could display lies in his Ku. Carmen was disgusted.

At the same time, she reminded herself that she needed to regulate her Ku. It would not do to get angry or to try to withhold emotions. She was not like Terret and could not pull off a lie; she would have to present an honest and gentle aura if she wanted to sway her judges.

"Carmen was assigned the sacred task of locating the Heir of Tullus," Terret continued as Carmen restrained herself from yelling out that he was lying again. "She was under my direct supervision to locate this man and bring him to us. When she found him, she deliberately withheld him. She told him valuable information that could harm the secret of our society. She protected him and kept him away from us. We believe she has fallen in love with this Crural and plans to keep him for herself. What they plan to do with our secrets, I do not have to tell you. One can only imagine the terror the two of them could inflict upon us."

Carmen was aghast. It was all so absurd. She knew what he was doing. He was winning his case by fear. He knew Pilou's aversion to Crurals, and every Serra had a deep fear that history would repeat itself if the secret of their existence was widely known. Pups from a very young age were taught the story of Nephira's capture and the subsequent years when the ocean was ravaged by land dwellers.

Carmen sat through it calmly and listened, though her Ku was quietly raging with fury for the entire room to feel.

Terret spoke for a moment longer, but Carmen didn't hear it. Her mind was too full of rage to hear his words. How could he sit before such esteemed Serras and lie to their Kus?

She was nearly shaking from her seat in the middle of the room. Finally, he wound down, and Pilou called for Fernando to speak. Carmen was snapped back to the present, anxious to hear what he would say.

Fernando swam to the front and positioned himself between Carmen and Pilou as he addressed the room.

"Carmen is my sister, but my son would not know it because he has never met her," Fernando began with a somber heart.

Carmen's eyes were wide, and she held her breath, afraid to move even the tiniest muscle.

*Why would he say such a thing?*

"My son is just over a year old now, and Carmen has not made any effort to meet him. She did send a gift when she heard the news… six months after he was born."

Carmen was perched on the edge of her seat in the middle of the room. If there hadn't been enough resistance in the water to hold her up, she surely would have fallen to the floor. He was not helping her case; he was portraying her as a terrible Serra. She needed to make him stop talking.

But Fernando continued.

"She has not been a good aunt—or sister—for a very long time. She has been so singularly focused as to abandon all her own pursuits, her family, and her happiness, in her desire to find this Heir. It has been her life's mission."

At this point, he paused and swam over to her, placing a hand on her shoulder. Carmen felt herself relax and take in a much-needed breath.

"Ocean Mother, it was Carmen's only desire to defeat Zitja and defend Serrakind. If she says she has been unable to do her duty, it is not for lack of trying, I can assure you."

Fernando looked at Carmen now for the first time, and she looked back at him. A small tick passed between their Kus. Gratitude, love, and trust were conveyed, and Carmen smiled. Though she would also have liked to tell him that he played a risky game with her reputation.

Fernando made a few more small claims about Carmen's loyalty, and then he was through.

Samir was called to speak next. After Fernando's dicey strategy, Carmen worried what Samir had in store. The two bucks were taking a different approach than what the three of them discussed the night before. Samir was often so thoroughly ruled by his emotions to the point where he didn't see reality for what it was that there was a very real possibility he would tell the chamber that he wanted her to run away with the Heir and leave everyone to Zitja.

After greeting the Cor and Ocean Mother warmly and charmingly, Samir jumped in, and Carmen held her breath again.

"I am Bound to the Crural woman who was Carmen's assistant."

Carmen let out her breath with such force it would have echoed were the chamber filled with air and not water. He was taking a terrible approach for this audience. Surely Samir knew how Pilou felt about Crural/Serra relations. Carmen thought maybe she should leave the chamber now and see herself back into the prison cell.

"My Bondmate, Jolene, worked with Carmen for years on different land masses, toiling away to find this Heir for us. Jolene told me that she would often bring Carmen genealogical books to look through for information. When it became late, Jolene would excuse herself and go home, but when she returned in the morning, Carmen was still sitting on the beach perusing the information."

Samir reached out his entire left arm, stretching it purposefully, and pointed at Carmen. He raised his voice just a bit, but his tone became much more firm.

"This Serra dam has labored diligently for this her entire life. She is accused today of withholding the Heir and with collusion with Crurals. Or maybe collusion with the Sirens themselves, the way Terret would have you believe it. But I challenge you: would Carmen do either of those things after all the work she put in to find him?"

Carmen's hands were clenched so tightly that her fingernails were cutting into her skin. He shouldn't have been so forceful to the Cor and Ocean Mother. He shouldn't have accused Terret of being devious. He was being just as risky as her brother.

*Are these the only two I have to speak for me?* she wondered.

If nothing else, she could say that these two bucks were right about her. She was a terrible Serra. No friends? Ignoring her family? Disinterest in any pursuits other than finding a Crural? She truly did not know how to be happy.

Carmen hung her head and waited for the verdict.

"Carmen," Ocean Mother Pilou said, not unkindly. "You may speak in defense of yourself now."

Carmen looked up abruptly. She hadn't known she would have the opportunity. She pushed herself up from her seat and tread the water between her chair and the dais, where the three bucks before her had made their statements.

"I…"

But she didn't know what to say. In her cell, there were a million things she would have said to Terret or to the Ocean Mother, but none of them were appropriate here. She hadn't thought of anything eloquent to say, and all she had was the idea she had been trying to tell Terret since her last failed attempt to bring Santiago down.

"I do not have much more to say than what Samir and Fernando have shared with everyone." She filled her Ku with humility. "The things they say are true. They portray me in a horrible and wonderful light. I am a terrible Serra, it would seem. But I am also very dedicated to this one pursuit. The only thing I can tell you now is that I failed to bring the Heir under the surface, but that I have a plan. If I can be given another chance, I know I can do it."

She turned to Terret, who had nothing to do with the outcome of her trial but whom she felt duty-bound to address.

"I can do it. Give me one last chance to try something that I know will work. If not, I will accept life imprisonment."

She sat back down in her seat like a scolded child. She hadn't done a good job of defending herself, but she didn't have more to say.

"Is that all?" Pilou asked. "It is highly unusual for a Serra to agree to imprisonment during their trial. You would not rather say something more?"

Carmen raised her head proudly and straightened her back.

"No, Ocean Mother. It is kind of you to show concern. Samir and Fernando have accurately shown my character, and I have presented a proposal for my future. Any more would be pandering and dishonest, I feel. I will accept whatever judgment you choose."

Her confidence waivered. She wasn't sure she liked the Serra she had become, but she had created this for herself. All she could do was stand by her choices in this moment. In the future, she could create someone she would like.

"Then we will confer," Pilou responded and waved to a guard at the back of the chamber.

The guard escorted Carmen out of the room and locked her back in the cell where she would wait for her fate to be decided. She looked around the tiny space and imagined spending the rest of her life in this room. Abruptly, she brought her hand up to her chest.

These were not the cells of life-time prisoners. These were temporary cells for the accused to wait in until their trial. In her life, Carmen had only heard of one Serra sentenced to a life of imprisonment. That Serra was taken to the caves under the old Siren lair at Anthemoessa. She put her hands to her face and lay down on the nest. At least this cell was brightly lit, and often there were Sentinels roaming the halls that she could talk to. In the darkness of the caves, she would surely go mad.

Carmen rolled over onto her side and faced the wall. She had gotten herself into a mess. The worst part was that she still felt conflict about the whole situation. It was her own fault. If she hadn't been so single-minded her entire life, if she had allowed herself to enjoy what her world had to offer, she wouldn't have been so enticed by her unique day with Santiago. She had truly felt happiness and freedom lighten the weight of her responsibilities while in his presence. What had she done to herself?

"Carmen." The voice came from behind her.

She slowly turned over to look out the bars. She had felt this Sentinel coming down the hallway but hoped he would pass by. She sent up a prayer to Nephira that he wasn't coming for her already. They hadn't even been discussing her evidence for ten minutes yet. It was too soon to make a decision in her favor.

"They are ready to present your verdict."

# *Chapter 10*

## Carmen

"He is so tiny and darling. It is taking every bit of restraint I have not to smother him with love," Carmen sighed.

She sat in her shelter in the Najilian chatting easily with Samir and Jolene while cuddling their small child in her arms.

"I cannot believe I have not seen you in over nine months!" Carmen exclaimed to Jolene.

She was still reeling from her trial but couldn't decide what made her more incredulous: the fact that they actually put her through the trial or that they detained her in Daris another three months with countless strategy meetings, flimsy excuses to delay proceeding, and endless threats. Terret was still convinced she was devious or underhanded.

She had a lot to accomplish if she wanted to prove him wrong and avoid imprisonment.

"Carmen!" Jolene nearly cried, "I'm just so happy to be seeing you at all."

She wasn't exaggerating. The moment they had heard that Carmen had been set free, she and Samir had traveled directly from their home in the Tipua, despite their new baby being so young.

Carmen's Ku filled the room with expressed gratitude. She looked to Samir.

"Thank you so much for speaking on my behalf, Samir. It meant everything to have you there."

"I would have done more, if I could. I do not feel as though I said enough."

"Such is the way with these things, sometimes," Carmen said, trying to brush it off but still feeling bitter about having undergone such an embarrassment. "Terret is an intimidator who will have his way. That is really the only reason I succeeded in my trial: I appealed to Terret's interests."

The Ocean Mother and Cor had not even had a chance to convene before Terret approached them to drop his pursuit of punishment. His desire to get his hands on the Heir outweighed his greed for Carmen's punishment.

"Although, if he had only given me the opportunity to tell him my idea nine months ago, before we even arrived in Daris, the trial would have been rendered unnecessary. I did not tell him anything during my trial that I would not have told him before."

Carmen sighed. The whole thing frustrated her.

# Surface Tension

"The thing is," Carmen said unleashing her anger on her undeserving friends, "Terret has thusly made things so much more difficult for me—for us all—because of this trial. Nine months is such a long time to be away! What if I cannot find Santiago again?"

"I can help you, of course!" Jolene offered. "We could get the old team back together to track him down!" she said lightly, trying to brighten Carmen's mood. "What is this new plan? What do you have to do?"

Carmen couldn't help smiling.

"I told Terret I could not coerce the Heir into the water and that I was not strong enough to overpower him. I told him that I could bring Santiago very close to the water, touching it, in fact, but that they would have to be the ones to bring him under. I told them that if they were not capable of it, it could not be done. Terret was very eager for the challenge. The troublesome part is that after nine months, and leaving Santiago so angrily, I worry I will not be able to draw him to the water again."

"If I know anything about men," Samir piped in, "he will come running when you call."

"And I will help you in any way I can!" Jolene said. "I owe you so much for changing my life."

She gave Samir's hand a loving squeeze.

"It will all work out," Carmen said, more to the baby than anyone else. She cooed to him as she bounced him in her arms. "It just has to work out."

Carmen gave the baby a squeeze, glad to feel normalcy after so long away. If she had been taken prisoner for life, she may never have been able to meet this child.

"He is the smallest thing I have ever seen," Carmen exclaimed. "His scales are still up to his neck. I do not think I have ever encountered a pup so young."

"Surely you have friends who have had pups?" Samir asked.

"No," Carmen said, completely detached from the question. Her entire focus was on this beautiful brown skinned baby.

"With my kinsmates who have pups, I did not meet them until at least their chest and shoulders were exposed."

"But, Carmen!" Samir exclaimed, "it is around the first year that the scale hegira exposes an infant's chest. Surely you visited your kinsmates sooner than a year after their birth?"

It was Serra custom for a Kinship to rally around a new mother and ease her in healing in the first months. Carmen scowled at him before her facial features softened.

"I know how I was before. I have great regret for taking my kinsmates, my family, and my friends for granted. Once I am free," she indicated the Sentinel standing guard just outside of her shelter, "I will make reparations for my past. If I learned nothing else while imprisoned, it is that I have had my priorities wrong my entire life."

Samir let the subject drop, and Carmen resumed cooing and coddling the baby. She had wanted nothing more than to save her people, to bring Santiago to the Sentinels, and to make him pay for causing her to look like a fool and a traitor. Whatever silly feelings she might have had for him had happened so long ago that they were easy to detach from. She had a mission right now. She had to save her people, and that was what mattered. But after that, after she was done with all of this for good, she would take Samir's advice. She would visit her family, she would find happiness, and—just maybe—she would fall in love herself.

The baby reached up and grabbed her nose, and Carmen smiled widely at the child. She had never had an interest in pups before, but this one seemed special to her. He was the only child she had ever felt was important.

Suddenly, she looked up.

"He is a month old now! Will you tell me his name?"

"Oh…" Samir hesitated, "his Naming Consecration is next week. That is why we must leave tonight. We have to return to the Tipua for it."

"But you know I cannot make it to the Consecration. Can you not tell me? Just me. I will keep it to myself, I promise." She smiled at them, knowing that they knew she had no one to tell.

Jolene spoke up. "I know it is considered bad luck to share a child's name with anyone before the Consecration, but where I come from we do not have the same superstition." She looked at Samir as if to ask permission.

A shadow of anger passed his countenance as he evaluated the question. Then, with a frown, he said, "No. This is an important event for our family and a special occasion for Serras. Carmen should be there if she wants to know."

Jolene looked at Carmen and bit her lips in agreement.

Carmen sighed, looking up and seeing her friends watching her. She tried to brush off the accusation.

"Ok, I will be there."

She could do it. She would bring Santiago down tomorrow, and then he would be Terret's property. She wasn't even allowed to help prepare him for his upcoming duties. She could make it to the Naming Consecration by then. She felt Samir's Ku lighten, and the tension in the room cleared.

She looked back down at the tiny thing looking up at her with big brown eyes. Her heart nearly melted out of her chest.

"He is beautiful!" Carmen said, cooing at the baby and holding him tightly. "I'm very happy for you two"

"Carmen, look at you!" Samir said, swimming over to her and cupping her face in his hands. "I have never seen you behave this way. You are not only interested in something besides your work, but you seem almost…"

"Carefree." Jolene answered where Samir faltered. "I haven't known you nearly as long, but I have never seen you so free from your constant worrying. You used to resemble humans so much in your manner and your preoccupation. This is the first time I've ever felt your Ku to be so light."

Carmen couldn't help but laugh. She did feel better than she had in a very long time. She was finally going to be free from her constant plight to find the Heir. Her people would be saved. She could do things for herself.

"You are excited to see Santiago tomorrow," Jolene assumed. "He has a place in your heart."

"No!" Carmen interjected forcefully. "You misinterpret my feelings. I am very happy to see Santiago again, but not for the reason you assume. I am happy to finally be done with this. I will turn him over to the Sentinels tomorrow and finally be freed. This is not about love. It is about success. I feel free knowing that I have finally done it."

The pair in front of her looked at each other and then Samir spoke to her in a soft, patronizing voice. "Carmen, *you* are the one deceived. You cannot hide the truth in your Ku from us. We know you too well. Even if you have convinced yourself otherwise, you love him."

"I certainly do not!"

"Use your Ku instead of your head or you are going to turn into a Crural and lose the important things about being a Serra," he rebutted.

Carmen was hurt by his accusations. She absentmindedly handed the baby back and said, "Good night. I will see you in the morning."

Carmen drifted through her bedtime routine in a haze. She unwound her hair while angrily brushing out the tangles, thinking how infuriating it was that Samir insisted on seeing all things in a romantic light. She cleaned her teeth while scoffing at Jolene's allegations. Samir's words continued to haunt Carmen. She knew how nonsensical it was for her to be in love.

*It is ludicrous,* she convinced herself.

She wanted to go back out and tell Samir that she hardly knew Santiago. She was also very angry with him for all of the trouble he had gotten her into with Terret. However, while she stripped off her chest wrappings and untied her loin covering, her thoughts shifted without her realizing. Her head had been full of Santiago for too long. By the time she was wrapping a nightshift around her body, she could think of nothing but his face and handsome voice. Her feelings about the man had shifted so completely that as she curled up in bed she was filled with genuine excitement to see him.

The next day, after the sun had barely been up for ten minutes, she was meeting with Terret, still trying to shake the sleepiness from her limbs.

"I do not have to tell you what it means if you return without him, do I?"

"But I am sure you will," Carmen replied with recklessness.

This was his favorite way of threatening: telling Carmen that he didn't need to tell her what would happen, and then telling her anyway. It infuriated her.

"You will be imprisoned immediately," he said, as if he hadn't noticed her cheekiness. "You have chosen to forfeit another trial this time if you fail. If you are to shield him from us again, you will be believed to be in collusion with the Sirens in order to subject Serras to genocide."

"Yes, of course. I agreed to it."

It was her idea, after all, but she kept that part to herself. Terret did not like Carmen taking credit for her own ideas.

"And this is a plan you can follow through on? There will be no excuses if you do not bring him below."

"It is a plan I cannot fail, I assure you."

She thought she very well could fail to bring Santiago. She could easily never find him again, but she kept that part to herself as well.

"May I ask how you are going to keep him from drowning the minute you pull him under if I do not teach him to breathe water first?"

# Surface Tension

Terret looked as if he would not answer her, but finally he relented.

"We have a way to convince Crurals that they can breathe water immediately. We shock them into it."

Carmen's Ku was filled with skepticism, and that skepticism urged Terret to reassure her. "It is nearly one hundred percent effective."

"And what about when it isn't effective?"

"Those Crurals drown. We will not let that happen, of course. The Heir is much too important to be haphazard with. We will bring him back to the surface for air as many times as it takes to get the process done."

Carmen was shocked. With eyes wide she asked, "And how do you know you will be able to do it?"

"Sirens have been doing it for thousands of years. I merely took what they had been doing and improved on their methods. It will work."

Carmen felt her stomach turn over. She feared she would be sick in the water, but it didn't matter. Terret was getting tired of her interrogation.

"You are excused, then. Bring him down today. *Today*," he emphasized.

She left Terret's sealskin temporary shelter and made her way towards the surface. Terret was using strategies to force Crurals to breathe water that he had learned from the Sirens? She felt a wave of revulsion for her supposed leader wash over her. Carmen kicked her fin harder. She needed to be done with this. It had consumed too much of her time and emotion, and she wanted to put it all behind her.

Once she met with Santiago, her plan could not fail, and she would be finished with the whole thing. It was perfectly plausible that she wouldn't be able to find him today, and that made her nervous about her future. Thankfully, Jolene had convinced Samir to postpone their trip back to the Tipua for one day. But if Jolene could not find Santiago today, Carmen was as good as imprisoned.

Carmen waited on the beach in the exact spot where she had first met him almost a year before while Jolene went to find him. Carmen had to admire Jolene's tenacity. As soon as she emerged from the water, the younger girl barely had time to call over her shoulder, "I'll bring him back in a jiffy," before she scampered off to retrieve him. What vehicle a "jiffy" was Carmen did not know, but she hoped it was fast.

Carmen's fears were instantly appeased. Only a moment passed before she saw the two running along the sand towards her.

*Great Nephira! She did it,* Carmen silently praised, breathing a sigh of relief and feeling chills wash over her. Santiago ran down the beach towards her, determined, wearing his military outfit and looking as though he were coming to save her. He looked as though he were coming to save them all.

The sun beat down on the white sand around him, making everything shine gold like Daris. He was a talisman of hope for her and her people, and her stomach flipped over with relief and excitement.

She had barely a moment to register her feelings when he came charging over to her and scooped her up in his arms and planted an impassioned kiss on her startled lips. She kissed him back eagerly. In that moment, forgotten were the Sentinels, her anger, her plan. Her head and heart were full of him.

# Surface Tension

He only pulled away for a flash to say, "I am so sorry, Carmen," before he smothered her in kisses again.

Finally, when he could free himself from her, Santiago set her back on the beach gently and held her hands in his and professed, "Please forgive me. I am afraid of the water and I am ashamed of that fear. When you wanted me to join you, I allowed my pride to rule my actions, and I reacted callously to you. I did not give any consideration for your feelings towards your home. I am truly sorry."

"No, please do not be sorry."

His humility and protestations were causing her Ku to swell uncomfortably with guilt and regret.

"I said harsh things and called you undeserved names. For that I am sorry."

She truly felt it. This man had the Ku of a Serra, sincere and genuine, yet he possessed a humble awareness of his Ku, like a new pup. He was so noble, so remorseful; she began to feel guilt at nothing and everything.

"Do not be sorry, my love," he cooed at her. "I was wrong. I have thought about our last encounter every day since you left. I have come to the beach every day in the hopes that you will come back and allow me to explain."

Carmen looked up at Jolene, who was just joining them, and the latter nodded, smiling vigorously.

"He was already headed to the beach when I was my way to his house." She laughed out loud as she finished, "He saw me on the street and took off running."

"It is true. I saw your friend and knew you had come back. You left me waiting so long I feared I would have to jump in the water myself to find you again. May I please explain what happened? I want you to understand."

Carmen was getting distracted from her purpose. She was easily swayed by his magnetism, and that made her think herself weak. But he was so pleasant to be with, so eager for her company. She had never enjoyed anyone so much.

But she had a duty to her people.

"Ok, yes," she responded eagerly. "You can explain whatever you would like, but first can we go somewhere? I want to show you something."

She had to keep to the plan. She had to use him to save her people.

And save herself from a lifetime of imprisonment.

"Of course! I will follow you anywhere. You make me happy, and I will follow happiness anywhere."

He picked her up, and she pointed in the direction he was to take her.

She was struck by Santiago's words. Hadn't Samir told her to find happiness and follow it anywhere?

But where was that? Happiness hit her periodically with Santiago, when she allowed herself to feel it, but how did she follow it? She pointed around some rocks and up onto a small cliff that sat just a few feet above the water. The further they went, the more contentment abandoned her. She was surely not following happiness now, but her objective wasn't to follow happiness. She was following the plan. The plan was what was important, right? To end the Sirens and Zitja, that was most important.

When the destination was in sight, Carmen felt a lump of dread growing in her gut. It sat there, heavy and uncomfortable, and she would have cried out in frustration if Santiago weren't carrying her.

# Surface Tension

Jolene followed behind. She was aware of the purpose for the change in location, and she was willing to help, but she could also feel Carmen's Ku and was confused.

"Carmen," Jolene spoke directly to her Ku. "This is not right. You are deceiving yourself if you think you don't love him. Run away from here and never come back."

Carmen's first thought was to scold Jolene. Speaking to one person's Ku in the presence of another was not polite. Most Serras would never consider doing it. But Jolene did not grow up with Serra values. Crurals told secrets all the time without regard for others' feelings. Carmen responded anyway, despite being devious.

"Jolene, I must follow through with the plan. I must save my people."

"But--"

"No!"

After that, Jolene remained quiet. While Santiago set Carmen on the edge of a rock that jutted out over the water, Jolene sat away from them, giving them privacy but at the ready to spring into action if Carmen called.

Santiago and Carmen sat on the ledge dangling their lower extremities. Her golden tail dangled over the cliff and fanned out widely on both sides of her. Santiago bent his knees over the edge and his feet almost touched the water. *Perfect,* Carmen thought. This was close enough. This would work.

When she had first proposed to Terret that she couldn't bring Santiago down but that she could bring him close enough to be pulled in, he was against it. Terret had refused to make the Sentinels vulnerable by exposing themselves above the surface. He argued that if they were to fail, they were risking many lives and possibly compromising the promise that the Heir had made to keep their existence a secret.

"He will not keep quiet about a race of underwater creatures that tried to kidnap and possibly kill him," Terret had told her.

Carmen persisted, and eventually Terret's greed had persuaded him—as long as she knew a place that would put Santiago in arm's reach without causing the troops to have to crawl on land.

This was such a place. Her tail flicked the water. Although she was a head shorter than Santiago while they sat on their bottoms, her tail was longer, and it dipped beneath the surface. Just enough to be able to signal the army of Sentinels waiting below when the time was right and the Heir was most vulnerable.

"I want to tell you why the water scares me so," Santiago said as soon as they sat down, "and then, if you wish, I will jump right into the water and spend the rest of my life with you down there if it will make you happy."

As he said this, he pulled his legs up onto the cliff and folded them underneath his body.

Carmen swore to herself. He was too far out of reach now, but with his promise to jump in himself, Carmen prodded him.

"I am listening."

"When I was fifteen, I was planning a fishing trip with my father. It was a small boat but well equipped, so we wanted to take it far out to sea and spend the whole weekend on the water. My mother got wind of our adventurous plans, and instead of forbidding it like we thought she would, she said we could not go without her. My father did not think it was a good idea, and besides, what would we do with the baby—my brother was four at the time—and he was sure we would drive each other crazy on the small boat. My mother told him that was nonsense and that we could all have a great weekend together.

"There was no swaying her. We set out early on Saturday morning and things were beautiful. It was perfection. The weather was superb and the fish were biting. We caught as many fish as we could possibly want right away and then spent the rest of the day relaxing and enjoying the stillness of the water. The whole of Saturday was spent lazily enjoying the open water and the salty air.

"That night things got too relaxed. Everything had gone so perfectly that we were all completely off our guard and allowed ourselves to be a little reckless. My brother took off his lifejacket for what had to be the hundredth time, and finally my parents were tired of fighting it back on to him. He had been out of the jacket for a couple hours when, suddenly, he was no longer on the boat. My mom saw him go over—though my father and I did not know how it happened—and she jumped in after him."

Carmen was touched by the story. She could feel the heartache in Santiago's Ku. It was an old memory but felt as fresh as the day it happened. She did not understand how he could be so saddened by the sea. She could not imagine being so upset by the place she had grown up.

Santiago was quiet for a moment as he stretched out and dangled his legs over the cliff again. His feet were now just inches above the water. He was in the perfect position. She could signal the Sentinels below and they would jump up and grab his legs while she pushed him over from above. The combination would bring him under the water before he even knew what hit him.

"That was the last time we ever saw them again."

"What?" Carmen nearly shouted. She was completely startled by his statement, and guilt washed over her again.

"That was the last time we saw them. Both of their heads were in front of us. My father was turning the boat towards them while I was getting rope ready to pull them in when my brother's head went under. My mother screamed out and then dove under as well. And that was it. Neither of them resurfaced."

"Ever? They just went down and did not come up?"

Carmen's stomach twisted, and she thought she might be sick. To just lose sight of a family member and have no idea where they went would be the most devastating feeling. He would always wonder where they were and how they could have just disappeared.

"Never. They were just gone."

"But why?" Carmen said. "How do two people just disappear?" But as she asked, she knew.

"My father screamed and cried and jumped in the water. He began swimming to the spot where their heads went under. He dove and resurfaced. Dove deeper and resurfaced.

"I yelled and yelled for him to come back in the boat, but he wouldn't. He kept going under to find them, but he couldn't see them anywhere. Over and over he would dive down, resurface, and then dive again. I thought I'd lose him in the same way, so I finally convinced him to tie the rope around his waist. He continued swimming and diving, tethered to the boat, until he grew so tired that with each dive he was merely lowering his face under water and searching with his eyes until he needed another breath."

Santiago stood up as if he just couldn't take the memory anymore and had to get away from it. He stared out into the ocean far into the distance.

"By this time, it was so dark he wouldn't have been able to see them if they had been swimming next to him. I pulled him in by the rope despite his protests."

Santiago paused and looked away while he wiped a tear from his eye. Carmen looked out upon the water to give him privacy.

The sun was bright in the sky, and the Sentinels would be growing antsy below, but with every word Santiago spoke about his family, she forgot about her duty and focused on the broken heart of the man before her.

He sat back down and looked at her earnestly.

"That night, my father and I lay soaking wet, clutching each other and crying until the sun came up. That was the second worst night in all my thirty-two years."

"The *second* worst?" Carmen choked out, his emotions overflowing her Ku and bringing a catch to her voice. "How could you have had a worse night than that?"

"The next day we could not make ourselves leave. We could not possibly turn the boat around and return home without them. What if they had merely drifted away and were waiting in anguish for us to pick them up? I mean," he paused and gave her a look so forlorn, so desperate for an answer, it looked like everything he believed was being tested with his next question, "How can two people completely disappear in an instant?"

## S.R. Atkinson

He was quiet, as if he expected her to answer.

Carmen was torn between giving him the answer he sought and protecting him from the truth. She knew exactly where they had gone. They weren't the first, and certainly not the last Crurals to be pulled under the surface and dragged away. Sirens often brought their prisoners under the water and tortured them for a long time before killing them. Carmen was not unaware of the similar situation she was putting Santiago in right now.

Carmen sat quietly; it was best that she did not tell him what had happened to his family.

Finally he spoke again, and Carmen was freed from having to answer.

"We took that boat all over the water until it ran out of gas, and then we pulled out the oars and continued the search—although they were hardly effective in moving the boat very far. As the sun was setting, a storm began to roll in. We put on our life jackets, but we had made a fatal mistake. The sea was going to take our entire family that weekend.

"We fought valiantly against the storm for many hours. We struggled to keep the boat above water, to stay inside of it, to stay alive. Exhaustion set in, and we clung to each other in desperation. At one point in the night, I was hit in the head by flying debris and was knocked unconscious.

"When I awoke, the sun was beating on me. I was in the water, the boat was nowhere to be seen, and I was alone. For hours I floated in the water, too defeated and exhausted to move. It was probably my immobility that saved me from the dangers of the sea, floating lifelessly, supported by my jacket. A few times, I saw dorsal fins in the distance. I was scared, but at that point I was so dulled from exhaustion and heartache that I almost welcomed death. I had lost my entire family and all hope.

"A few hours later, I was picked up by a fishing boat. I had drifted all the way to Brazil. My journey back home I hardly remember, so lost was I in my own grief."

Carmen sympathized with his heartache so thoroughly she knew she could never make him go underwater against his will. What was she to do?

Carmen was holding his hand without realizing it, and now she lifted it up to her heart. It was a sign to comfort him, and even though he was unfamiliar with Serra customs, he seemed to understand.

"I haven't been in the water since. I still wake in a sweat after having nightmares of that weekend, and I often find myself lost in thought about what could have happened to my family. The ocean haunts me."

"Santiago."

Carmen was going to say something comforting, but at that moment she looked into the water and the sight before her was terrifying.

Directly below their dangling limbs were dozens of eyes looking up at them. The Sentinels were ready. If Santiago were to look over now he would be haunted by this new sight. So many faces were peering up at them with menacing expressions, ready to pounce on her signal. She knew the Sentinels were aware of the Heir's presence and would soon make a move with or without her sign.

She knew she had to act fast because once she made up her mind, they would sense her change of Ku immediately.

"Santiago," she yelled at him forcefully. "Pick me up, now. Don't argue with me," she said when she suspected he was going to question her.

"Pick me up and run. RUN!" she yelled as the Sentinels began to leap out of the water.

# *Chapter 11*

## Santiago

Santi put her head in her hands and leaned onto her desk as frustration consumed her. She was two months into the semester, and for the last two weeks had experienced absolutely no hearing. This was probably it. Amed had warned her that it would almost certainly be gone for good.

She looked up through her fingers at her professor talking away, telling the class all about the social construct of the indigenous people in Papua New Guinea. The school had worked with her hearing troubles rather flawlessly, as most major universities were legally obligated to do, but it had been a struggle for her to accept her new way of life.

So much had to change during her bouts of deafness, and she wasn't sure she could handle the way her friends treated her during that time. They displayed more frustration than empathy, and when she discussed learning sign language with them, none of them seemed inclined to learn it for her sake. Not that she considered any of them to be serious friendships, but it still hurt. Her friend and roommate, Shelbie, was the most understanding about it, but she was still very impatient with the strain on their friendship.

That evening Santi texted her mom.

> I think I want to come to California.
> Need Dr. apmt and mom time.

What about school?
> Maybe I'll check out.

Santiago. What is going on? I'll call you.

> You can't. Ever. My hearing is gone.

I'll get you a flight for tomorrow.
> Thx.

Santi knew she was being dramatic, but it was true. Her hearing was gone. She had been thinking about checking out of school anyway, and her hearing was the last straw. That alone was not enough to solidify the decision, of course, but she found she couldn't focus on land life.

It was all coming to a head lately. Living as a Serra had been calling to her more and more fiercely the longer she was away from it. And, when she took the time—without distractions—to think, what was the point of finishing college when she would just start over with a Serra education? She had always been adamant that she finish college—an old belief her mom had ingrained into her. It was an important time for her to learn and experience life, but she could do all that underwater. And, now with her hearing gone, it would make things easier.

It was time to visit her mom and sort things out. Celia would be passionate about keeping Santi close, but she had never held her daughter back from making her own choices. The last thing holding Santi back now was the dilemma about her mom. The two of them had been through many tumultuous years when Santi was young and had grown together so much; she couldn't go backwards in their relationship. They would work it out together.

The luminescent orb Santi carried for light was great at brightening the space around it but not very good at shining a ray of light into a small space. She scratched her ten-year-old head and wondered if there was such a thing as an underwater flashlight. If she brought one down here, everyone would be so impressed. And their investigating would be so much easier.

"What are you looking at, Santiago?" the tiny Tizz asked, obscuring Santi's view of the hole with her big blonde head.

"Something cool just went into that little tunnel. I don't know what it is, but I want to check it out."

"So reach in and get it!" Tizz responded, but Santi yelled at her quickly.

"No, Amaratizz! You don't know what's in there."

Maybe Santi was more cautious on their adventures because she wasn't as comfortable in the water, or maybe it was because Tizz was only six and didn't think of the consequences, but whatever it was, Tizz was fearless during their explorations.

"Don't be silly," Tizz said now as she reached her hand inside. "I got it!" she exclaimed before screaming out so piercingly that Santi burst into tears immediately.

"What happened?" she said through tears of fear. "Are you just trying to scare me?"

Tizz was still screaming as she pulled her hand out of the hole. Latched on to the tip of her finger was a small snake, no longer than the length of Santi's forearm. It wasn't very foreboding, and they had come across snakes that were much more deadly, but this one was latched on to Tizz with teeth larger than its head.

Tizz was still screaming both in her Ku and loudly through the water when Santi snapped out of her stupor. She quickly rummaged in her bag and pulled out a small-handled knife Rogan had given her after she got tangled in seaweed a few weeks ago. Just then, Rogan and Sully swam up to the two girls with panic-stricken faces asking what had happened and rushing to their sides. Feeling emboldened by their presence and wanting to show them how brave she was, Santi grabbed the snake around the middle and chopped off its head. Tizz shook the detached head off her finger and examined her wound.

"Oh no!" Sully said from Santi's side.

"What?" Santi asked, holding up the rest of the snake in her hand. "I'm sorry I killed the snake, but I didn't think I had much choice!"

"No, it is not that, Santi," Sully said, cautiously reaching out his hand to take the snake.

# Surface Tension

"We had better take this to my father," Rogan said with urgency. "Tizz, empty out your bag."

"Why?" Tizz responded, clutching her bag tightly, her finger forgotten under the threat of upheaving her possessions.

"It is too late!" Sully yelled, leaping for the dismembered snake in Santi's hand.

Santi looked at the source of the commotion in disbelief and terror. The tiny wriggling snake in her hand was pushing against her fingers with the strain of growth as it expanded its girth. Then, to her horror, the gaping neck-hole began to wiggle and writhe as two heads sprouted where the one used to be. She released it immediately, which caused Sully to jump back from the creature. At the same moment, Rogan grabbed Santi's bag and turned it upside-down, spilling its contents to the sand five feet below.

Santi lifted up her knife to attack the creature again, but Sully and Rogan both shouted, "No!",", and the two boys wrestled the gnashing creature into Santi's empty bag.

Once they had it tied shut and the creature was contained, Sully explained, "That wasn't a snake. That was a hydra."

When Santi and Tizz merely looked on in confusion Rogan explained.

"Every time one of its appendages are cut off, it grows bigger and two more grow in its place. The only way to kill it is to cut out its heart."

"Since we don't know how to do that," Sully continued, "we will take it to Amed. You have to be careful because if you miss its heart and just slice it in half, it could grow double torsos—or even feet. Some of them have gotten really big and dangerous before they were able to be killed."

Santi felt sufficiently stupid. She would have just kept slicing away as the beast grew and grew. She was always making a fool of herself underwater, and this time she had put not only little Tizz but all of them in danger.

Sully felt the shift in her Ku and responded, "It is fine. Do not even worry. I have done plenty of reckless things myself."

Santi nodded, but she didn't necessarily feel any less foolish. It didn't help when Rogan said, "Amaratizz, this is why you must always feel for something's Ku to know what it is. Especially if you are going to go reaching into dark caverns."

"That's my fault, too," Santi answered. "I felt its Ku and I'd never felt anything like it before, so I wanted to investigate. I'm sorry, Tizz. I shouldn't have been so curious."

It wasn't until years after the experience with the baby hydra that Santi watched a movie about Hercules with some kids from school. She told them that the many-headed beast was real but was so thoroughly contradicted by the others that she pushed the hydra from her memory, convincing herself that she had made it up. Remembering it now, she couldn't help but feel a little vindicated about that miserable sleepover and all of the girls laughing at her for believing in ancient Greek mythology.

The memory of the hydra had been running through Santi's mind ever since Rogan had shown her the cryptids. She had forgotten all about it, but seeing the mythical beasts brought back this and many other memories. And now that she sat on a plane full of people all headed to California, cramped in her tiny coach seat, she wished very much that she were traveling by cryptid again.

She shifted on the table and tore at the thin tissue paper with her fingers while she waited for the doctor to come back. Celia was smiling in the corner, trying to be encouraging, but they both knew what the news would be. The doctor emerged from behind the closed door, and Celia jumped up from her chair along the wall and came over to hold Santi's hand.

He spoke to her mother for a minute—which Santiago thought was very rude considering he knew she was there for hearing trouble. He then leaned over his clipboard, scribbled a note and handed it to her.

*Miss Morales,*

*Your loss of hearing is permanent.*

His handwriting was so bad she wasn't sure she had even read it correctly. How cliché. Then he handed her a pamphlet for the California Hearing Center in San Mateo, California. The cover showed an elderly couple sitting on the beach, laughing at a shared joke. A joke they could both hear, no doubt, thanks to the hearing center.

He also gave her a pamphlet for hearing aids, cochlear implants, and one on dealing with grief. He began talking to Celia again, explaining something that Santi could only guess was related to the pamphlets. He then began handing her information for a specialist and something on learning sign language as an adult. He held up the one for the specialist and waggled it around, pointing to it; she got the idea that he felt this one was particularly important.

As they walked through the parking lot to find their silver Mazda in the sea of silver sedans, they were quiet. Neither of them could think of what to say, even if both of them could have heard it. They didn't know how to process the information. Deaf. That was the last word he jotted down, as if to punctuate his point. She had suspected it, and Amed hard warned her it was coming, but somehow it seemed so final.

Santi had read the word in his messy handwriting and a cold pinch stabbed her gut. She felt devastated and angry for a while. She fumed and worried through half of the drive before her feelings started to shift to something else. Santi's quiet contemplation filled the car as they made their way to Celia's home.

When they finally arrived at home, the women sat at the kitchen table with two cups of tea, a notepad, and all of Dr. Excellent-Bedside-Manner's pamphlets. Celia carefully wrote down all that he had told her so that Santi could read it. She explained the diagnosis and all of Santi's options. The bottom line: the puncture was more serious than anything he had ever seen before—thanks only to herself for being so vicious with the fishbone—and there was also severe damage that he had never seen before.

The doctor was suggesting that another specialist could possibly account for it, but that he was at a loss.

Santi didn't need another specialist. It was Siren Song's damage. That was clear to Santi.

# Surface Tension

On and on Celia wrote until Santi gently put her hand on her mother's to make her stop writing.

Celia looked up at her daughter questioningly, pen poised to write the question on her mind. Santi braced herself. She didn't know what her mom would think of this. Celia wasn't usually one for strange things. She liked to be in control and did not like surprises.

Santiago reached deep within her and connected to her mother's heart with ease. It was exactly what she thought it would feel like. It seemed to be very busy, as if she were taking care of everyone's concerns in the world, and it was a little scattered because she was thinking about too many things at once. More than anything, it was comfortable. It felt like her mother's love, only magnified to an extent she would never be able to feel without her Ku. Santi wondered why she had never done this before.

Santi spoke through their connection.

"Mommi, it's ok." And then she waited.

She looked at her mom and waited some more, but Celia seemed to be completely paralyzed. Santi felt her mom's Ku go from chaos to pinpoint focus. Celia didn't seem to be scared, but she also didn't seem to accept hearing her daughter's voice inside her head.

Santi waited a bit longer before she decided she'd better explain.

"This is how Serras communicate underwater. Every person has a Ku. There isn't a human word for it—or even something that humans could relate to—but it's like your heart, or even your soul. This is how they link to one another. It's how they communicate, but it also keeps them honest and…" Santi paused not knowing how to explain it. "Real," she finished. "It keeps them real with one another."

When her mom still didn't say anything, Santi continued. It was the longest she had ever held her mom's attention without being interrupted, and she was not going to take it for granted.

"See, speaking this way requires no ears or hearing!"

She smiled, trying to make a joke, but her mom was still motionless.

On an on, Santi explained all about how the Ku worked and how Serras communicated. Her mother was still silent, so she just rambled and rambled. She told her mother all about last August—although she left out the part about being kidnapped—she figured her mother didn't need to know about that in this moment—and she told her all about Rogan again and the decision she had been contemplating.

"I had been wondering what I would do now that I found Rogan again. Would I finish college? Would I remain in Florida? Would I live with Rogan underwater? So many things are unclear and confusing. Ultimately, I had decided I'd come back to school but… Mom?"

Finally—after the longest time Celia had ever gone without speaking that Santi could remember—Celia spoke timidly with her heart so that Santi could understand.

"I know this feeling."

Santi froze.

"How do you know how to do this?"

She had been talking and explaining for a long time, but she never actually told her mom how to do it.

"Jor abuela would touch my… Ku." Celia hesitated with the new word. "She used to sit on my bed at night and sing to me. It was so comforting, and I felt so close wit her. When joo did it, I recognized the feeling. She always connected to me."

Celia had tears in her eyes as she thought about her mother.

Suddenly, Santi smiled. Her mother's voice and accent, so familiar and precious in Santi's opinion, was exactly as it was with her voice. She had never thought about it before. Rogan was the only other person she had talked to with voices as well as Kus, and she had never realized that they both sounded exactly the same. It made sense. Her smile grew. Celia's lullaby accent was one thing she did not want to give up with her deafness.

She encouraged her mom to keep speaking.

They talked late into the night. Celia had so many questions about the Serra world, questions she had always wanted to ask her mother but wasn't able to do so. Santi was so glad to be able to tell her mother everything about the world that she was half part of and hadn't known.

Santi used their intense conversation as an opportunity to discuss the decision she was planning.

"Mommi, I am thinking about living underwater. Permanently. I…. I want to see where things lead with Rogan, and I think want to be a part of the world under the surface."

Celia nodded. "I could feel that in jor Ku, Santee. Joo love him and the water."

Santi wasn't surprised that her mom had sensed all of that. Celia had always been so intuitive, and the use of her Ku only magnified it.

Before going to bed, they discussed Celia going with Santi some time to meet Rogan and his family. They also discussed the possibility of finding Carmen's relatives and meeting their own family members—a prospect that excited both women. On land, they were the only two Moraleses left in their family, but under water they might have aunts and uncles and cousins. After Abuelo's death, the thought of still having family out there was very exciting.

Santi stayed with her mom for a few more weeks—putting off the decision to check out of school for good or not—and read more of her abuela's journals. They were a calming distraction from her hearing issues and a remarkably helpful tool to help her make decisions about her future.

Ostensibly, Carmen had made the very same choice that Santi was making. She had wrestled a great deal with the decision to give up the world she came from for Santiago. Santi could feel the internal struggle played out through the pages as she read about the things Carmen had given up to be with the man she loved. Santi learned, without a doubt, that Carmen felt the benefit of losing her former self was great enough to outweigh any loss. Santi learned a lot about herself as she pondered the struggle she shared with her abuela.

Sitting in the sunshine on her mother's porch one afternoon, Santi read a passage that made her sit up in her chair. She slammed the journal shut and placed a hand on her beating heart, thinking about the implications of what she had just learned. It appeared to Santi that everyone was dangerously mistaken about the facts. Suddenly, she was consumed with worry for Amed's safety. He was putting himself needlessly in harm's way.

# Surface Tension

It was in that moment, reading her abuela's words, that Santi knew what she had to do with her life. There was no deciding about it. The choice was made for her, and she almost had a responsibility to the Serras to live amongst them.

That's how she viewed it anyway.

Santi's heart beat, and she felt a bond with her abuela that she had never felt before; she and Carmen made their choices for the same reason. They both needed to live in the other's world.

By the beginning of March, Santi was ready to take the plunge—laughing to herself at her witty puns—and checked out of college. Before she left California, Santi taught her mother how to use a nuntium, and arrangements were made so that Celia would check the beach frequently so that the two of them could stay in touch.

Once Santi got to Florida, she bustled around campus, thinking intently about what her life might be like under water as she went through the process of checking out of school. She thought about the implications of her life change as she sold her belongings online. She imagined what she would say to Rogan and his family as she emptied out her dorm room and deliberated back and forth about what she would need for a life under water. The entire process took a few nerve-wracking weeks. Anxiety about getting underwater quickly enough consumed her, and she was so preoccupied that whole days would pass where she didn't remember what she had actually done, only what she had thought about.

For clothing, she kept only her swimming suits and a water resistant windbreaker—an extra layer was helpful in some colder waters. She packed her hairbrush, nail clippers, and toothbrush for toiletries. Then she filled her vinyl satchel with other objects that wouldn't get damaged under water.

Finally, she sent the text her mom had been waiting for.

"I'm going to see Rogan now. I'll let you know how it goes."

After she sent her text, she put her phone on airplane mode as the flight attendant came out to demonstrate safety during their trip from Florida to Delaware.

As she began to think of Rogan with the frame of mind that she was living underwater permanently, she started to be more honest with herself about what he meant to her. He had always been her best friend, but now she was allowing herself to love him for the first time without her previous reservations. She had been so busy grappling with the huge decision to make about where to live that she hadn't allowed herself to dive in to her feelings too deeply.

Now, as she allowed herself to examine her feelings about Rogan, she was surprisingly feeling ready to be Bound to him and, in time, have a family of their own in the Nhori Clan. She blushed at the thought, remembering how long and muscular he had grown, how he came to rescue her, and how his giant hands seemed to reach all the way around her waist. She began to grow embarrassed thinking about him in this way.

On the other hand, Santiago wondered what Rogan had thought about and decided during their time apart. Maybe his thoughts had gone in the exact opposite way as hers? Maybe he and Caliapi were already Bound? The thought made her sick to her stomach, but it didn't dissuade her in the slightest. Regardless of what happened between her and Rogan, she had decided to make a life underwater for herself. It was her destiny, although the word seemed cheesy to her. She had made her decision, she had a job to do, and she would see it through despite whatever Rogan decided.

Even the overcast, gray Delaware sky couldn't dampen her mood as she stepped into the familiar pond. The wind did its best to throw her off course, but she trudged through, determined and driven by the news she had to share with Amed and Rogan. She hoped it would be well received, but either way, she could not keep the smile from her face, and her heart was bursting with anticipation.

Santi leapt into the water and left the ugly weather above her as she dove down to meet him.

"I think I have very bad news for you, Amed." Santi hung her head. "This may be hard to hear."

She was disappointed that Rogan was still in Daris for Sentinel training and that Amed wasn't sure when to expect him to return. She would just have to be content to wait until their scheduled meeting in June. She shook it off, and reminded herself that she was down here for a purpose that had nothing to do with him, anyway.

"What is it?" Coral said, with concern bursting from her Ku.

Santi explained to them all she had learned during while reading her abuela's journals. She finished with a heavy heart.

"So, what I'm trying to say is my abuela learned that her husband, Santiago, was a descendant of Tullus. THE Tullus. The Heir."

Santi waited for the news to sink in, but when they were silent, she continued.

"My mom and I did further research because the Internet provided tools my abuela didn't have before. It turns out that all of her research was, in fact, correct.

"I won't bore you with the details, but he is nearly the hundredth great-grandson of a woman who came to South America from Rome hundreds of years ago. So we scoured the Internet and found that woman was the… the many great-great-grandaughter of one of Tullus's bastard-born daughters. Anyway, the genealogy is a mess—as it always is going that far back—but we were able to find the link thanks to some dedicated old ladies in a church office in Utah. Can you believe it?"

She tried to sound light-hearted because she was getting nothing from Amed's Ku, and she was growing more anxious.

"I realize this is bad news. You have dedicated your entire life to this, only to learn that it's wrong. I'm sorry."

She was beginning to feel guilty for bearing such bad news and had to remind herself that none of it was her fault.

Amed almost laughed.

"No, actually. I really cannot believe it. You learned this all with an *Internet*? Interesting."

Santi laughed along with him. *I should bring him on land,* she thought to herself and imagined how his face would look if she showed him all of the amazing technologies that he knew nothing about.

# Surface Tension

The three of them sat in a circle in the sparsely but beautifully decorated main room of the shelter. Flowers grew directly on the walls, and the sand was pressed on the floor in intricate designs.

"And you are sure of this?" Amed questioned. "You are definitely the descendant of Tullus?"

"Well, as sure as anyone can be about this type of thing. My mother is, as well. Isn't it odd?"

She had thought frequently since learning the news that her mother could have very well finished the job long ago, had she only known. Santi wondered what a different state both her life and the world underwater would be like had her mother taken on the task of defeating Zitja.

Amed's expression and Ku were unreadable, as was usual with his Sentinel-trained demeanor, and Santi waited. Surely he was going to rebuff her. Amed had grown up knowing he was the one who could defeat Zitja. He wasn't just about to put that all aside and accept her explanation so simply.

Finally, Amed made a motion that looked like a sigh of relief and said, "I always hoped this day would come. I hoped that the true Heir would make their way down here because I did not know what else to do."

Santi was too confused to even ask a question for clarification, but luckily she didn't have to as Amed continued.

"I know that I am not the Heir. I have always known."

"You did?" Santi said in shock, eyes wide. "But then why did you pretend?"

"For hope."

S.R. Atkinson

He paused, as if that was all the explanation necessary. When Coral and Santi continued looking at him with bewilderment, he continued. "To give our people hope that one day Zitja could be defeated. Do you know that since my birth, the ocean has shifted from what it once was? Before then, it had become so miserable and dangerous because Serras did not believe there was any chance of change. But now I am able to keep the Sirens in line so effectively merely because of Zitja's fear of me."

Santiago let the information roll around in her mind.

Coral seemed to be just as stunned as Santi.

"How have you kept this from me?" Coral's Ku was sad, but Santi noticed she didn't seem angry. "I knew you kept secrets from me because of your Opus but... but this seems so huge."

"For that, I am sorry, Coral. I have hated everything I have had to keep from you. I hope one day to not be in this position."

Coral seemed to accept it, but she still looked hurt. This changed all of the beliefs she held about her Bondmate—and even her children.

Suddenly, Santi felt very sad for Rogan. This changed his life, too. He was training to be a Sentinel right now to take over if his father failed. If it was her destiny to defeat Zitja, not theirs, then everything Rogan knew about himself was a lie. It made her feel uneasy that Rogan didn't know this, and she hoped she would be able to talk to him soon.

Finally, Coral asked, "How do you know all this, Amed?" Her Ku still held traces of hurt at being in the dark about this. "More importantly, if Santiago's grandfather was the Heir, how did you come to be believed as such?"

# Surface Tension

"Let me start at the beginning," Amed answered in a thoughtful tone. "I have always told the story about how my father, Samir, and his assistant were the ones that tracked down the Heir and that my father was Bound to the Heir. You now know that this is not true."

Turning to Santi, Amed said, "The one who tracked down the Heir was your grandmother—though I never knew who she was. It was her assistant, Jolene, not the Heir, who was my mother.

"Jolene met Samir merely on a fluke because he and your grandmother were friends. My parents fell instantly in love and were Bound. Your grandmother fell in love with the real heir. When your grandparents ran away together, my mother threw herself into the hands of the Sentinels, claiming that she was the sister to the Heir. The Sentinels she turned herself over to didn't know any better. Nor did they care to know the truth."

Santi's eyes widened. She had read about a close friend named Samir in her abuela's journals: the friend who fell in love with her research assistant and ostensibly traded places with Carmen. One woman gave up a life under the ocean to follow her love on land while the other did the exact opposite. Everything Santi had read in her abuela's journals was falling in line perfectly with the story Amed told. Santi could do nothing more than try to prevent her eyes from popping out of her skull.

"No one questioned Jolene's story, and your grandmother was left in peace. Though I do not think she knew what my mother had done, because she never returned to the ocean—to my knowledge, at least.

"My mother was treated as the Heir—but poorly, since she was a Crural and deemed incapable by their standards—for only a short time until my father came to her rescue. He knew that she was not the Heir and could not be used to fight Zitja. He intervened and tried to sort things out, but ultimately they decided to keep Carmen's secret. Once the Sentinel Commander found out that Jolene had a son who was Serra, things changed for my mother, and they stopped combatting my father to use her.

"The prospect of raising me up to be a glorious warrior, or symbol of sorts, was more than the Sentinel commander could have dreamed of. He agreed to allow me to be raised by my parents until the age of Daristor, and then I would begin my training.

"We had always planned to make the truth known, but over the years I had become the very symbol of hope that the commander had wanted. We delayed telling the truth because the ocean was changing with merely the simple thought of having the Heir underwater.

"As you know, my parents were killed when I was very young, and I was sent to live with my aunts. They did not know the truth, and by that time, I did not care about the truth, either. I had lived in the lie for so long that a part of me believed I could kill Zitja. I knew I couldn't, mind you, but it didn't seem to matter to me anymore. Besides that, it was Sirens that had killed my parents for fear of who I was, and I wanted to do all that I could to avenge them."

"But," Coral interrupted, "Zitja killed your parents because she believed you were the one that could kill her. Does that not make you angry? Knowing that your parents could still be alive had they not told such a lie?"

"There are many things to be angry about over the course of a lifetime; does it do any good by holding on to them?"

"Why would your mom want to sacrifice you like that, though?" Santi asked with concern in her voice. The whole situation seemed unreal, almost.

"She never thought she was sacrificing me. You have to remember that she had lived down here for a while by this point and was just as traumatized by the Sirens as anyone else. She wanted what was best for everyone, and loving your grandmother so dearly, wanted her to be happy on land. She felt this was a way for everyone to seemingly get what they wanted.

"You have to also understand that just my presence in the ocean seemed to shift the tides. A new energy took hold in the water now that the Siren problem did not seem bleak. Sentinels trained harder and took their positions more seriously, the Sentinel Commander made plans that were not self-serving for the first time, and the Siren problem seemed not to threaten everyday life for the common Serra anymore. My father saw this and encouraged it with the lie—of course, he never felt as comfortable lying as my Crural mother, but it was something he grew accustomed to."

"How have you kept up the lie for so long?" Coral asked, sounding bewildered.

"It is like I told you. I had said, been told, and heard I was the one to defeat Zitja so often that I believed it. I still do believe it for the way that it maintains my determination. Have I not effected much change where the Sirens are concerned? They are quite sufficiently maintained in their new location and hardly cause much trouble at all.

"The only time I really recognize the truth is when I am face-to-face with Zitja herself. Santiago, you remember when I did not kill Zitja last year as she pursued us away from the battle and you wondered why? Well, now you have your true answer. I actually cannot."

Everyone was silent for a moment before Amed's look of concentration melted away as a large grin broke across his face.

"But, Santiago, you being here is the best news the ocean has received since Nephira herself returned. We can set things straight and effect real change. One day, you will have a child who can do the job that I cannot."

This statement shook Santi from the calm that listening to Amed's story had created within her. She had been so excited to tell him the news she had gleaned from her abuela's journals, as if Amed might find relief from the burden of needing to save the ocean, but she hadn't yet gotten to her point.

"I want to do it!" Santi said forcefully. "That's why I'm down here. I've decided to make my life here, and in doing so, I want to help with the cause to get rid of the Sirens."

"Oh, Santiago!" Coral said, raising her hand to her chest. Santi could feel the disapproval in her Ku.

"Are you sure about this?" Amed said reassuringly. His fatherly protective air engulfed her. "It is very dangerous. We have waited thousands of years to find someone. We can wait longer."

Santi was hurt by their dismissal.

"No, I want to do this. You said that if I chose to stay down here that I could choose my Opus. I choose Sentinel. I know we all have our doubts about my abilities, but I want to try! I want to be there to face whatever needs to be faced. I've seen so much, and you even said that I handled my Siren encounters very well."

Amed was quiet, but Santi could feel him coming up with a rebuttal, so she pressed on.

"I was held captive by the Sirens. I was at their mercy and saw what they were capable of. For weeks!" she emphasized. "Can you say that? I don't mean to be disrespectful, but please let me learn. Please let me try!"

Amed gave in, albeit reluctantly, and said, "Tizz is constantly telling me that I try to hold her back in my desire to be protective. I am realizing that my little girls are not little girls anymore. You are right. This is your choice. We have never decided another's Opus for them, why should I start with you?"

Santi was overcome by emotion and still reeling from his sentiment about his "little girls." She said, "You have been the only father I've ever known, and I love you as such."

And then she enveloped him in a giant hug before she became too embarrassed. Amed hugged her back—a custom that she had brought under water and that was still an awkward gesture for him.

Then he said almost in a whisper, "Rogan is going to be very angry with me."

# Chapter 12

## Santiago

The day after Santi told Amed she wanted to be a Sentinel, the water was filled with debris from an overhead storm that was churning up the surface. She sat on the Healer's table—a large stone that had been cut flat and polished smooth—while the Healer, Tilda, strategically placed starfish on her ankle.

Santiago had not had a good session with Grendor, and in her sloppiness, instead of kicking him squarely in the chest as she had intended, she slid her leg along the edge of his blade. Grendor felt terrible that she was hurt but tried to tell her that it was part of the process, and she would learn from it. The cut was her first serious injury during training, and it was simply because of careless maneuvering. Santi wanted to blame it on the distractions in the water. The current was hectic, and the debris was in the way. But she knew battle could be worse than a little shrubbery and litter floating around. The truth was, she felt discouraged and was letting it effect her concentration.

Without warning, Amed swam into Tilda's shelter, where she did her work in the large front room. He approached Santi with a sense of urgency and reproach.

"Remember to keep your Ku open to your surroundings or anything can sneak up on you."

Santi looked up from watching Tilda, and her heart sank. She wasn't doing much right today.

"I know, I'm so sorry. It's so hard to focus on what I'm doing while my Ku is open to my surrounding. Sometimes I just can't focus."

Amed just shook his head, but he didn't seem too upset.

"I've come to talk to you when you are finished."

"Excellent timing, Amed," Tilda proclaimed. "Santi is finished."

Tilda looked at Santi and said, "Come back tomorrow so that I can check on this, but otherwise, the starfish will do all the work, and you should heal up nicely."

"Thank you, Tilda," Santi said before following Amed out of the cavern so they could talk in private without being rude.

They made their way to the garden, where Santi was due for her turn at weeding. Luckily, swimming didn't seem to bother her cut so long as she kicked from her hips and knees and kept her ankle still.

"I came to tell you that I will be going to Daris tomorrow. I am going to fill Rogan in on all we have discussed. I had better find Tizz and tell her, too. She deserves to know. You should make a lot of progress by the time I return, Santiago. I may be gone a few months because I will also meet with my Sentinels to create a plan for you."

Santi's stomach flipped over in her belly. They had agreed that she could not begin training to be a Sentinel until she had learned all she would have if she were raised as a Serra. Amed decided that he would be leaving Grendor behind to teach Santi. Coral had agreed to put her work as an Artisan on hiatus and assume the position of Magister to Santiago, just as she had done when Rogan and Amaratizz were young. Between the two of them, they would catch Santi up on all she should have learned from her beginning lessons and Daristor, if she had been raised as a Serra.

"If you are diligent, we could possibly be ready for Zitja within the year."

Amed paused as if contemplating whether to tell Santi what he was thinking before he gave a nearly imperceptible nod of his head and continued.

"While I am there, I will work with my first in command and top generals to create a strategy to attack the Sirens and give you an optimal chance of success against Zitja. We have been working on an assault of the Siren camp to happen later this year. If we strategize it just right, it could be the opportunity we need to end this problem once and for all. Remember that this is important not to tell anyone about. We cannot compromise the upper hand we have. "

Santi blinked rapidly. She was still reeling from finding out she was the Heir, and this statement made it all very real. *One day, I will actually face Zitja*, she reminded herself.

Santi had a lot to do, and she hadn't been taking it serious enough. Abruptly she felt very inadequate.

Amed, sensing her dread, reassured her.

"This is still a long ways off. We will make sure you are ready. If you are still up for it? You do not have to do this."

"No."

She knew this was her idea, and she stood by it, but discussing it directly made the reality extremely intense. Like looking at the sunlight after sitting in the dark.

"If only you were the true Heir, it would be much simpler."

She tried to joke, to shake it off, but Amed's Ku was suddenly more grave than before.

"Santiago." Amed grabbed her arm to stop her from swimming. He suddenly sounded worried. "Someone is connected to your Ku."

"What?" She was confused. "No, I'm only connected to yours."

"Yes, but someone else…"

He trailed off, and Santi was left to wonder what was happening. She always wanted to impress Amed, but he had just caught her sitting HaruKu, and now someone was connected to her without her awareness. That meant the person could hear everything she was saying. *So much for impressing Amed today*, she thought, frustrated with herself for not doing anything correctly. Trying to make up for her shortcomings, Santi found the other Ku in her chest and reached out to it.

"Caliapi!" Santi nearly shouted.

S.R. Atkinson

Suddenly, the turquoise-tailed dam swam up to where they had stopped in the middle of the kinship, surrounded by plants, fish, and shelters. Amed confronted her.

"Making a connection without the other's awareness is—"

"No, Amed." Caliapi was speaking fast and her heart was racing. "I connected to her only a moment ago."

Santi didn't quite know all of Serra law, but she could guess how inappropriate that would be—like eavesdropping. Whatever the consequences, Caliapi was clearly afraid of Amed's authority.

"Santi didn't notice. I just connected, but she was talking, and I didn't want to interrupt."

Amed only stared at her fiercely. Santi wracked her brain to remember what they had just been talking about and became very nervous. Caliapi could have overheard that Santi was the Heir. Santi wasn't worried that Caliapi would use the information against her, but she might tell someone without knowing how important it was to keep it a secret.

"I…" Caliapi hesitated, almost cowering before Amed. "I have come to make amends."

Amed gave one of his nearly imperceptible nods before saying, "This should have been done long ago. As it is, find me next week in Daris to finish your punishment."

Caliapi hung her head. Amed said goodbye to Santi and left the two women to speak.

Santi's eyes widened. She did not like being left alone with Caliapi. A nervous chill ran down Santi's spine. Her last nuntium from Rogan had been both confusing and mysterious. All he said was, "I sorted things out with Caliapi and learned something I have to talk to you about." Was this the thing he needed to tell her, only Caliapi got to Santiago first?

Santi felt foolish hovering low amongst the plants, feeling like her injury made her look weak, unsure what was happening. She looked up at Caliapi, who was in the water above her, and the dam raised her head, a fierce look in her eyes.

"As I said, I have come to make amends."

Santi only scowled further, squinting her eyes and grinding her teeth. Caliapi wasn't speaking with the tone of someone who wished to apologize.

"For what?" Santi asked, a hint of defiance in her voice.

Caliapi had an air of confusion mingled with condescension.

"Rogan did not tell you? Or Amed? It was his decision that I am even here. As part of my punishment."

She was starting to sound exasperated.

"If I had my way, I would really rather not talk to you again."

The urgent need to fling herself at the arrogant dam consumed Santiago. She dropped her fear of the girl and took a more offensive stance that she had learned in training. She did not like Caliapi hovering above her, sounding threatening and superior.

"Listen," Caliapi said as if she'd rather turn and leave, "Rogan always loved you. I knew that, but you were gone so long that I figured he would forget you in time, if only I was patient. I was with him for a long time. We were in love, you know."

Jealousy resounded through Santi, but she knew Caliapi was only trying to goad her. Why she came here just for this, Santi didn't know, but she wasn't going to allow herself to be cajoled into a fight. She waited silently for the redhead to finish what she came here to say.

Caliapi let out a little growl.

"Fine, the truth is that I loved him, but he was still completely wrapped up in you. He knew how I felt and did not dissuade me from pursuing him. I took it as encouragement that things would change eventually. If only I had the luxury of being HaruKu like Crurals. Save myself a little embarrassment."

This took Santi by surprise. She had always felt like Crurals were at a disadvantage and that using one's Ku was the luxury. She didn't say so, but she thought Caliapi was wrong about this.

"While training to be Crural Guardians," Caliapi continued, "one day, he said to me that maybe he needed to forget you. That he was starting to put his life on hold for love of you. After that… things changed between us. They were finally headed in the direction I had been hoping. I thought we would be Bound. It seemed to me that was the course our relationship was taking."

Santi didn't like hearing any of this and wanted to shake the stupid girl and tell her to get to the point, but Caliapi continued.

"When it never happened, I knew that he would never forget you. I was exceedingly angry. I felt that I had wasted valuable time on him that could have been spent on other pursuits.

# Surface Tension

"That is when he decided to go to the Liscon Region for a while to 'collect himself,' as he said. We were to meet back up later and see if time had changed his heart and if we might be Bound after that. I again allowed myself to put my life on hold to wait for him to make a decision."

Santi felt uncomfortable with the heartbreak she sensed in Caliapi's Ku—as real as if it were her own. Santi didn't want to feel empathy for Caliapi, and she didn't want the dam to feel just how upset her words were making her. She kicked her feet and swam up to meet Caliapi eye-to-eye.

"Why are you here, Caliapi? If you're trying to tell me that Rogan has chosen you, I don't—"

"That is not why I am here. But I can certainly relay that message while I am here, since he hasn't told you already."

Santi kicked her feet to swim just a little above Caliapi so that she could look down on her for the first time in this conversation.

Santi spoke with confidence, having learned the truth from Rogan's nuntium.

"I know that you and Rogan are done. In fact, he told me that he would rather never see your face again as long as he lives."

The last bit was an elaboration of what he had said, but Rogan had made it clear he and Caliapi were through, and Santi was growing irritated with Caliapi's lies and hostility.

"So tell me now, why are you here?"

Caliapi looked like she would argue after having been caught in her lie, but she pulled herself together and carried on with her explanation.

"You stumbled on Sully, Torren, and me just days after my last interaction with Rogan. He was on his way to the Liscon, and I was on my way to pathetically wait for him to return. When we ran into you..." She paused and disconnected her Ku before immediately reconnecting.

Santi had never experienced anything like that before in conversation and wondered what it meant.

"I was not myself. I was rude to you where you deserved nothing but kindness, and I did things I am very ashamed of. I am sorry for that."

"Well, sure," Santi said.

She looked around the water at the plants, towards the garden where she had been headed, back towards the shelter where she could seek solace from this miserable conversation, avoiding eye contact in any way she could.

*That must be the Crural equivalent to disconnecting Kus for a moment*, Santi thought.

Finally, she looked back at the dam.

"I can understand why you were rude. I forgive you."

Caliapi's Ku grew more intense, and Santi realized she had not said everything she had come to say. Dread filled her once again.

"No, you misunderstand me. I have not told you what I am here to apologize for."

Santi looked at Caliapi with confusion as her heart began to pound harder. Dread from an unknown source filled her with the anticipation of the upcoming information. Caliapi's Ku was clobbering the water around them with angst and jealousy. Caliapi kicked her tail almost imperceptively and swam to look down at Santi. The water became suffocating from the emotion from both women.

# Surface Tension

Sometimes, it was too much to feel as a Serra felt and, for the first time since knowing this world, Santi understood the luxury of having a hidden Ku. Santi scratched a nonexistent itch on her left arm, if only to give herself something to do.

"What didn't Rogan tell me?"

"You see, when we stumbled upon you, Sully already knew he would take you to the Sirens. I assume he had been planning the scheme in his head long before we saw you that day. When you wandered off, I knew what he was going to do, and I did not stop you."

Caliapi's regret washed over them, drowning all other feelings. But where Caliapi began to lose her anger towards Santi, Santi's rage grew stronger.

"I then kept it a secret for an entire day before I did anything about it. I am ashamed to have let this happen. Rogan said that if you had died, it would be as much my fault as it was Sully's."

"And he's right!" Santi shouted, kicking her feet so that she was looking down on Caliapi. "I was nearly killed! I was kidnapped and starved and Sung to for over a week! And you could have prevented the whole thing."

She balled her hands into fists.

"I do not expect you to forgive me," Caliapi said without losing any of her previous haughtiness, "but only know that I do regret my actions."

Santi did not know Caliapi had anything to do with the events surrounding her kidnapping nearly a year ago, and now she had was boiling with anger.

"You put Rogan, Amed, and a lot of Sentinels in danger coming to get me."

Santi sounded admonishing, but the truth was, she had a lot of guilt over the situation herself. A lot of people had risked their lives for her.

"I know, and I truly regret it. I have already had to answer for my actions to them, but I am here to tell you I am sorry."

Santi wanted to punch Caliapi in her smug Ku. She was not apologizing because she felt truly sorry for it—though, if Santi were honest with herself, she could feel true regret mingled in with the indignation and jealousy emanating from Caliapi's Ku—but mostly Caliapi was here because it was part of her punishment. Santi was all too familiar with the Serra custom of making amends after having done wrong. As children, Rogan, Sully, Tizz, and she were always getting into trouble and having this very same consequence.

"When Sully told me of his plan to kidnap you and take you to the Sirens as bait for Amed and that you would eventually be killed, freeing up Rogan for me, I am ashamed to say I relished the thought. I went along with his devious plan, though I do regret it. I do."

Santi kicked her feet carelessly,, sending a shot of pain through her ankle. She ignored it and swam closer to Caliapi, fists balled. Santi was sure that Caliapi was only sorry things had turned out the way they had and not with Santi dead and Caliapi in Rogan's company.

"I take small pride in saying that I was supposed to wait longer to tell Rogan—to make sure that Sully had sufficient time to make arrangements—but I told him after one day instead of two."

# Surface Tension

"Oh, thank you," Santiago sneered. "You saved me a whole extra day of torture by your sudden stroke of conscience."

"Listen, I am sorry," Caliapi shot back, not sounding sorry at all. She flicked her tail in the water to rise a few inches. "I'm sorry for a whole lot of things that happened over the past few years. I wish many things would have turned out differently."

"Just stay away from us now," Santi said, climbing in the water to look down on Caliapi. "We hate you for what you've done. Are you working with the Sirens and Sully still? You seem devious enough. I'm surprised you haven't made the transformation into Siren yourself."

Most of that wasn't true. Santi didn't know how Rogan felt, and she didn't think Caliapi was very evil—mostly stupid and jealous—but Santi was angry and wanted to hurt her. Being taken to the Sirens by her childhood friend was the worst thing she had ever been through. It still gave her nightmares.

Santi realized she was very close to Caliapi and was on the verge of hitting her. She did not want this to devolve into a cat fight, Amed would be very disappointed in her. She kicked herself backwards and looked around. The two of them were nearly at the surface and would have been having this conversation with their voices if they kept trying to look down on the other for much longer.

Caliapi filled herself with all her former haughtiness and rage.

"I have said what I came to say."

Then she turned to leave.

"You've hardly made amends!" Santi shouted.

"I will do double punishment with Amed, then," Caliapi said as she swam away.

Santi felt the nearly imperceptible pop of Caliapi disconnecting, and she let out a scream of frustration in the water. She was boiling. Caliapi could have stopped everything from happening. With two small kicks of her feet, her head broke the surface, and she expelled the water from her lungs. The cool breeze felt nice on her face as she tried to shake off the encounter. Santi let out another scream for the wide-open ocean to hear.

# Chapter 13

## Carmen

Carmen looked behind her as the Sentinels jumped from the water to grab Santiago. They called for Carmen in her Ku as he ran swiftly, carrying her away from the scene of her betrayal.

Had she made a horrible mistake? She had committed treason. She was abandoning her world and the people she loved, dooming them to live with Sirens forever. For what?

This was essentially the turning point in her life; she had chosen to take a proverbial leap with Santiago, and she could never return to the water again. She was now a hunted dam. The bucks on the front line were declaring treason and contemplating how to bring her down to throw into prison. Luckily, she was too far away to hear Terret, for surely he would have heard about her betrayal by now.

Carmen closed off her Ku to them. She had made her choice; that wasn't her life anymore.

"Where am I going?" Santiago asked after he had been running for a few minutes.

"Huh? Oh!" She had been completely distracted, listening to the conversations in the water. "You can stop running now."

Truly, he only needed to get away from the edge of the water, but she was carried away by her desire to put a chasm between them and the ocean.

The moment she had yelled at Santiago to run, the Sentinels under the surface knew her intentions. They felt the moment her Ku had shifted, and they leapt from the water, attempting to catch Santiago before Carmen had the chance to ruin everything. It was lucky for them both that Santiago had unquestioning faith in her, and he didn't hesitate to jump up and run. He had been running ever since.

"What happened back there?" he said as he sat her down in the sand. "You scared me. Are you ok?"

Carmen thought fast. She couldn't tell him the truth. There would be so much to explain and even more to avoid in her explanation.

"There are Serras after me."

"After you?"

"Yes. They want to capture me." It wasn't a lie, after all.

Carmen looked up into his dark brown eyes and tried to use her face—untrained in expressing emotions—to convey the desperation she felt in her Ku.

"I cannot go back."

# Surface Tension

"You don't have to," he said as he picked her up and started walking again. They walked silently across the beach, neither knowing quite what to say.

When he got to the edge of the beach, she saw that he had been waiting, or at least hoping, for this very thing to happen.

Santiago set Carmen on her wheelchair—the same one he had used to take her to the fair—and covered her tail with a blanket. He leaned down and kissed her on the cheek before pushing her away.

Carmen's heart pounded loudly in her ears. What had she just done? What was she going to do now? She was breathing heavily and looking around as if any moment Terret was going to show up and take her away. Santiago reached down and touched her face gently, and Carmen took a calming breath. She would figure it all out. It seemed they would figure it out together as Santiago took her to his home.

Carmen spent the first few days riddled with worry and guilt. At night, she dreamed that the Sentinels had found her and had come to take her back. They would pull her from her bed. In her dream, the floor of her room turned into water, and they dragged her under the surface. Every night she awoke in a panicked sweat. She felt fear as real as if she were being attacked by Sirens, and no amount of calm breathing could make her believe they couldn't reach her on land. But every night, Santiago stroked her hair, reassuring her that she was safe.

Where the nights were tumultuous, the days were blissful. Samir would be proud of how happy she was. In the mornings, Carmen and Santiago would laugh together and share ideas. While he was at work, she would go to the library in her wheelchair—which she found easy to maneuver, though she was still mostly clumsy and awkward—and learn all she could about Crural history. Santiago urged her to take as much time as she needed to get used to the way things were done on land, but she wanted to start right away. She needed to strengthen her arms for the wheelchair, and trips to the library were the perfect opportunity. She was able to learn so much from the books that helped her in understanding her new home. Often times, she would bring home works of fiction to read until Santiago returned, and then they would spend the evening talking or watching the television, a device that fascinated Carmen to no end.

Santiago was nothing but patient and the embodiment of care. Together, they figured out how she could navigate his home and how she could hide her tail when she was around town. It was Santiago who sewed her a type of bag that she could slide into so that her fin wouldn't peek out from under a blanket. He bought her long-sleeve shirts and Crural hair pieces. She felt mildly nervous about her webbed fingers, but he told her that once in a while Crurals were born with them, and it would not be viewed suspiciously. By the end of the first month, they had built the beginnings of a life.

They didn't find the need to discuss what was happening. Both slipped right into their new roles in their relationship as if they had been waiting for it to happen. Being with Santiago felt to Carmen as if she was always meant to live this way. If she were supposed to have lived underwater for the rest of her days, she would never have guessed it. She felt more at home amongst the Crurals than she ever had in Serra life.

Even her guilt started to dissipate. Maybe it was selfish of her to be so happy while her people continued to suffer at the hands of the Sirens when she could have done something about it, but Carmen was finding it harder and harder to care. Not that she had turned her back on her people, but she had learned to justify it in her mind. She deserved happiness, and Santiago did not deserve to die at the hands of the Sirens because of her, and maybe one day her posterity would eventually find their way underwater and defeat the Sirens. She thought of ways to make sure there was a record left for them. Maybe she would try using the typewriter.

One morning, after living on land for six months, Carmen woke up and gasped loudly.

"Santiago!" she cried, reaching over to him.

He awoke instantly.

"What is it? Are you all right?"

"Santiago, I… I just… slept. That is all." Carmen laughed out loud. "I did not have a bad dream or wake in fright. I just slept."

She leaned over and kissed him before sitting up.

"I feel so…"

She leaned over the bed and put her hands on her wheelchair.

"I just feel free and light."

Carmen pulled herself from the bed to her chair as she sighed with happiness.

"Carmen that is wonderful."

"I know. Maybe I am finally done being scared of my old life."

But as she said it, her wheelchair rolled away from the bed. She leaned harder on it and tried to pull it back, but her tail started slipping, and she couldn't regain control. She hit the floor with her hands, then face. Finally her chest hit the ground, and her tail flipped over her body.

"Carmen!" Santiago shouted and propelled himself out of bed, jumped down to the floor, and gathered her in his arms.

Carmen only laughed.

Santiago laughed.

"No more nightmares. I just have to remember to put the brake on my chair. A problem I will gladly deal with."

They sat on the floor together, Carmen finally feeling unconcerned with what once was. For the first time in her life, something was motivating her to action other than duty; she felt a purpose beyond retaliation. She was driven to fit into Crural life and find a new purpose. It was a relief. She was ready to forget everything in her life about being a Serra and be one with the Crurals.

There was just one thing that bothered her; one thing she truly missed besides her friends and family, the one thing she *could* bring on land with her. She wanted to remedy that loss.

That afternoon, she sat down on the couch with a purpose.

"Santiago, I need to teach you something that is very important to me."

She sat Santiago down on his soft, brown couch. It was the first place she had sat when he brought her home, and she stroked the cushion fondly. Carmen looked around at the simply decorated room with its wide windows and oddly shaped doorways. It had seemed like a peculiar dwelling when she first arrived, but now it was home. She breathed out a quick breath and held his hand.

"After living away from the Serra world—the only world I have known—I want to have a piece of that home here on land."

She had embraced everything about Crural culture wholeheartedly, but this was something she could not live without.

"Anything" he answered eagerly as he took a seat beside her.

"I need you to be able to know the true feelings in my heart."

She felt his heart race and his love for her swell.

"Tell me everything."

"Not like that. I do not need to tell you. I know a better way."

When he remained silent, she proceeded, "Serras communicate through their Kus. It is like the essence of their heart. We connect them together and our feelings are known to one another without discussion."

"Some sort of Serra magic?"

Carmen smiled. "Not magic, no. Magic—I guess you would call it—used to be part of our world. It was called Vis. But no one knows what happened to it. The Ku is just a way of life for us."

He was quiet, and she could feel him wrestling to grasp the concept. He looked out the window through the sheer white curtains for a full minute before turning to her and saying, "Teach me."

Carmen smiled widely.

"You have to be aware of your own Ku before you can be aware of another's. First, I want you to sit silently and focus in on your heart. Soon, you will have a heightened sense of awareness about it. You will be able to feel your desires and intentions inside your heart." When he looked skeptical she added, "Trust me."

"But I already know my desires and intentions," he said with a sly smile and squeezed her hand. There was no mistaking what he meant, but before he said more, Carmen quickly interrupted him.

"You *know* them, but you need to *feel* them. Go ahead. I will wait as long as it takes."

Santiago grew silent, but Carmen could feel him doing nothing more than waiting for her to say more. When she did not, he finally set himself to concentrating. A full five minutes passed in silence before his Ku made a slight shift from unawareness to understanding.

She saw it in his eyes as well as felt it in his Ku; he was beginning to understand that he had a deeper consciousness that he had never harnessed before. The notion seemed to excite him, and he focused harder and pushed himself.

After almost ten more minutes, he looked up at her with his eyes glistening with tears. He had it. He was aware of himself like he had never been before.

He whispered, "Thank you."

After a few more minutes, he nodded. She knew this was her sign to tell him what to do next. Carmen explained the concept of pushing his Ku out to feel all that was around him and to find her.

"It will feel almost like you bump into me, which, in a way, you will... with your Ku. Once you do, find my Ku and connect to it. That part I cannot explain, but it will make sense once it happens. It will seem natural."

He only nodded, so focused on not losing his progress thus far.

Carmen sat quietly and waited. She felt his Ku move outward and back towards his body again as he grew comfortable understanding how it worked. Finally, she felt him bump against her, and her heart soared. She knew he would grasp the next part quickly, and she was elated. She wanted him to feel what she felt, to know what she knew in a deeper way than words could explain. She was elated for him to finally know, truly and honestly know, how she felt about him.

Slowly, his Ku wrapped around her as he felt his way through this new phenomenon, and then, like a notch clicking into place, he connected their Kus. A jolt hit them. Their love was thick between them. They could feel it as if it were a tangible object to be picked up and examined.

Carmen placed her hand on his heart and, without question, he did the same to her. No words were needed to express what had just happened. The feeling—the overwhelming feeling of love and commitment—told it all. They were Bound in that moment.

"Enjoy that book! I sure did!" Carmen called out as she ushered the last patron—an old man with white hair protruding from his nose and ears—out of the library and locked the door behind him.

"I thought that guy would never choose a book and leave," she sighed to her coworker. "I finally handed him a book on fishing and told him it was my favorite one."

"He'll be back tomorrow," returned Blanca, a middle aged widow with a dazzling smile and quick wit. "He'll be telling you that he loved the book and it is now his favorite as well. He only comes here because he is in love with you, Carmen. Everyone is. You should sell cars or something. You'd make a fortune."

Carmen laughed, and the two women set about closing up the library.

She had come so frequently to the library and had such a passion for books and knowledge that they offered her a job after one particularly intense all-day visit amongst the stacks.

For the past five years, Carmen used her advantage as a librarian to steamroll her one-woman mission to read every book ever written. She would often get distracted by reading during her shift and could only be pulled out of a book by a patron needing her assistance. Every night she would bring stacks of books home with her, and Santiago was starting to wonder if she was going to start her own library at home.

"Here, let me help you with that, dear."

Blanca swept the stack of books out of Carmen's hands and began putting them up on the higher shelves.

"It is fine, I can reach them," Carmen said in defense. "I have worked out a system."

Her tail wasn't completely useless; she could put pressure on it and have it support her weight—albeit awkwardly—to reach up to the higher shelves if she was quick enough. She had only fallen once but recovered before anyone noticed.

But as she reached up to grab the books from Blanca, she paused so suddenly she nearly toppled over. That terrible, ugly feeling touched her again. It came from so many people she encountered that she was tempted to close off her Ku in the Crural world so that she would never have to feel it again.

"Don't be silly," Blanca cooed in a motherly way. "We're about done here if you want to get home. I think Santiago is in the parking lot already."

And there was that feeling again.

Pity.

Carmen wanted to recoil and shudder from the older woman's well-intentioned benevolence.

Blanca thought very highly of Carmen, she knew, but the wheelchair made Carmen seem broken. An object to protect. No matter what, Blanca would never view Carmen as fully capable.

"Ok, goodnight," Carmen conceded.

It was easier than arguing, and Carmen didn't want to force Blanca into saying something unintentionally hurtful about Carmen's abilities.

Carmen gathered up her things and slipped on her sweater. She had never been the object of pity in her underwater life. It was an entirely new emotion for her. Serras hardly felt it because they either understood that the other was not one to be pitied, or they would seek to understand the Serra whom they might pity. She had only learned of the concept through reading and asking Santiago about it. And, of course, feeling it from every Crural she encountered. It was such a disrespectful emotion in Carmen's opinion. She didn't ask for it, yet they showered it on her at every turn.

Carmen shut the back door and saw Santiago's truck in the parking lot. As she pushed herself toward it, she wondered for the first time if she had made a mistake. Her love for him was stronger than she could have imagined feeling towards another person. She didn't feel even a hint of disappointment from him, only love and admiration. He didn't care in the slightest how she got around. But was that enough for her to deal with the constant barrage of kindhearted condescension because of her chair?

He greeted her with a smile that instantly fell when he connected to her Ku.

"Carmen?" He crunched through the leaves and squatted down to look her in the eyes.

"What's wrong?"

Carmen wheeled herself over to the passenger side, opened the door, and hoisted herself inside.

"I don't like the way people react to me being in a wheelchair."

She flicked her tail so that the bag Santiago made—which they jokingly called her "pants"—swung inside the truck.

"I am capable—fully capable—of anything other people are capable of... except walking."

She slammed the door closed.

Santiago put her chair in the bed of the truck and came around to his side. He started the car and drove out of the parking lot before he spoke.

"Ok! What do we do? Let's fix this."

# Surface Tension

"Santiago! There is nothing to fix."

She didn't know why she was letting her anger get the better of her. Usually, she loved his productive attitude, but right now she used his optimism to fuel her fury, as if it was all his fault somehow.

"We cannot live underwater for numerous reasons, but I cannot live feeling the Kus of strangers who think I am pathetic.

"You know, I used to be something. I was important. I was in training to have the most respected Opus—job—that one can have. I only ever stopped training because I had a special assignment. But I was not even given that assignment."

She yelled the last sentence, allowing her rage to snowball and take over completely.

"I had to work hard to *prove* that I could do the task. I learned things that no other Serra knows how to do. Do you know that I speak four languages? Or that reading and writing are not things Serras know how to do? I taught myself all of that. And so much more. All to prove I could do what no other Serra has ever done before."

"And did you do it?"

"Yes! I did, I... Wait, what?"

"Did you do it? The thing that no other Serra had ever done before. Your special assignment."

Yes. Technically she had found him.

All the fury she had been building deflated like a popped balloon. She wanted to tell him that she had found the Heir—him. She would have told him that she could have saved her people, but instead she fell in love. She had chosen to save his life instead of everyone else's. She selfishly placed her happiness over the safety and freedom of her people. But she had decided long ago never to trouble him with the burden of knowing the part he played in all of this.

And it hit her what was really bothering her. She didn't hate being pitied. She didn't like it, sure, but every time someone did something for her that she could do herself, it reminded her that she wasn't living up to her potential. She didn't do the one thing everyone was counting on her to do.

"No," she whispered to him. "I failed."

She let the guilt wash over her. Carmen had let go of the guilt years ago, pushed it to the background and convinced herself it wasn't real anymore. Or so she thought. Guilt, she decided, was the worst feeling one could ever harbor. It felt worse than the pity.

"Carmen," he said quietly, but stopped. There was nothing to say. He could feel her broken Ku, and although he didn't understand why she felt it, he knew she needed to feel it in this moment, so he sat quietly.

"Santiago, I failed my people. That is why I cannot return. I had a job to do. The most important job anyone has ever had in thousands of years. Since nearly the beginning of our spoken language, no other has sought to do what I have done. And I failed."

"Is it too late? Can you try again? I'll help you. I will do whatever you need me to do. As a team we are stronger, more capable. Can I help you with this?"

*Yes, you can sacrifice yourself. You can be a martyr for my people and ultimately die.*

Carmen thought long and hard. Maybe if she could train him to fight before they went down there. But she didn't have the skill. Or maybe if she brought him down and together they sought Terret and convinced him to train Santiago. He wouldn't need to die if they only explained.

Terret was so convinced that the Heir would have to be a sacrifice—that a Crural couldn't possibly stand up against the most powerful Siren—but what if he was wrong?

"Santy?" She started her question. What if he could save her people and they could be together? She had thought it might be possible in the beginning, and now that Carmen loved him so much more, she believed she could have both. She wanted to believe it. She would simply explain the situation to Santiago and ask him to help.

But she never had the chance. Suddenly, inside the cab of the truck, they felt the presence of another Ku, and they were both stunned into silence as the good news sank in.

# *Chapter 14*

## Santiago

"Yes, Flora, I know you feel that way." Santi smiled sincerely at the old dam. "And it's not that I don't agree with you, it's just that I haven't seen Rogan in a very long time."

"You two were meant for each other," Flora repeated.

"You'll be Bound as soon as he returns," Delany, Flora's partner in crime, chimed in. "You two have been in love since you were children." Flora and Delany were like the kinship's grandmothers, matchmaking and chatting about the events of the kinship.

Santi pursed her lips. "You two are trouble." Flora particularly had been a big proponent of Rogan and Santi's Bonding and used to accost Santi during her produce delivery to tell her to give up the Crural life and decide in her Ku that Rogan was her future.

# Surface Tension

It was a week after the encounter with Caliapi, and Santi's head was still full of the news she had learned about her kidnapping. She was having a hard time shaking off the anger she felt, and she didn't want to talk with Flora and Delany about their disappointment in Santi's lack of Binding with Rogan. She usually liked her interactions with these two because it was fun to talk about him.

Today, however, she was preoccupied by other thoughts. She couldn't believe the whole kidnapping could have been avoided if Caliapi hadn't been such a jealous coward.

Santi looked at the two of them as they hovered above her good-naturedly. She was working in the community garden after an intense training session with Grendor, and she felt infinitely tired. Gardening was usually a good reprieve for Santi, and she knew the two had her best interests in mind.

"I promise that as soon as Rogan returns, he and I will have a chat about this." Then she added with a smile, "And then you two will be the first to know."

This seemed to satisfy Flora and Delany, and the two of them floated off to pester someone else.

Santi smiled to herself. She pretended to be more annoyed than she was. The fact was, they were a good distraction. It seemed that every waking moment these days was spent doing lessons with Coral as if she was just a pup or training with Grendor. During her limited free time, she would take extra turns in the garden and tend to the plants or volunteer around the kinship. She would be sure to bring some vegetables over to the dams this evening to make up for her dismissal of them.

While she was checking on her carrots—an idea of hers she was pleased to see was working out—she was hit roughly on the side of her body and flung across the soil. She rolled across the green tops and landed on her stomach. Santi reached to her belt but realized she had not brought her sai to the garden. That was her second mistake. The first was not keeping her Ku open to her surroundings. Rogan and Amed were always telling her that she must be aware of her environment at all times, but she enjoyed the solitude in the garden and often closed off her Ku for some reprieve.

Santi scrambled to a lunge position on her hands and feet, readying herself for defense the way Grendor had taught her, when she was barreled into again. Santi yelped, then sprung to her feet to face her attacker. Suddenly, she laughed and squealed, "Amphitrite!" She flung her arms around the neck of her reptilian friend. "You're back! Did you lay your eggs, girl?" she asked lovingly.

She looked affectionately at her massive pet. "Remember how small you used to be!" Santi laughed and put her hand under Amphitrite's belly. "You fit in the palm of my hand! And now you are bigger than any green turtle in the ocean. There is something mysterious about you, isn't there?"

Santi often wondered if Amphitrite was magical; or, more likely, Celia had something to do with it. When Santi was a child, she used to bring the turtle home every night and then all through the winter when she wasn't allowed down at the beach. That was the reason why Rogan had given Amphitrite to Santi for Sariahdiem—to have the ocean with her when she could not be in the ocean. Celia had loved the tiny turtle so much she spoiled little Amphitrite and fed her to excess. As a child, Santiago always admonished her mother that she was going to make the turtle fat. Santi wished her mother were here for this reunion. Celia would love to see Amphitrite again.

Amed had been gone for two months before he returned to the kinship. And not a moment too soon, in Santi's opinion; she was getting impatient. Mostly, she kept busy learning from Coral or training with Grendor throughout the day. Then Coral would fill their evenings with more lessons in an attempt to get Santiago caught up quickly on all she needed to know. Santi found it fascinating to learn about Serra history and customs. She never found herself daydreaming or losing interest as she had in college. Just the day before, Coral had explained about the social faux pas of unintentional eavesdropping.

It was often hard for Serras who were not Sentinel-trained to perceive a Ku that was connected to them if they did not speak right away. Santi was right that it was not punishable, but it was extremely looked down upon. The things she learned with Coral weren't always useful in combat training with Grendor, but she made connections at times and asked him about this same principle of listening to other's conversations.

*Aucupium*, Grendor called it, a good tool for Sentinels but very offensive in Serra culture.

"So can I learn to sense a Ku connecting to me?"

"You can teach yourself easily. Whenever you are connecting with someone, let them go first and try to notice the connection. It takes a while, but you will soon start to notice it."

Santi had implemented his suggestion into all of her interactions around the kinship. It was difficult, but she was slowly noticing others' connections to her.

Her lessons were interesting, and her training was intense, but as time passed, she was growing weary of the same activities and was riddled with curiosity about what Amed had in store for her. As soon as he returned, she pounced on him for information.

"It is nearly time, Santiago," Amed said in answer to her question.

Santi's stomach clenched painfully, and she felt herself break out into a sweat that gave her the chills as it hit the water around her. "What… What's the plan, then?" she asked, trying to sound ready and brave but knowing she failed miserably.

Amed had gone to Daris to tell Rogan everything about Santi being the Heir and training to be a Sentinel. Rogan promptly sent a nuntium to Santi that sounded supportive but was riddled with worry and doubt. Amed had also sent her a nuntium telling her that he and his top bucks were creating a plan of attack that was sure to succeed in ridding the waters of Sirens once and for all. He told her to keep training and learning all she could, and that he would tell her everything in person.

Now she floated in the water across from Amed, ready to show him what she had learned with Grendor while he was away. Amed looked at her intently. Santi noticed just how much he looked like Rogan: the same dark blue tail and tan skin, the same eyes and mouth; but where Amed's was usually serious and determined, Rogan was always smiling and silly. Rogan wore his hair short and shaggy, which was unusual for a Serra, while Amed's hairstyle was more customary. It floated around his shoulders and he wore it simply tied out of his face by two braids that started at each temple and secured behind his head.

Santi took her mind away from the comparison and focused on the task before her. Amed liked to talk with her while she practiced. He said it was good for her to sometimes train with distractions to simulate battle environments.

He took an easy swipe at her, fighting at the level at which she had been when he left. Santi easily flicked his arm aside with her foot while using the momentum to push herself towards his neck with her sai. Amed's eyes went wide in surprise, but he immediately recovered with a proud smile as he grabbed her wrist and flung her to the side.

"Good," was all he said before he answered her question. "I do not think it is a good idea to tell you the whole plan—not because I do not trust you, of course, but because it is not strategically wise."

Santi lunged at him, but he deflected her with insulting ease. She was not discouraged and charged again. This time when she punched—and he blocked—she immediately followed up with a swipe of her sai. He was still able to stop her, but only just barely this time. She kicked off his chest to give herself space, then quickly righted her body to use her sai against him.

"But I will tell you the next step in the plan," Amed said as he came at Santi's neck. She barely got her sai up in time to deflect the blow. She knew Amed would never have landed his khert in her neck, but her heart pounded furiously nonetheless.

"Ok," Santi said when she had collected herself. "What is the next step? Coral says I'm doing well with her lessons and that she'll need to bring in other Magisters soon because she'll have taught me everything from beginning lessons."

"That means you are almost ready for Daristor lessons. This is perfect timing."

Amed grabbed Santi around the neck with his free hand and held her extended in front of him.

"Perfect timing for what?" Santiago said, grabbing his fingers with her hand as she flipped her body around his arm, freeing herself and sending Amed off balance for a moment.

"When Rogan returns, the three of us are going to go to Daris to finish your training. It is time for the final preparations for our attack on the Sirens."

Santi stopped, shocked, just as Amed brought his fist up and punched Santi firmly in the face. She soared through the water nearly ten feet before she stopped herself, and Amed swooped down on her.

"Santi! I am so sorry. Never stop fighting an opponent."

"I know! I'm sorry. It's just... you're taking me to Daris? When?"

Amed smiled kindly. "Rogan should be home in two months and will be due to return a couple weeks after. We will all go back together."

"And..." She wasn't sure she wanted to know the answer to her next question. "And how long after we arrive in Daris are we planning to attack the Sirens?"

Amed weighed the question. Santi knew he didn't want to tell her too much in case someone tried to get the information from her, but he also wanted her to be prepared. "I would say once we get to Daris you will have less than two months to be ready."

Santi's eyes went wide, and she felt slightly dizzy.

"Do you think you can do it?" Amed asked sincerely.

"Yes." She nodded confidently though she didn't feel so. "Yes, I can do it."

Amed seemed to sigh in his Ku, as if he wished she would say she had changed her mind. She knew he didn't like that she was putting herself in such a position, but he said, "Then I will do everything I can to help you prepare."

Santi wanted to hug Amed, but she also wanted to find a cave to hide in forever. She settled on giving him a weak smile. Amed excused himself, and Santi sank down into the sand. This little combat and chat with Amed had been her second training session of the day, and she felt too fatigued even to stand in the water.

She had already worked out with Grendor earlier that morning, and although he sometimes let her get the upper hand to build her confidence, today was not one of those times. He continually bested her again and again, keeping her moving and defending herself until he deemed the session over. And now, after her session with Amed—combined with the reveal that her time for training was coming to an end— Santi felt exhausted and wrecked. Her body was so tired she would have crawled home if she were close enough.

Santi perked up a little with an idea. "Amphitrite," she said to her friend, who was always close by. She wrapped her arms around the giant turtle's neck. "Take us home."

Amphitrite took off swimming towards the shelter, and Santi could barely hold on with her weak arms. She must have looked very foolish hanging off the neck of a speeding green bullet, but she couldn't muster up the feeling to care. She was finding herself getting rather discouraged, and she just hoped she had the fortitude to last two more months until Rogan returned. She was feeling like she needed the kind of bolstering she could only find from his easy smile and playful teasing.

Santi was pleased to find that the separation had made her yearn for his company, and she wanted his presence in a painful way that she could feel in her chest. It answered many questions for her about how important Rogan was to her. She also realized she was missing her mother terribly. Celia also had an encouraging effect on Santi, and she could really use her positive outlook when faced with a challenge.

When Amphitrite stopped at the shelter, Santi was tempted to go inside and curl into a ball in bed and sleep the rest of the day. But sleeping felt like defeat. It was a bright day, with the sunlight reaching all the way to the ocean floor. Now seemed like a good time to send a nuntium to her mother.

The plan was for Celia to check the beach in the back of her house nightly for a nuntium—like checking the messages on an answering machine. Santi and her mother had been sending nuntiums back and forth successfully, and she was glad they were able to stay in touch. With her move to Daris coming up so soon, Santi thought they should arrange a visit beforehand. She intended to use this message to tell Celia she was missed, and maybe they could discuss a visit so Santi could show Celia around.

# Surface Tension

When Rogan was due to return within the week, Santi started getting anxious. She filled up her time and her mind with learning and practicing. She was particularly proud of her success with feeling outwardly with her Ku, and it was paying off in unexpected ways. She was amazed to find how well her combat skills had improved by being more in touch with her Ku, and she wanted to show Rogan that she was finally more aware of her surroundings. He wasn't going to be able to sneak up on her anymore and tickle her unsuspecting feet. She was really proud of the progress she had made towards being more Serra and less Crural. The anticipation of getting to show him everything was killing her.

She had received a nuntium the day before telling her that he was leaving Daris—which was a four-day journey when swum—so now she just had to wait while the butterflies of excitement distracted her at every turn.

Santi decided to go to the garden to weed out the pesky fish and plants and have some alone time. The garden was usually the place she allowed herself to be all Crural—closing off her Ku, so she could sit quietly and think—but she had learned from her surprise by Amphitrite. This time, she sat on her knees, carefully plucking away the pesky parasites that would kill her kelp. While she gardened, she worked on keeping her Ku open in the background. She was still struggling with this, but she no longer allowed herself to ever sit HaruKu. Grendor told her the best way to learn to do this was to actively think of one thing while simultaneously pushing her Ku out further and further.

She focused her active mind on thoughts about how much her life had changed in the last year—and how much more it would probably change. Literally nothing was the same as it had been just last year. Before finding the pearl necklace in her keepsake box, she had been an eighteen-year-old going to college, planning to be an anthropologist. Now she was nearly twenty, learning to be a Serra, and training to defeat the most powerful foe the ocean had ever seen. She wasn't sure if laughing or crying was more appropriate.

As she thought, she forgot about her Ku and it began shrinking back into herself. It was much harder to do than she anticipated. Santi chastised herself and pushed her Ku back outward. When she did, she felt the nearby fish and Serras going about their business, she felt Amphitrite sleeping in the corner of the garden, she felt a few birds on the surface of the water, and she felt something that was moving swiftly appear in her range of awareness. She focused her attention on it and found it was swimming through the kinship faster than normal swimming speed. Santi stood up and readied herself to act in whatever way necessary once she learned what it was.

She slid her Ku around the object. It was a large entity, most likely a Serra or Siren by the shape of it. Santi reached into the leather strap around her waist and grabbed her sai. The being was coming directly at her at a speed that indicated something terrible had happened or was about to. She had learned a lot from her foolishness with the Amphitrite encounter and was ready this time. She lifted her sai to a defensive position as she connected to the Ku of the oncoming individual.

When their Kus touched, she felt a weird sensation she had never felt before. She dropped her sai in the dirt at her feet. Rogan was still approaching fast, but he was also taken off guard by their strange connection and staggered in the water. It was like a bubble popped in her chest and warm fizzy water flowed from it and poured through her entire body. She was numb and overcome with feeling at the same time. Euphoria erupted in her gut with an unwavering truth.

This was Bonding.

There wasn't a doubt about it. She was washed all over by such uncontainable giddiness that she couldn't help but let out a small laugh and smile from ear to ear.

He finally arrived in front of her, and the two of them placed their hands on each other's hearts with conviction driving them, as if touching each other's Ku's from the inside and outside was the only thing there was to do.

Her heart had connected with Rogan's and seemed to lock into place. She felt fulfilled, whole. She had been living some sort of half-life this entire time without even realizing it, and now she was complete. Rogan reached out and enveloped her in a fierce hug and then kissed her hard on the mouth. She responded with more passion than they had ever shared, and she felt more love for him than was humanly possible. The feeling was only something that could be shared between two Bound Serras. Santi felt very Serra in that moment. It was as if she had been waiting her whole life for this instant and she didn't even know it. She felt... right.

"Santiago, I love you." Rogan said.

She responded, placing her finger to the side of her eye. "Obviously."

# Chapter 15

## Santiago

"No!" Santi said fervently when Coral informed her of the Serra custom of having a Bonding celebration the day after a Bonding took place. "My mother needs to be here for this."

Coral chuckled and gave a wry smile. "You had better get to Flora and Delany quickly before the whole kinship is involved in preparations for the event."

Santi hadn't even been awake ten minutes when she went rushing from the shelter, finger-combing her hair to make it semi-presentable. She didn't have to search far to find them. The two old dams were sitting in the kinship center—a place where everyone gathered for parties or meetings—giggling like pups and weaving garlands of flowers.

# Surface Tension

"Flora!" Santi called before she could even see the dams. "Delany, please wait."

"No way, starfish. We have been waiting a long time for this," Flora responded.

Santi swooped down on the two grandmotherly figures, pleading in her eyes and Ku. "I want my mother to be here for this. She needs to be here, and you know it."

Delany gave what might be considered an eye-roll in her Ku. "How long will it take? Bonding celebrations can only be put off a day or two."

Santi was sure they could be put off as long as the Bound couple wanted, but she wasn't going to argue with these powerhouses of influence.

"Give me a week."

"A week!" Flora responded, looking like she'd argue, but then the old dam broke into a smile. "Fine, but any longer and we have the celebration without you! We've been waiting nearly ten years for this."

Santi gave Flora a side eye. "You cannot have been waiting for this since I was ten years old."

"We have," Flora answered firmly. "Since the first time that little pup brought you down here. Scrawny little legs you had."

" And a smile that never left your face," Delany added.

"We knew you would be together."

"But then," Delany interrupted, "you returned to us but needed to go to... college! It is nonsense."

"Nonsense. For sure," Flora agreed.

Santi swooped down and hugged the two of them. If she didn't have her own grandmother, these two would do.

"One week. Thank you!" And she swam away from them while Flora shouted at her.

"You had better send that nuntium right now, starfish!"

That was exactly where she was headed.

"Use your legs to your benefit," Grendor admonished Santi. "Stop thinking of them as a hindrance."

It had been ten days since she was Bound, and she was still waiting to hear back from her mother. It was the perfect time to be productive; Santi was feeling the pressure mounting as the time to be ready for Zitja dwindled.

"Grendor," Santi would have laughed if she weren't so frustrated. "They *are* a hindrance."

"Only because you are thinking about them as such. Look," he extended his arm, pointing the short sword at her. "If you were to get inside my reach," he waved his other hand to indicate she come towards him. Santi ducked under his sword arm and came in close to him.

"And wrapped your legs around my waist."

Again she did as she was told, but she began to feel uncomfortable.

"Now you have rendered my weapon ineffective by your close proximity, but your weapon is much smaller and can still be used in such a tight space. Show me how you could use it."

Pushing her discomfort aside, Santi squeezed her legs to try to cause him pain and hold on tightly if he were to attempt to fling her off. Then she pulled her body in closer and brought her sai down to the back of his neck.

"Excellent job," he praised her. "There is not much I can do with my sword. But…" Suddenly, he brought his free hand in between their bodies and grabbed her neck, pulling her to the side. Santi hung on with her legs while she twisted her torso to get out of his grasp. He tried to push her off or release her legs, but she held on tightly and fought back. They grappled like this for a moment—reminding Santi of some professional wrestling she had seen on TV—when Rogan swam up to them, eyes wide.

"This is an interesting fighting style," he said with a chuckle. "What do you call it?"

"I call it," Santi responded, stopping but not releasing her grip around Grendor's waist and neck, "using my legs to my advantage."

"We will have to try it out later," Rogan smiled slyly, making Santi self-conscious enough to release her grip on Grendor. Santi untangled herself and let out a small squeal of delight when she realized why Rogan had come. She clasped her hands together in excitement and then swooped down on him and grabbed the blue, glowing nuntium from his hands. She connected right away, and Celia's warm voice and familiar accent filled her head.

"I'll be there in the morning. Meet me at jor little pond. I can' wait."

The next morning, so early the sun hadn't even warmed the sand yet, Santi crawled out onto the bank of her old pond. Rogan had made a fuss about her going by herself, but she wouldn't let him accompany her. She had made the journey from kinship to pond a hundred times. She didn't need him hovering and worrying, and, now, as she emerged, she gave a self-satisfied nod.

Santi stood waiting for her mother, excited for the day to come. Holding Flora and Delany off from throwing the celebration without Celia had been hard, but Santi told them the extra time allowed Tizz to be able to get away from Daristor as well so that she could attend. The two dams would do anything to have Tizz back in their company. It also gave them so much time to prepare that Santi was sure she and Rogan would have a Bonding celebration to rival a Crural celebrity wedding.

When Celia arrived, running excitedly to see her daughter, the two women stood on the shore in a long embrace until Celia pulled away with tears in her eyes. "I can' believe my babee is married." She brushed a hand across Santi's forehead and tucked a strand of wet hair behind her ear.

Santi leaned over and kissed her mom on the cheek. "I'm so glad you're here Mommi! Everything is set to start tonight, and you'll get to meet Rogan's family this morning."

Celia pulled off her sneakers, pants, and t-shirt to reveal a blue one-piece swimsuit underneath. "I can' wait." She tucked her purse in between the folds of her pants and handed it to Santi. "Joo sure this will be here when I come back up?"

"Well, I can't be sure," Santi said as she stuck them in her usual hiding spot. "but so far, my clothes are still here if I ever need them." Celia nodded and began walking into the water. "Ok, so what you want to do—" Santi began to explain how to breathe water, but Celia dove into the pond and kicked herself down to the bottom while breathing in a lungful of water.

Santi stopped, poised on the verge of the pond and her explanation, mouth agape.

"Are joo coming in?" Celia called with her Ku.

"How did you learn to breathe water?" Santi asked as she followed her mother under, filling her lungs, and swimming to the mouth of the cave.

"Jor abuela left me instructions at the end of her journal. Joo need to finish dem sometime. I've been practicing in the ocean at home. Now," Celia said, kicking herself around the pond as if she'd been living underwater her whole life, "I think we have a party to get to."

Santi lead her mom to the mouth of the cave, and the two of them followed the tunnel towards the open water below.

When they broke through, Santi regaled her mom with instructions. "Remember, connect to the Kus of anyone who is speaking to you, and greet everyone with the word 'amicus.' Don't forget to hold on to as many Kus as you can when you're in a group. Oh, and Serras don't really hug or give cheek kisses when they meet but... well... I guess these ones would be open to it if you want. They're used to me. But what you should do is—"

"Santee!" Celia interrupted, grabbing Santi's bicep while they swam. "Stop. Joo're making me nervous."

"Oh, I'm so sorry!"

In her entire life, Santi had never known her mother to be nervous. She knew Celia had lead conferences and seminars and controlled a department of over a hundred employees, and Santi had seen first-hand how Celia could turn an ordinary get-together into a raucous party. Nervous was not in her repertoire. "Don't worry, mom. Everyone will love you."

"Well, jes. I'm not worried about that."

Santi laughed and reached out to give her mother a playful punch on the shoulder, but when she turned, she saw something that made her freeze in mid-motion.

"Swim faster!" Santi shouted at her mom as she grabbed her by the wrist and pulled her towards the kinship.

"What is it?" Celia could sense the overwhelming fear in Santi's Ku and looked back over her shoulder. "Who is that?" She asked as she kicked her legs harder.

But before Santi could answer, Sully ripped Celia out of her grasp and held her, knife poised at her neck. Celia screamed out, and Santi wasted no time jumping to the attack. She slid her sai out of its holster and charged at Sully, holding the largest tine of the sai to his gut.

"Let her go, Sully," Santi sneered. Her face was inches from his, but she wouldn't allow any fear in her Ku. "What are you going to do, kidnap every member of my family?"

She had not been this close to him, face to face, since the kidnapping. She was filled with a peculiar mixture of hatred for her tormenter and a deep-seated sadness for the loss of a good friend.

"Killing my mother will not bring yours back."

In one swift motion, Sully flicked his tail—almost lazily—and pushed Santi backwards while giving him space from her and her weapon.

# Surface Tension

"I've just come here to ask one question," he said, almost as if it didn't matter. "After that I'll leave your mother be."

Santi didn't believe that for a second. She looked at her mom, her fingers grasping Sully's hands at her throat. The look in her eyes was not as terrified as they should have been. Santi knew her mother had grown up much tougher than Santi and that Celia wasn't unaccustomed to defending herself, but she didn't know what she was up against with Sully. Santi hoped they could make it out of this together. She tried to push her Ku towards Rogan or Amed to call for help, but they were still too far for Santi to reach.

Sully pulled her attention back to him by saying, "Caliapi told me that Amed is not the one who can kill Zitja. And you know who can."

"I don't know what you're talking about," Santi said without hesitation. "Amed is the one that can kill her, and you know it."

"Liar!" Sully yelled at her. He pulled the knife away from Celia's neck and immediately thrust it into the top of her thigh. Celia screamed out loud, the last of the remaining air in her lungs escaping as small bubbles.

"No!" Santi yelled and lunged for him again, but he easily kicked his tail away from her. In all her training with Grendor, they had never practiced a situation where she would need to pursue an opponent. She wasn't fast enough to be able to reach him if he didn't want her to.

Sully pulled the knife out of Celia's thigh, and a small trickle of blood followed. Luckily, the knife was small, and Celia was tough. She remained stoic through the pain. Santi knew Celia would keep their secret if her own life was at risk, but Santi didn't think she had the same fortitude.

Sully shifted Celia to his other arm and switched the knife to the other hand. "Tell me the truth, Terrasite," Sully growled at her as he shifted the knife back to Celia's throat.

"I don't know anything you don't know. Sully, please let her go."

"Just tell me and she's free," Sully said and brought the knife away from her mother's neck. This time, he held it in front of her chest and pulled it back, poised to stab her again.

Celia had been motionless up to this point, but now she swiftly punched her arm upwards and connected her elbow with his nose. Sully released her for a second, and she kicked off of him.

But Sully was much too fast and used to dealing with Morales women trying to free themselves from his clutches. He grabbed Celia around the waist again and repositioned his knife over her heart.

"Tell me, Santiago," Sully yelled. He moved the knife away from her body and then brought it down towards Celia's chest.

Santi panicked. "It's me!" she screamed and hoped he wouldn't make the connection that the Heir was her mother as well.

"I thought so." Sully dropped Celia from his grasp and lunged at Santi.

She took a defensive stance, sai poised in front, her other arm to the side, fingers spread, ready to maneuver her like a rudder in whichever direction she needed. Sully charged carelessly, not knowing that Santi was much better trained than at their last encounter.

When he got close enough, Santi pulled her arm across her face and brought it back swiftly, her elbow connecting firmly with his cheekbone. She felt smug that both women had hit him in the face in the exact same fashion.

Sully pulled up short and looked at her, stunned. She knew she'd only get that one lucky strike. She was glad it hit its mark and was rewarded to see a tiny trickle of blood seeping from his cheek.

He came at her again, and Santi raised her sai. She deflected his first jab with the knife but missed a punch coming from his other fist. It hit her in the stomach, and Santi doubled over and drifted backwards through the water. Sully charged again. She was already curled in a ball, so when he came in close, she kicked out her feet and hit him in the chest, sending both of them flying in opposite directions.

Immediately, she knew that was a mistake. It didn't cause any pain or damage to Sully and only put space between them. Santi realized she always used this move on Grendor when she needed a moment's respite. Pushing Sully away like that would never give her the upper hand; she needed something stronger, something that connected and caused injury.

Sully returned quickly, and as his weapon came towards her face, Santi pushed herself below his swing, moving herself downward in an "L" shape as her bottom lead the way.

Suddenly, she was struck by an idea. Santi flung her upper body backwards, sending her head shooting towards the ocean floor. A second later, she brought her feet around swiftly, arcing to meet back up with her torso. As she deftly maneuvered the Landry Tuck, her feet smashed into Sully's neck, jarring him so violently and unexpectedly that he dropped his knife and faltered in the water. Santi used his hesitation to kick off his chest once more, but this time, she used the reprieve to grab her mom by the arm and swim away. Celia kicked fiercely alongside Santi, but Sully only needed a moment's recovery time before he resumed the chase.

Just as Santi was wondering how the two of them could possible get away from Sully on their own, Rogan swept them both up in his arms and swam them toward the kinship as Amed and Grendor took chase after Sully. Santi looked back to see the three of them headed swiftly towards the open ocean.

It didn't matter that Santi couldn't reach out and connect to Rogan. Their Bonding alerted him to her peril. Santi nearly sighed with relief. Rogan took the two of them directly to the Healer's shelter and deposited them on to the table.

"I am going back to help. I will be back soon."

Rogan quickly kissed Santi on the forehead, then rushed from the shelter. Santi hopped off the table and turned to her mother as she spoke to Tilda.

"I'm fine, but my mom was stabbed."

Tilda had already gotten to work examining the wound and assuring Celia that she'd be all right.

"I feel ok," Celia said. "He had such a small knife," she said, giving a wink that made Santi smile despite the worry she felt.

# Surface Tension

"My heart is pounding and I feel dizzy from adrenaline... and you're over there making jokes." Santi wasn't sure if she was angry or thankful.

But an instant later, Celia grew somber. "So that was *the* Sully, aye?"

Santi just nodded. "Caliapi must have overheard me talking to Amed about being the Heir and told Sully." Santi called the dam a name that made Tilda look at her in confusion and Celia's mouth drop open.

"Well, what happens next?" Celia asked.

Santi shook her head and shrugged.

Tilda continued to work on Celia, and the three of them were silent.

"The wound is really small," Tilda eventually said, trying to be encouraging. "It will not cause any long-term damage to your leg. The starfish will clean the wound and heal it with minimal scarring."

Rogan returned when Celia was almost finished.

"He is gone."

"Gone...?" Santi asked, "Like, dead?"

"No, more like chased off and lost. When I got back to where you were fighting him, Sully was gone, and my father and Grendor were returning."

Santi's heart pounded in her chest. "He's just gone?" She looked back at her mother, but Celia was chatting with Tilda, asking questions about the salve and starfish application that was being applied to her leg.

"My father has sent for Sentinel reinforcements, and he and Grendor are searching the perimeter now. I am going to join them. I just wanted you to know it is safe for now.

You can relax." Santi just stared incredulously. She could feel that Rogan wasn't taking his own advice.

Santi stared at him hard. Relaxing wasn't an option at the moment, but she changed the subject.

"Rogan, I don't know about my decision. Maybe I've made a mistake." She rushed on when it was clear Rogan was hurt by her statement. "I mean, in thinking I can cut it as a Sentinel. What even made me think I was capable? Against Sully alone, both my mother and I would have been killed if you hadn't shown up."

"Santiago," Rogan clasped both her shoulders in his hands. "It would bring me great pleasure if you did not want to be a Sentinel, to think that you would be safe and out of harm's way. But it is not really your style. And you would be very angry with yourself if you quit. You are just starting to train and learn."

"Just starting!" she exclaimed. "I've been at it for nearly five months. Your father wants me ready in just a couple more months. My time is almost up."

Rogan wrapped her in a tight embrace. "You are more ready than you think. Look how well you did against Sully. I hate that you had to go through that, but you did well. Besides, you will not be doing it on your own. We are a team. If this is what you want to do, I support you. But I will also be there all along the way. You are not alone in this. In anything."

Santi felt the tightness in her chest loosen. Somehow, she had felt like it all weighed on her shoulders, but she didn't have to do it alone. They were all with her, supporting, encouraging, and protecting her. Santi felt bolstered. She would train that much harder, and when the time came, she knew Amed and Rogan would be with her. She nodded up at him, and he smiled, though the worry was still behind his eyes.

When Tilda was finished with Celia, they went back to Rogan's shelter, where they found Coral arranging some flowers and pearls for a project she was working on for the bonding celebration.

"I am going to help with the perimeter check, and I will be back," Rogan said, and he left as soon as he set Celia down on a cushion.

Santi scrunched her eyebrows and said to Coral with an air of confusion that bordered on anger, "Why are you still preparing for the celebration?"

Coral looked at her, flower poised in her hand, and responded sincerely, "Why would I not? We are set to start this evening, and I still have to get your dress ready."

Wearing a white dress was not a Serra custom, but Santi had decided she wanted to incorporate a few Crural wedding customs, one of those being a white dress. Coral had insisted that she had just the fabric and an idea for it.

"But, surely we aren't still going to do it?" Santi said incredulously. When Coral still didn't seem to understand Santi continued, "But Sully is out there!"

"Sully has always been out there, and he will always be," Coral said calmly. "I have lived my entire life knowing that Sirens are out there. Sharks are out there. Danger is out there, Santiago. There will always be some Sully or another to worry about. We cannot stop living our lives because of the bad that *might* happen."

Santi bit the inside of her cheek and nodded while Celia said, "I am only here for three days, Santee, and I came for a party. I'm fine, really." When Santi still looked worried, she added, "Joo think I've never been stabbed?"

This made Santi laugh out loud, pushing the water from her lungs. Celia was always exaggerating her childhood. "I'm sure you've never been stabbed... right?"

Celia didn't answer, but she had achieved her purpose of lightening the mood. Celia pushed herself off the cushion and came over to Santi, holding her cheeks in her motherly hands.

"Santee, when we were in Venezuela, joo had to take care of me. I was a mess after Abuelo died. Joo did a very good job of taking care of me then. Now it's my turn to take care of joo. Well, someone else will have to actually protect joo," Celia winked, "But I'm going to be the mother, and joo are going to relax and enjoy jor weddi... um... Bonding."

Santi hugged her mother and gave Coral a nod.

She felt better about carrying on with the plans, and when Amed and Grendor returned to report the perimeter was secure, she felt she had their permission to enjoy the day. When Rogan returned an hour later to say that he had gathered Sentinels from surrounding kinships to be on guard in case Sully made an appearance, she felt ready to embrace her celebration.

A few hours later, Santi was on the edge of the kinship gathering sea flowers to make a bouquet. It wasn't a Serra custom, but, rather, something Celia felt would make a nice Crural addition to the celebration. The purple pom-pom-looking plants, pink leafy flowers, and yellow starburst were turning into a bouquet to make any florist envious. She was just tying the ends together when Coral arrived with a huge smile on her face.

"We had better get started or Flora will make good on her promise to throw this event without you. Go get Rogan and meet me at home."

"Ok," Santi laughed. Waiting this long had been a real test of Flora and Delany's patience. "Is Rogan at the new shelter?"

"He is," Coral confirmed and took the bouquet from Santi.

Clapping her hands together in excitement, Santi sprang up and took off in the opposite direction as Coral.

She swam up behind Rogan sitting on a pile of stones, talking languidly to some Serra bucks. He had been working with the Gragglers since their Bonding to hollow out a new cavern that would be their shelter. Once an opening was cut and the insides emptied out, more holes were cut out to let water flow through the shelter so that it didn't get stagnant and dirty. All debris was cleared from the inside, then the inner walls were smoothed out. Over the next week, Santi and Coral would press the floor and plant flowers on the walls. Eventually, Santi and Rogan could collect items from a mercatura to furnish the shelter. But they would be able to move in tonight once the messiest of the work was done.

"Rogan," Santi called when she was close enough to connect to him. She swam up to the site and quickly connected her to Ku the other bucks. They all offered greetings of "Amicus" to one another before she turned her attention back to Rogan. "It appears it's time to get ready."

"I am not quite done here," he said as he motioned to the pile of rubble around him.

Santi laughed at him relaxing on the rock. "Glad to see you're working so hard."

As they made their way to Rogan's parent's shelter, Santi found she had been sufficiently able to let the events of the morning drift away. Excitement and happiness were the only feelings in her Ku, and she was eager to have a fun evening with her friends and family. Coral was right: Sirens and Sully and danger would always be out there, and she couldn't let them take away the happiness she deserved.

They entered the shelter where Coral was ready with a wooden box and a white piece of fabric. Santi slipped the "dress" over her yellow bikini and almost laughed out loud.

"I saw a mermaid on TV wear the exact same thing!" Santi proclaimed, running her hands over the rough fabric of an old ship's sail. The dress was more like a toga or a sash, covering her right shoulder and chest before falling down her left side, a leather woven belt tied around her torso to hold it in place.

"There was a Serra on TV?" Rogan said with concern. Coral looked on in confusion; Rogan understood the concept of television, but Coral had never heard any such thing.

"Aye, no!" Celia interjected. "Santee is being a brat."

Santi immediately sobered up. "I love it, Coral. You did a wonderful job." Coral had sewn pearls along the hem and neckline, and fresh flowers were sewn onto the shoulder.

Next, Coral lifted the wooden box and opened it to reveal jewelry and flowers. She pulled out a wreath of blue, pink, green, and white flowers and draped them over Rogan's neck to hang down around his chest. Santi thought it complemented his dark skin and made his brown eyes pop in contrast. She had never seen him with any sort of adornment, only ever wearing the chest piece that held his short swords on his back. Next, Coral pulled out a similar but much smaller circle of pearls and geodes woven with flowers and wrapped it around Rogan's tail at the base, just before his fin spread out wide. To see Rogan covered in flowers and jewelry almost made Santi giggle. She liked the look of his masculine build adorned with bright colors.

Coral pulled out the last item and handed it to Celia. As her mother tied the matching piece of jewelry around Santi's right foot, Coral explained, "This is a simul. Hundreds of years ago, a Bound couple would be tied together at the base of their tail with a simul for their Bonding celebration. It was a visual manifestation of being Bound. These days, it is customary to wear, but it is merely symbolic."

Santi reached down and fingered the anklet. It had blue geodes and pearls tied securely together with what looked like fishing line and adorned afterwards with the same pink, blue, and green flowers that made up Rogan's neck wreath.

"In a few days, the flowers will die and fall off, but the simul will stay." Coral flicked her blue-green tail upwards to show Santi. "I have not taken mine off since my Bonding celebration. There is no custom that dictates a rule on the matter—Amed does not wear his at all—so you can do whatever you would like with yours."

Santi nodded. "It's beautiful, thank you." She had noticed Coral's simul before but had assumed it was an ordinary piece of jewelry like any other Coral wore. Now that she thought about it, she had noticed other Serras in the kinship wearing them as well. Santi knew she would be one who never took it off.

# *Chapter 16*

## Santiago

The Bonding celebration was in full swing with inhabitants of their own and surrounding kinships in attendance. Tizz had even arrived just as things were starting, and Santi wasted no time smothering her new sister in attention, nearly forgetting Rogan's existence.

"Tizz!" Santi squealed when she saw her and gathered her in a tight hug. "Look at you. You are so old."

"Oh, thanks so much, Santiago," Tizz teased as she returned Santi's hug with fervor. Of all the people Santi's hugging influence had rubbed off on, Tizz hugged with the most sincerity and exuberance. The last time Santi had seen Amaratizz, she was a scrawny nine-year-old with scales up to her stomach and just barely wearing chest coverings. Now, at sixteen, she was nearly full grown, wearing what looked more like one of Santi's bikini bottoms than a loincloth. She still had large, curly, unruly hair and a strong aura around her, but the frantically moving Ku of her youth had been replaced by a calm fierceness. Her torso was as long as Santi's, but now her tail reached far beyond Santi's feet, leaving her to feel small compared to the younger girl.

"I hear you are head of the class and so wise."

Tizz placed a finger next to her eye and said, "I was always smarter than you."

The two girls hugged again before being separated by other guests wanting to speak to the newly-Bound couple. Amaratizz floated away to find her parents with promises to talk soon.

"I knew without a doubt that you two would be Bound," Darly, the little old Serra dam that Santi brought vegetables to every week, told them. "Never has there been a more perfect match. Well, except for me and my Bondmate, of course." Darly nodded agreeably.

"Of course," Santi told her. Darly's Bondmate had been dead for over five years, and the elderly dam still mourned him as if it were yesterday.

Now Santi understood just how intense those feelings were and why someone wouldn't be able to let go. The feeling of Rogan's Ku in her chest was as strong as hers. His death would feel like her own. The thought of losing him brought an involuntary tear to her eye. He wasn't anywhere close to dying, but she already heartbroken at the thought.

Almost elbowing Darly out of the way to greet them was their oldest friend, Wayne. He was wearing the cowboy hat Santi had brought down when she came to stay. Santi told him that with a name like Wayne, he had to have one. He greeted them now by placing his fingers on the brim and giving them a little nod of his head, just as Santi had shown him.

"Hello, Wayne. You look sharp," Santi smiled.

"I brought you a very special gift," he said, extending his shaky hands. Wayne was very late in years now, and he hadn't recovered well from the Siren attack seven years ago. He was scarred and tattered on the outside, but on the inside he was still as sweet and Crural-obsessed as ever.

Santi laughed out loud at the gift, and felt she could never be happier than she was at this moment.

"What… what is it?" Rogan asked, looking perplexed.

"Rogan!" Santi replied with mock chastisement, "it is the traditional Crural wedding gift."

"Oh, right. Ok," he said as though he understood. "But what does it do?"

For this, Santi looked at Wayne to answer. She always loved to hear what he came up with for the function of Crural items. She was nearly giddy with anticipation to hear what he saw as the purpose of a toaster.

"It's a game," Wayne answered matter-of-factly. "See, you put the clams in here"—he indicated towards the two slots for the bread—"and press down this lever. Then you and your friend fling the lever back up and try to see who can catch the most clams! It's very exciting. And this is a convenient strap to carry as you swim." He held up the cord and nodded happily.

"It *is* very exciting," Santi agreed with a smile she could not contain. "But what I don't understand is how you knew that this is a typical Crural wedding gift."

"Oh, I read it in a magazine once."

"You… you read it in a magazine?" Santi was incredulous. Wayne would never cease to amaze her. Not even Amed could read, but it made sense: Wayne spent a lot of time on the shore scavenging items and learning what he could. Santi seemed to recall he used to be a Thaed when Santi was a girl.

Wayne made his way towards the food, leaving Rogan and Santi with matching looks of confusion and amusement.

Santi was delirious with excitement; the more Serras who greeted and congratulated her, the more her head and heart seemed to leave her body. She couldn't focus on anything or anyone; her only awareness was a growing excitement that bordered on mania. The feeling of being connected so thoroughly to someone she loved so deeply was a glorious high no one could ever imitate with drugs. Rogan's heart pounded in her chest along with hers, and every small beat felt like a secret glance between lovers.

The party would be nearly a twelve-hour event, she was told. Starting in the early evening, it would last well into the next morning. A Bonding was a sacred and wonderful occasion for Serras. Coral had told her that Bound Serras—because of their personal knowledge of how wonderful a Binding was—celebrated a Bonding with as much fervor as if it were their own.

The excitement in the water between the members of the kinship was palpable. Flora and Delany had had plenty of time to prepare, and it seemed they filled the entire time while they waited for Celia with celebration arrangements. Flora had set a couple of the Dumkes to gathering as much bioluminescent bacteria as they could and place them in orbs that Coral made. The luminescents were placed around the center of the kinship, making it glow beautifully. After the party, they would use the influx in luminescents to trade with the mercatera, and the Dumkes would make out better because of the party. Santi was glad that their Bonding wasn't a wasteful event like many weddings on land often were. The effect of the added lighting was like twinkling stars on a black sky. Along with lighting and flowers, Flora and Delany had assigned the Magisters to prepare food and had gathered Cantors from around the Nhori. It seemed everyone had a hand in the event.

Santi had observed Cantors before at other celebrations and was always mesmerized by the beauty of their music and a bit awed by the fact that the sound could travel through water so brilliantly. She had seen Cantors before who used Crural instruments they had found and taught themselves to play, but these Cantors were playing Serra-made instruments. Santi had never seen them before, although one looked suspiciously like a harp. Another instrument caused Santi to stop all merriment and stare at it for a full five minutes. It was the largest shell she had ever seen, carved with intricate designs and strategically placed holes to change the sound and pitch. A seal-pelt bag full of air was attached at the back, and when squeezed, sound rang through the water as the Serra moved her fingers across the holes. Most interesting of all was that out of the back of the air bag, a wide tube ran all the way up to the surface to refill the contraption with air. Santi couldn't hear the specific tune, but she could feel the beat in her chest and reminded her of the feelings she'd had when listening to music in the past. The whole thing left her feeling dazed and in awe.

The entire scene was striking, and later, when the Serras began to dance, it was like nothing she had ever seen before. They moved so gracefully, twisting and turning through the ocean. The water allowed for movement not possible on land, and often times, their dancing took them tail over head or floating horizontally. Santi laughed with glee as Serras were dancing upside down for several movements. Amphitrite was in the mix, too, swooping down on the children and doing her own kind of dance. The turtle was clearly as happy as everyone else for this long awaited occasion.

A burst of laughter escaped her lips as she pointed to her mother in the middle of the crowd dancing with Grendor. Santi had never seen him look so carefree and relaxed. Her mother had that effect on people. At one point, he threw her out for a twirl that got out of hand, and she ran into another dancing couple. She laughed, squeezed them tightly, and began twirling and swaying with the Serra dam until Grendor came back to collect her to resume their dance.

Santi thought she could sit and watch the beautiful smoothness of it all for the rest of the night. She was mesmerized. She didn't want to miss a moment of it, but Rogan was pulling her towards the dancers, and he meant for her to learn.

"Oh, no!" she proclaimed in self-conscious preservation. "I don't know how."

"I will teach you."

He was a strong leader, and she was a floppy follower. He pushed and pulled in lovely movements meant to be an elegant dance, but Santi sort of kicked around and flailed about trying to keep up. She must have looked a fool.

*But it's my party!* she admonished herself. No one watching could think she was anything less than the happiest woman alive. Rogan grabbed her around the waist and flung her to the side, causing her to free-flip round and round what felt like a hundred times, but was probably no more than twice. Santi smiled blissfully, and Rogan grabbed her tight and whispered, "You are beautiful."

"Thank you." Santi had never really mastered the art of doing her own hair; even on land it usually fell in natural curls or was pulled up in a sloppy ponytail. But today, Coral had woven and braided it beautifully. A crown of pearls encircled her head, and loops of braids and twists cascaded down her back. She truly felt beautiful with her hair and dress and simul, but mostly she felt so because of the happiness radiating from her.

She looked up at him and locked his gaze. Never before had she seen a pair of eyes so intent on looking into her soul. Her heart fluttered, and she wrapped her arms around Rogan's neck. Her husband's neck. No, her *Bondmate's* neck. The connection was so much more than a husband could ever be. Santi never thought such thorough joy existed. On and on they danced as the night turned late and dark.

Through the entire night, Santi danced with everyone: Celia, Wayne, Amed, and even Tizz had a turn, and Santi and Tizz spent most of the time giggling and talking about the young dam's adventures in Daristor. Santi was so glad her mother and Tizz had been able to make it, she would have been heartbroken if either of them had missed this celebration. Through it all, no one was happier for Rogan and Santi than Celia had been, and there wasn't time for worry or concern about living in separate worlds. They both vowed to stay in touch and to have many visits.

Santi didn't notice the passing of time and had no awareness of the lateness of the hour. Everyone seemed content to share in the couple's joy until they dropped from fatigue sometime tomorrow. Her happiness was all consuming. She was sure that if she never woke up tomorrow, she could not regret a minute of her life.

Finally, Rogan gave her a little smirk and said, "Let's go home. It's time to be alone."

She nodded vigorously and snuck a peak down at his hip where the wide leather strap of his loin coverings crossed over his dark blue scales. She took in the deep V his muscles made between his hip scales and appraised the brown, smooth skin.

"Can we go to *our* shelter now? Is it finished?"

Rogan nodded, and she gave him a sly grin. Since their Binding, they had still been at his parents' shelter while theirs was being excavated. Of course she loved Coral and Amed, but she was looking forward to having much more privacy. She kicked her legs vigorously and was soon out-swimming Rogan's speed in her eagerness.

Suddenly, Rogan grabbed her wrist and stopped her with a jerk. "Oh, no! We cannot do this now."

"What!" She had said this very thing to boys many times as a teenager, and she fully understood their disappointment now. "What do you-"

He cut her off. "Santi, expand your Ku. Really push it out." He was angry with her.

# Surface Tension

She had been working with Grendor for the past three months on this skill and was able to do it with ease and efficiency once she tried. She felt what he was indicating, and a cold sweat made her shiver. Her Ku expanded in a wide circle. She felt the excitement from the party that everyone was still enjoying; fish and animals in the area eating and carrying on their business; birds sitting on top of the water resting their wings. But none of that was what caused her fear.

"Sirens! A lot of them."

He grabbed her wrist and began pulling her back to the party.

"How far away was that?" she asked.

"About two miles."

Her momentary pleasure at having reached so far was instantly dashed when she realized what that meant. "They'll be here in less than ten minutes."

"I know."

When they returned to the others, Rogan set to work right away commanding the mothers with children to seek shelter as far away from the kinship as possible. The others he ordered to arm themselves and prepare for battle. His natural command and leadership left Santi in awe. After setting up a perimeter and going to get his short-swords from his shelter, strapping his holster across his chest, he returned to Santi. "Where would you like to go? To seek shelter or to fight?"

"To fight," she said without missing a beat.

Rogan's face was a combination of worry for her safety and pride in her courage. "Then you'll need this," he said as he handed her the raggedy little sai. "Please stay close to me, though."

"I will never leave you again."

Santi only had a moment to look over her shoulder at the mob of Sirens, over a hundred, all wielding weapons and evil expressions. They swarmed upon the kinship like bees on a hive. Rolling through the water, they spread out among the crowd of celebrators. They wove through the shelters and took on any Serra in their path. They were clearly there for no other purpose than to attack and kill any who stood in their way. Amed's Sentinel backups had not arrived yet; the only ones in the area were him were Grendor and the few others that lived in the kinship. The rest of the Serras poised to fight were regular Serras who were bold enough to face the Sirens. This also meant that they were untrained and susceptible to the Song. Santi saw glimpses of Serras writhing in pain while she fought her first opponent.

Santi tried to fight a beautifully adorned Siren dam as she would fight Grendor. She kept her Ku open to sense the Siren's movements, with her sai poised at her side and never extended herself too far. She had learned from her mistake with Sully and didn't try to kick the Siren for a reprieve. But the dam met every swipe through the water with her short sword, and every blow that Santi blocked was followed by another right after. She was tiring quickly and exerting herself more than she should—exactly the opposite of what Grendor had instructed her to do. She soon realized that when she fought Grendor, her open Ku had been an advantage because he would also keep his Ku open to her. This Siren beast was like fighting against a wall; in fact, she seemed to anticipate Santi's every movement.

# Surface Tension

That's when Santi remembered Grendor's instruction to fight HaruKu. All Sentinels learned to close off their Kus tightly during battle so as not to give away their motives. HaruKu was not a lesson Santi needed to learn. It was time for her to be a little more Crural. She immediately shrank her Ku down and closed it off to the dam. The difference was immediate. The Siren lost her advantage. Now when Santi struck a punch or kick, they landed more often than missed. Santi brought her arm up, striking the dam with her elbow across the face, and then she struck her foe with the backside of her elbow as she brought her arm back. The successive double hits knocked the Siren off balance. Her eyes flared with rage, and she lashed back at Santi sloppily.

This time when the Siren slashed at Santi, she leaned backwards quickly and brought her foot up. It was time to use her legs as an advantage.

She brought her foot around the back of the dam's neck and hooked her with the top of her toes, then pulled her forward. She successfully knocked the Siren's head towards the ocean floor and made her flail helplessly. Santi moved to follow up with a kick, but as she tried to pull her foot away, she became entangled in the dam's necklaces. Santi kicked and struggled and was soon filled with panic. The Siren was recovering, and as she righted herself, Santi kicked her foot frantically to release herself. Adrenaline coursing through her body, heartbeat pounding in her ears, Santi barely raised her sai in time to catch the Siren's blade as she brought it up to swipe at Santi's gut. With the dam's blade between two of the tines of her sai, Santi twisted her wrist and flung the sword out of the Siren's hand. She was elated. That move had never worked in all the times she'd practiced it, no matter how many times Grendor or Amed showed her. Right after casting the sword away, Santi kicked her heel down fiercely, ripping all of the jewelry from the Siren's neck. Then she followed up by sinking her sai into the Siren's shoulder.

The combination of it all was enough to shock the Siren so that Santi could remove the sai and strike her in the other shoulder. The last strand of green gems wound around the Siren's neck glimmered beautifully as the dam fled, both arms streaking blood in her wake.

Santiago didn't know what it was about the Siren dam, but she could not kill her. All of the Siren's beautiful jewelry was distracting in a way that made her too real. The Siren had deliberately put those beads on this morning. She had the same desire for beauty as any Serra or Crural; it wasn't some thoughtless beast Santi was fighting. They were real, with purposes and desires for self-preservation as much as anyone else.

Santi looked to her left and saw Rogan was battling with two Sirens of his own. He was doing a serviceable job, but she wanted to help him, and she *had* promised to stay close. But as she was rushing towards him, she saw a pair of legs in the crowd. *Another Crural?*

"Mommi!!" she shouted. How had she forgotten that her mother was at the party? Santi left Rogan quickly and made her way towards her mother. She connected her Ku and practically shouted at her. "What are you doing here? Why didn't you leave with the others?"

Her mother looked terrified and grabbed Santi on both shoulders. "I couldn' leave joo. I though'… maybe I could get joo and we could leave together."

"You need to get to safety."

"Jes, I see dat now, but you must come with me."

The look of total fear and concern for her daughter made Santi feel a little guilty for saying, "I can't. This is what I have been training for. I'm the one that can kill Zitja." Santi hadn't seen the ancient dam yet but assumed she would be here.

"I am too, Santiago, but this is no place for us."

Santi couldn't argue the truth of it, but this was not the time to discuss such matters. The bottom line was that her mother was not prepared for this, and the longer she stuck around, the more apparent that would become.

"This is why I'm here. This is what I'm training for. You have to go." And as if to prove her point, a gaunt-looking Siren buck swam up to them, mouth open, pointy teeth bared down at Celia.

Santi watched in horror as her mother shrieked out loud and clutched herself around the middle. Then Celia began pulling at her hair and writhing in the water. Without thinking, Santi thrust her sai into the belly of the Siren until the hilt caught skin.

Startled, the buck stopped his Song. At once, he went from looking like a malnourished, ghostly buck to a young, scared pup. He grabbed Santi's hand that was still holding the sai in his belly and pulled it out, releasing him.

Santi turned to look at her mother, confident he was no longer a threat, and grabbed her by the shoulders as she tried to recover.

"Mom, please go."

Celia nodded, convinced she had to leave the battle. "Please come too." she pleaded with her eyes. "We can seek shelter together."

Her mother's stubbornness was infuriating.

And that's when she saw *her*.

Surely the news of Santi's heritage had reached the one-armed Siren, and she sought to do away with her only threats here and now.

Zitja came at Santi with her moon-shaped blade in hand. Santi parried the first blow, but she knew she would be no match for this well-trained Siren queen for more than a few more lucky escapes.

As she fought with Santi, Zitja opened her mouth and Sang, her Song directed at Celia. Santi knew that the Song could cause death in minutes or inflict pain indefinitely. She didn't know how long she had to fight against Zitja before the dam would choose to kill her mother. Santi hoped that Singing would be enough of a distraction to allow Santi to get the upper hand and give her time to call to Amed. If this was Santi's opportunity to kill Zitja, she would need his help. She could never get the upper hand on her own.

Slowly, Celia began bleeding from her pores and Santi knew that her death would soon follow. Zitja suddenly thrust her blade in a tight arc and sliced Santi across her left bicep, and with a second swipe just as quickly, her right. The wounds were so deep, Santi struggled to fight back. Her arms were severely weakened, and she was losing blood quickly. Santi haphazardly reached out to Amed and called for his help. She was sure she hadn't connected with him directly, but someone could get the message to him—or, possibly, Amed was linked to her without her awareness.

# Surface Tension

Zitja raised her blade above her head and brought it down with a swiftness that Santi knew her weakened arms wouldn't be able to deflect. This was the blow that would kill her, and she could merely watch it happen.

Suddenly, from her right side, a blur of a Serra tackled Zitja so forcefully that she was knocked away into a pair of other fighting bodies. With that swift collision, Santi had been protected from Zitja's blade and Celia released from the Song. In one fell swoop, Amed had just saved both of their lives.

Santi quickly pulled herself together and turned to her mother, who was floating to the floor, unconscious. *Or dead?*

Santi dipped down and snagged Celia out of her fall, cringing from the pain in her arms. Celia was still breathing, albeit weakly, as Santiago hefted her limp body around the waist and dragged her all the way to the shelter. Once safely inside, she laid her on a cushion in the main room. Celia opened her eyes as Santi roused her.

With a look of concern, Santi whispered urgently, "I'll be right back, Mommi."

This stirred Celia back to life better than anything else could have. Without sitting up she said firmly,, "No, don'. Joo're not going back out dere."

"I have to help them. Mom, Zitja is out there. This is my chance to do what I moved down here to do."

Celia sat up and pointed a finger at Santi. "Let dem take care of this. It's not safe for us with legs."

"No." Santi hated to be so rude, but she was wasting time.

"Fine, but joo are losing so much blood." Celia ripped Santi's dress off and quickly wound strips of it around the gashes in her arms. The loss of Coral's lovely gift and the turn the evening had taken tugged at Santi's heart.

In only a few minutes, Celia was finished, and Santi had to admit that her arms felt much better. She quickly leaned over and kissed her mom on the cheek before turning and kicking herself out of the shelter and back towards the fray.

When Santi emerged from the shelter, she was surprised to see the area was quite cleared out. She couldn't see a Siren anywhere in the kinship, though the water was murky and hard to see through. The calmness felt eerie after the chaos only moments ago.

In fact, the further she swam towards where the fighting had been, the more eerie she began to feel. Not only was there no combat, there were no Sirens or Serras anywhere to be found. Her stomach clenched with dread. How could everyone have disappeared so quickly? With her Ku closed for the fight with her opponents, she hadn't felt the shift in the fighting.

When she expanded her Ku around the perimeter, she felt the Sirens retreating with Amed's men on their tails. Santi sighed with relief, and her stomach released a little. The Sentinels had arrived in large enough numbers to scare off the entire hoard or Sirens. She kept expanding her Ku to find the remaining Serras in the kinship. She still didn't know where everyone had gone.

And then Santi felt something that made her heart rip in two.

*No!* She whispered to herself. *It can't be.*

She swam with all her might, ignoring the searing pain in both of her arms that caused blood to soak through the bandages. She pushed and kicked, wishing that she had a tail so that she could reach the center of the kinship faster.

After what seemed like an unendurable amount of time, Santiago finally reached the square where just hours ago she had been enjoying her Bonding celebration. She stopped outside the kinship center and saw a group of Serras sitting on the ocean floor, huddled around a body. Santi broke down, tears blurring her eyes, her stomach tied in a tight knot. The lump that sat solidly in her throat prohibited her from breathing, and she coughed twice to clear it.

Gingerly, she made her way through the crowd, pushing Serras aside without consequence in her desire to reach him. She sank down to the sand, letting her toes take purchase, and she began walking towards Coral.

Santi was crying hard now, moisture running out of her eyes and nose, mixing with the water around her, but she took no notice of it. Her heart was tugging in her chest with a tight sharpness. The water was thick from the fight, but her tears obstructed her vision more than the gore. She wiped them away, and her chin quivered. Finally, she reached the group and sank down beside Coral, who was broken in her grief and cradling him in her arms, his head nestled against her tail. Santi reached out and touched the lifeless form of the only father she had ever known.

# *Chapter 17*

## Carmen

Carmen screamed out in pain so loud she woke up Santiago. He immediately jumped out of bed and ran into the kitchen. She heard the water run, and a moment later he was back in their bedroom with a cold, wet towel. She peeled back the covers, well aware of what she was going to see, but was still as shocked and horrified as the first time.

The scene laid out on their sheets was gruesome. Blood and golden scales littered their bed and the floor. Dark red blood soaked through the bottom sheet, while fragile golden scales clung to the top sheet, dried out and crusted to the fabric. Her "legs" were now bare down to her knees and covered in scabs. She reached down and touched her thigh but quickly recoiled at the sharp pains that pierced her from her freshly exposed skin. The slightest touch sent her into a dizzying spiral nowadays.

# Surface Tension

"It's moving faster," Santiago said in awe as he gingerly placed the soaking towel on her thighs. The pain was almost unbearable until the cool water began to ease her tender nerves.

The hegira was moving much faster now. In the first three or four years after being away from the ocean, she had barely lost more than a handful of scales from the sides of her hips each year, and those merely flaked off in much the same manner that Serra pups experienced hegira—in a staggered manner without much pain. When it first happened, she had been curious and almost excited to see what might result. Would she actually have legs? Would she be able to walk around one day? During the last year, the hegira-like change had increased in speed and pain, but in the three months since learning she was pregnant, she began losing scales in bloody, painful, and ghastly chunks.

"Look at my fin," she said as grief tugged at her heart. The end of her tail, which used to be wider than their bed and powerfully strong, was now shriveled and frayed so that it was no wider than her hips and as ragged as an old cloth. "It hurts so much!" she cried as he wrapped another towel around her newly revealed knees and stroked her hair.

"Do your hips hurt anymore?"

She smoothed her hand over the tight pink skin on her hip. "No, thankfully." She moved her hand down her thigh and stopped mid-way. "It does not hurt until here. And then it is only to the touch. But the new skin hurts without touching it."

"Ok, my love," he gave her an encouraging smile. "At least we know the skin is healing. Hopefully, soon you will be finished with all of this. I wish I could take your pain away from you." He gave her a look of such genuine anguish that she couldn't help but smile in gratitude for his concern.

Carmen grabbed his hand in hers. He had been so wonderful through all of this and so helpful. He had tried everything to ease her pain and came home most nights with a new remedy to try. Their cabinets were full of bottles of ointments and oils and tubes of creams and lotions, all to alleviate skin pain and irritation. The problem was that he couldn't find anything to relieve the pain of a Serra dam losing her tale scales.

Santiago raised Carmen's arm by the wrist. "These scales are completely gone now." He gingerly rubbed a finger across her forearm. "Do your arms hurt?"

"No!" she said in exasperation. "These all fell off in one day like it was nothing and have not caused me a bit of trouble. I am glad for it, but why couldn't my legs go through the same process?" Carmen had been rather excited when her arm scales fell off; she was getting dreadfully sick of wearing long sleeves. "And look," she said, sticking her opened hand in his face, the back of her hand nearly touching his nose, "my finger webbings are shrinking, as well. My fingers are rather stiff and sore, but it isn't painful."

She let out another scream as a ripping pain shot through what would soon be her calves. "Nothing like these legs, though."

"Maybe we shouldn't go today. Maybe we should wait until you are done with this process and you feel better."

"No!" she almost cried—a new thing that she had started doing since living on land for so long. In thirty-five years of life she had never cried, had no need to do so because of her Ku, but now she seemed to be crying at least once a day. "I cannot stand the thought of putting it off. I want to be in the water so badly. I yearn to be swimming again. I will risk anything. Obviously."

"I know, but that's another thing…"

"No. I know what you are going to say," she interrupted, causing an expression of worry to cross his face. "I want to go now," she nearly pleaded, "while I still have a semblance of a tail. If there is trouble, I have a greater possibility of escape with this little fin than without. And if I wait too much longer, I will not be telling Samir our good news so much as I will be showing him our new baby. I think it is much too risky to bring our child under the surface."

She shuddered to think what the Sentinels would do if they got their hands on a small, easily manipulated child. They could raise up the Heir to be their own personal Siren killer.

"No, I had better do it now while I am still small in my belly, and--" she gestured to the horror scene in their bed, "look like a Serra for the most part."

"Ok, my love," he said, smiling despite the reluctance she felt in his Ku. He always treated her like an equal team member, and when she made a decision, he never felt it was his place to presume he knew better. "Let's go to the airport. Do you think you can put on your pants?"

They worked together to slide her into her blanket sack. Over the last few years, they had gone through several different designs and patterns until they finally came up with the one she now wore. It fastened around her waist and was cut and sewn together in such a way that it looked like a flowing skirt made from material that was trendy amongst women. Only one small layer on the inside was sewn together to keep her tail from accidentally slipping out. And now that she didn't have any arm scales, she slipped on a tank top and blended in with the other humans. She barely got a second look except for the chair she sat in, but even that didn't stop Carmen from being as functional as she possibly could.

Carmen hoisted herself out of the bed and into her wheelchair with the ease and grace of a maneuver practiced a thousand times. Once she was situated in her chair, her lower body settled down and became more of a throbbing ache than a stabbing pain. She could deal with that and hoped the security screening process at the airport didn't send her back into fits of pain.

"Our flight leaves in an hour," Santiago said with his hand on a travel bag,. "Are you ready to go?"

Carmen nodded. It was her first time on an airplane and her first time diving deeply into the ocean in over five years. She had sat in the water a few times and swum in the shallows to find jellyfish, but this would be a deep dive, and she'd have to immerse herself back into the Serra world. She didn't know if she'd truly feel ready for it.

Santiago helped her out of her chair and set her on the sand. They had had a hard time finding a private beach in India, so they ended up renting an entire house with its own beach so that they could have an excluded spot to meet at night. She pulled off her tail-hiding bag and tightened the straps on the red swimsuit Jolene had given her so long ago. Carmen hadn't worn it since the day it was given to her, and she found it comforting to be wearing a relic of the day she met Santiago.

# Surface Tension

Santiago folded up her pants and collected her discarded shirt.

"Did you tell Jolene about the baby?"

Carmen smiled up at him. She had sent a nuntium two month ago in preparation for the visit.

"Jolene had many expletives of incredulity, but ultimately, she cannot wait to see our 'mer-baby,' as she called it. As you know, their baby was born with a tail, so she is very curious to see how ours will be born. She is going to come visit us in Venezuela after the birth." Carmen kept her Ku as light as she could so that Santiago wouldn't feel her concern, but Jolene's curiosity had resonated too much with Carmen.

While working in the library, Carmen took the opportunity to do a little research on the matter. She read everything she could about what Crurals thought about mermaids, wanting to know what they knew—or thought they knew—and filled her head with all the folklore she could find. She enjoyed the research because it was usually terribly funny to hear what Crurals thought, but eventually all the stories caused her to worry.

Every one of them seemed to be very tragic, and the endings were horrifying. The mermaids in the stories never survived, and usually they learned a horrible lesson in the process. It wasn't until Carmen became pregnant and read a particularly awful tale that she grew legitimately concerned. In this story, the mermaid had to go back to the ocean every night to ward off a curse, but when she failed to do so, her children were born as mutated animals. The whole story was so gruesome Carmen had to leave early from work that day for fear she was going to be sick.

*S.R. Atkinson*

That night she decided that she needed to visit home. Carmen hoped to find reassurance from Samir that she was being irrational. He and Jolene always had a way of making her worries seem trivial. And besides, she missed them terribly.

"I hope she does come to visit," Santiago laughed, breaking her from her ugly thoughts. He handed over her bag that was brimming with presents for Samir, Jolene and the baby. "Our flight home leaves in a week. I will be at the water's edge waiting for you every night... but our house is right there," he said pointing to the bungalow that was a mere ten feet up the coast, "and I'll probably be glued to the window watching for you." He hesitated before adding, "I wish I could go with you. I wish that I could go with you and that by doing so I could keep you safe."

She placed her hand on his heart. "I know."

They had agreed that this quick trip was not the time for him to conquer his ocean demons and that his slow swimming would put them at a disadvantage if they were to run into the Sentinels—or worse. In all this time, she had never even told him about Sirens. "I will be ok! I will be back tonight, and if not, I'll send you a nuntium. You remember what to look for and how it works?"

"Yes."

"Ok, then. I know exactly where his family lives, and I should be at their shelter in a couple hours." They had found a rental house as close to Samir's family as possible so that she would have to spend minimal time traveling. "Now, *where* Samir lives exactly, I don't know, but his mother or the Tipua clan will help me out easily. If I do not return tonight, do not panic! It simply means I have to travel a longer distance to their shelter," she told him reassuringly.

It wasn't necessarily true. It was possible, but not the only option. However, there was nothing he could do from his position on land, so she didn't want him to be burdened with anxiety while she was gone.

"I'll see you soon," he said, leaning down to her level in the water and kissing her. "I'll check for a nuntium right here, every day."

"I'll see you soon." She smiled reassuringly and dove into the water.

Carmen was swimming up to Samir's family's shelter in a little over an hour, elated by how quickly she had gotten there and relieved that she remembered where it was after all these years. She reached out and connected with his mother before entering their kinship, but she was confused by what she felt in the older dam's Ku.

"Carmen?" Kikona proclaimed, a feeling of excitement, confusion, and sadness filled her Ku.

"Jolene did not tell you I was coming?"

She entered the shelter and placed her hand on Kikona's chest. Kikona returned the gesture and whispered, "Amicus."

"I am sorry I have not made it here in a long time," Carmen said, true regret filling her heart. Being with Samir's mother felt as if no time had passed since she was a child. It made her wonder how she could have ever stayed away so long. She had only to look at the lines in the woman's face to realize that, although she had lived on land for nearly six years, she hadn't seen anyone she had known as a child except Samir and Fernando for far longer. "I let my priorities get completely misaligned. And then I decided to live on land. As you can see," she said, making a sweeping motion to her almost non-existent tail. "But I could not stay away any longer, and I miss Samir so much. Does he live close?"

At these words, Kikona's Ku darkened. Her heart filled up with so much anguish and remorse that Carmen could not question its meaning. She clutched her hand to her chest. Kikona's extreme despair and sorrow felt physically painful in Carmen's chest.

Carmen's spirits dropped and fresh Crural tears appeared in her eyes. "How?" Carmen said, thunderstruck. She held her hand tightly to her chest, as if to stop her heart from falling out altogether. "And Jolene? The baby? When? How?"

"It was the Sirens. They attacked their kinship three weeks ago. Jolene, too."

Carmen let out a gasp as if she were still on land. It felt hard to breathe, and her entire chest constricted.

She had received a nuntium from Jolene nearly that long ago. It must have happened right after. Carmen ran her fingers through her long, loose hair. She had not remembered to pull it up after being away for so long. How could she have kept herself from her home all this time?

"And the baby?" Carmen asked.

"He survived," Kikona answered, "though Amed is hardly a baby anymore."

"Amed." Carmen rolled the name around in her head. She had missed the Naming Consecration that she promised to attend.

# Surface Tension

Kikona continued, "He was found underneath Jolene's body, wrapped up in a pelt to stay hidden. But the Sirens killed Samir and Jolene and all of their guards."

Both women sat quietly absorbing Kikona's words and letting their implications make the water grow stale around them. *Her friends were dead. They were dead because of the Sirens.*

Guilt consumed Carmen like a raging fire. Everything she had pushed aside these last years came rushing back up to punch her in the gut. She had done what was best. Hadn't she?

"Where is Amed now?" Carmen asked.

"He is living with Samir's sister and her Bondmate. I can take you, if you would like to see him. Their kinship is not far."

"I'd like to see Rikka again," Carmen responded. She had not seen Samir's sister since they were all children living in the Najilian.

They set off for the kinship at a slow pace. Carmen's tail wasn't as swift as other Serras, but at least the pain was gone. Being in the salt water—being home—made her wounds seem nonexistent. The skin was healing up and her scales filled with water. She felt like herself again. She felt whole except for the gaping pain in her chest where her friends should be.

The journey took a while, and it pushed them out further into the open ocean. It made Carmen nervous to be so exposed, but she wouldn't give up this meeting for anything. Rikka and her Bondmate's kinship was a bustling metropolis that made Carmen very nervous. Serras were moving about visiting with each other and working their Opuses, and mothers watched while their pups played. It felt risky to be surrounded by so many; surely Sentinels were stationed or lived in this kinship. Carmen was relieved when they made it to the shelter without being spotted. The two dams entered the shelter and met Samir's sister, Rikka, and her Bondmate, Ma'leah, with a melancholy, "Amicus."

Carmen greeted Amed and hugged him in her arms with a heavy heart. Although he wouldn't remember her, he didn't seem hesitant at all to meet her and show off just a bit. Amed was a big six year old who seemed to exude a confidence and certainty not often found in the young. He had the same dark but brilliant blue scales that Samir, Kikona, and Rikka all shared, and the resemblance to her dear friend in the pup's face was almost more than she could bear.

"He has Samir's dark eyes and thick hair," she said somberly.

"Starfish," Kikona said with a smile, "we all have dark eyes and thick hair."

Carmen looked up at the three dams and couldn't help but laugh. "You are right. Look at you!" They all let out a laugh that eased the tension. Gently, the sadness in the water drifted away, and they spent the evening reminiscing about their loved ones.

As often happens when losing someone dear, they gained strength from each other, knowing that they all missed their loved ones. Carmen welcomed the stories these women had to tell. Amed talked with the women and told stories about his parents along with them until he grew tired and settled quietly on Carmen's lap. He was a big child, but not so much so that she didn't relish squeezing him tightly in his sleep. After spending the day in such a way, she felt that if she could just hug Amed a little more, it might be as if Samir and Jolene were right in the room with them.

Late in the evening, the conversation somehow made its way back around to the tragedy at hand. Rikka offered to take the sleeping Amed from Carmen and put him in bed, but she refused, saying she wanted to hold him a little longer.

This seemed to make Ma'leah ignite, and she said, "He exudes a sense of security, doesn't he?"

"I..." Carmen didn't understand what she meant by this odd statement.

"It all rides on Amed now. A big burden for such a small pup."

Carmen was silent and barely uttered a faint, "What?" before Rikka chimed in.

"You do not know, Carmen?"

"Know what?"

"Jolene, she was the Heir we had all been searching for. She was the one who could have killed Zitja."

"Samir and Jolene were not killed by a random band of Sirens," Kikona chimed in, "which is why she had the guards stationed to protect her. The Sirens targeted her because she could kill Zitja. But she was ill-equipped to defend herself. Amed will be different."

Carmen's head was spinning. What were these women saying? She wanted them to slow down or start over; someone needed to make sense of it all because it sounded like they were telling her that Amed was a descendant of Tullus. But she couldn't formulate a question to ask them because they were all talking so quickly in their excitement.

Ma'leah continued briskly, "The Sentinel Commander had the idea when Amed was just a baby to train him up properly. They are not taking any risks with him. He is our last hope."

"Wait a minute," Carmen said as she tried to bring the conversation back to reality, "Amed is… he is not the Heir. Is that what you think? Jolene was not."

"Oh! But she was," Ma'leah interrupted. "I cannot believe Samir never told you. He found her and brought her here! It was merely fate that they fell in love and brought such a blessing into our world." She nodded towards Amed to indicate the blessing she meant.

"Who told you all of this?" Carmen asked. "Does Terret know?" *What has happened while I have been away?* Carmen ruminated. *I should have come down sooner. This is a disaster.*

"Jolene told us everything. She told us how Samir found her and told her that she was a descendant of Tullus and what that meant to us. She was very willing to help. She was such a dear, sweet thing," Ma'leah gushed.

Kikona took over the story from Ma'leah. "Terret did not think it proper for Jolene to do the task. He knew that, as a Crural, she was much too weak to be able to defeat Zitja."

Rikka added, "And he decided that Amed would be more useful than Jolene. She was honored to have her son be raised to defeat Zitja."

"Just as we are honored," Ma'leah interjected, "to be the ones chosen to raise him until he goes off to Daristor."

In an instant, Carmen was back to her old self. The Heir-seeking, duty-bound Serra dam personality she had fought so hard to shed rushed back into her countenance.

# Surface Tension

*How did I let this happen?* she rebuked herself. *How have I let so much go wrong?*

It was Carmen's fault Samir and Jolene were killed. It was her fault anyone in the last six years had died at the hands of the Sirens while she was off living blissfully on land with the real Heir. She had possessed the way to end everything this entire time and had let her people down.

And now what? An innocent pup, her best friends' child, was going to be trained for a destiny he could not possibly fulfill? The weight of responsibility sat heavily in her stomach. What had she done to her fellow Serra? Conviction filled her; she had to discuss this with Santiago. She had to tell him the truth she had been hiding from him all this time. Together, they would decide what was best. She had to go right away. If she discussed it with Santiago tonight, they could set things right by tomorrow.

As soon as she could politely excuse herself, Carmen made her apologies for leaving.

"Oh you must stay the night now," Ma'leah offered. "It is getting late."

"No, it's fine," Carmen reassured her. "My husband... Bondmate... is on the shore. He'll be expecting me. However, I think I will be back tomorrow."

Carmen made her goodbyes and insisted she could travel alone and they should relax. The dams bade her farewell and urged her to return.

Carmen swam from their shelter, her mind foggy with guilt and planning as she made her way back towards land. Things had gotten so messed up because of her greed. *My poor friends!* Carmen was wracked with shame.

She looked forward as she tried to remember the way she had come, but she noticed something that made her pick up her pace. A Sentinel had noticed her scraggly tail and seemed particularly interested in watching her swimming alone. The Sentinel didn't bother to connect with her Ku to find out who she was, but he kept watching her. Carmen picked up her pace. The Sentinel followed behind at a slow pace. And then another Sentinel joined the slow pursuit. Carmen grew agitated. *What are they waiting for?* she wondered to herself, wishing she had her wide, powerful tail back. Swimming was remarkably slow, and it felt as though they were toying with her.

Another Sentinel joined the first two, and then the three of them stopped their languid swimming and charged at her full speed.

"Let go of me!" Carmen shouted when they grabbed her from all sides.

"There has been a mandate out for you for six years," the first Sentinel said. "Clearly, you believed living on land would save you from your punishment," he added, looking almost disgustedly at her disintegrating tail. "But if you do not pay for your crime, the ocean would have no order."

"This is crazy. It's been so long," she said.

Another of the bucks spoke, though much gentler. "Terret's orders still stand. We have to take you in. I am sorry."

Carmen didn't have the strength to fight the three of them off, and even if she were to get out of their grip, she could never swim away fast enough. She had to resign herself to letting them pull her to their destination, but she refused to swim on her own accord.

# Surface Tension

They made their way opposite the landmass towards which she was headed and out into the open ocean. After several hours, they eventually dragged her between continents and into the shallower sea. They were swimming deep, and she knew they would take her through the tunnel that connected the Tipua and the Afiti. She would be put in the caves, where she would spend her life sentence. Carmen only hoped she would be able to speak to anyone she could talk sense into. She knew they'd never believe her if she said she'd bring the Heir down this time, but if she could just talk to Santiago, they could figure something out.

Her Sentinel escorts were not interested in conversation or compromise, so eventually Carmen grew weary of trying to convince them to let her go. For hours they swam in silence until, finally, early the next afternoon, they emerged from the tunnel between clans, and she was taken to the caves.

"Please, you don't need to lock me up," she said as they arrived. She was too tired to put up a fight. They were perched before an opening to a small dark chamber. "Please, if I could—"

But the buck gave her an argument-ending push and threw her into the small round opening before he dropped metal bars from above, locking her inside.

"You will have to answer to Terret for your treason." He turned and left towards the center of the large, open room from which they had come.

Carmen could not believe she was in this position. She could help, set things straight after years of dissonance, but to be treated thusly was insulting to her. What was worse was that they clearly held a grudge, and she would have to be clever to talk them into giving her another chance.

Carmen had to wait several agonizing hours before she felt Terret's Ku enter the vicinity, but when he arrived, he came right to her, anger burning in him. He stopped abruptly in front of the bars of her prison, looking haughty and severe. Carmen was almost relieved to have the bars between them. Terret was not the kind to be duped.

Carmen steeled herself. She was here for a purpose. She was here to right her wrongs. She could still save them if she kept her head and thought carefully. As a last resort, she could offer her child—not as a sacrifice, but for the same duty and responsibility that mistakenly weighed upon Amed. On the way here, she had decided that if Jolene could offer up her son as hero—knowing that he was not what she claimed—then Carmen could do the same with her child. She had to make an effort to finish the job she had started and quite possibly save their race.

Carmen tried to overlook his pomp and intention to intimidate her. He was not going to give her much time, so she rushed with the important information.

"Terret, I know that what I have done is a bad thing, punishable, but you do not know the whole truth. Amed is not the Heir. My husb… bondmate is the Heir. I have been with him on land these last six years. I carry his child now."

Terret was silent. She could tell by his demeanor that he wasn't often taken by surprise, nor did he care for the bold way with which she spoke to him. She watched him intently, hands on the bars to steady herself, as she felt his Ku wrestle between scoffing at her and accepting her explanation.

# Surface Tension

"Terret, you know what I say is true. I had always told you that I found the Heir and I'd bring *him* down. The Heir was not a woman." When he was still silent, she pressed on. "We cannot let Amed continue with a responsibility he will not be able to accomplish.

It didn't seem possible, but Terret's anger increased. "I told the Sentinels that brought her in they had the wrong Crural, but she swore it was her. And the other one, her Bondmate, he confirmed her story. They willingly offered their son to our services." He silently fumed.

Carmen knew she would pay dearly for all of the tricks that had been played on Terret. If Jolene were still alive, her life would have been in danger. Carmen was sure of it.

"I ask you to let my child do the same thing. Let me return to my home. When she is old enough, then—"

But he cut her off. "You are not leaving my sight," he announced. "You will stay here until you deliver, and we will take the pup and use it to do the job you selfishly prevented us from doing long ago."

"No!" she said firmly. "We can train her to be strong and brave, and she can defeat Zitja. But I will not have her taken from me."

Carmen was proud of the child she carried, thinking of all it would accomplish. Somehow, the death of her best friends had made her feel a little reckless with her promises for her future, but she would not have her daughter taken from her.

"We are not going to wait for that pup to reach adulthood," Terret responded, more irritated than angry. "If what you claim is true, we will be resigned to wait until you have delivered, of course, but no longer."

She spat sarcastically, "And just how do you intend for a child to fight against the most powerful force we have ever encountered?"

"We have waited long enough. We do not need it to fight. It is merely a weapon."

Carmen was appalled. "That is not... You are not sacrificing Amed in this way."

"Would you prefer that we did?"

"I would not!" she answered, incensed. "Why can you not do the same for my child?"

He scoffed and looked as though he wouldn't answer her and then said, "How do we know your child will be born with a tail or legs? Besides, there has been enough waiting and too many promises made by you. I'm taking things into my own hands."

Just then, the fluttering Ku in her womb stroked Carmen from the inside, as if to remind her of its existence. Carmen snapped. Spurred on by an uncontrollable need to protect her child Carmen shouted, "You will not take my daughter from me!"

She was so full of rage she was shaking as Terret laughed and simply said, "Think what you will."

He swam away, leaving a stern-faced guard behind. She shouted at him and taunted his Ku until he was too far away for her to hold the connection.

Carmen swam frantic circles around her cell. The bars in front of her allowed her to view the goings on of the large chamber where Terret held council while he was away from Daris. Other than that, there was only a small opening at the top of the cave that let her see what time of day it was. She reached her hand out and felt air. She was so close to the surface, but the hole was only large enough for her hand. There was no way she could get out through it.

As the day turned to night, Carmen sat slumped against the wall of the cave, looking out towards the great room in front of her. Everyone began disappearing as they made their way to their sleeping quarters, and, eventually, Carmen could see only one lone Sentinel at the far end of the open room. She thought about calling out to him, but what would she say? Would she plead to be let go? Would she barter with him? There was nothing she could say to this Sentinel that would make him go against orders. Most Sentinels were reasonable and decent, but she doubted one of those sensible bucks would be left as her only guard. This one would surely be trusted by Terret to watch her closely.

Just then, a blue jellyfish came gliding its way through the bars of her cage, and Carmen leapt up to snatch it and hide the blue light from her guard. Thankfully, he hadn't noticed. It was late, and she had seen him looking sleepy-eyed. She immediately connected her Ku with the nuntium, and Santiago's voice filled her being.

"Carmen." His voice was full of worry. "Is everything all right? I didn't hear from you yesterday. Shall I come down there? If I don't receive word from you soon, I will find you. Please let me know what has happened."

*Oh no!* Carmen was filled with worry for Santiago's safety. If he came down here, the Sentinels would surely get a hold of him, and Terret would put Carmen's confessions to the test. He was ill-equipped to fight, and they would lash a knife to his hand and wield it for him, just as they would her daughter. There would be nothing she could do.

She calmed herself. She could not let him hear her panic. She cleared the nuntium of his message to leave her own. She took a soothing breath, connected to the jellyfish, and began, "Do not come down. I am ok. I am sorry I didn't send word, I had to travel to the Afiti. I am in the… um Medeter… the Mediterranean Sea." She hoped that's what it was called. "I left quickly to see my friend. I have much to tell you. I will see you soon." She almost ended her message but decided to add, "We will not even miss our flight home. I love you."

She ended her message and hoped it would prevent him from coming into the water. Carmen released the nuntium, but as it glided past the wall of the cave, she saw something etched upon it, lit up by the bluish hue. She grabbed the nuntium quickly by the tentacles before it got away and dragged it closer to the wall. She swept the luminous creature back and forth to capture the whole scene. Carmen stood there, mouth agape, as she tried to understand what she was seeing.

It was apparent the etching had been in this cave for thousands of years. At some places, the drawing was worn away, and in others, she had to scrape off debris, but she was certain she could see enough.

In the center was a rough etching of a Serra dam with arms outstretched. She was in this same cell that Carmen sat in now, and Sirens surrounded her prison—in the midst of them, the one-armed Siren queen herself. Carmen studied it for hours until she realized that the great hall would again be filling up with Sentinels and she would never be able to get her message to Santiago. She finally released the nuntium and watched as it traveled through the bars, headed towards its destination on the shore.

Carmen sat herself back down on the gravelly bottom of the cave and looked out at the hall without really seeing anything. Her mind was working frantically as she reviewed her memory of the markings, trying to decipher what they meant. It looked like Nephira was using her KuVis, but how? As far as Carmen knew, Vis left the water when the Sirens were created. She thought hard about what she had seen and began to piece things together.

Finally, when the guard brought her breakfast, she asked him in as nonchalant a tone as she could muster, "Did this stronghold used to belong to the Sirens?"

He deliberated responding, but when he decided the answer was harmless he said, "The Sirens were banished from here long ago." With that, he left her with a nugget of information that seemed to be of no consequence.

But Carmen had been studying the drawing over and over so long that the nugget was all she needed to put it together. *This is the island Anthemoessa.* She was sure of it. This was where Sirens lived for thousands of years after their transformation. If Nephira's drawings—for she was sure these had been drawn by Nephira herself—were correct, there was Vis to be found among the walls of these caves. In the drawing, little lines were etched around Nephira's chest, and it seemed to be swelling. All around the cell and the Sirens, these same lines were leaving the rocks and bodies. She thought back to what she had seen by blue nuntium light. Nephira was absorbing the Vis into her Ku.

Carmen's Ku had been open and aware while she was imprisoned. She was on guard and anxious for Terret's return, but now she expanded and explored with her Ku. She tried to concentration on the prison cell deep into the walls and surrounding water—not just the Serras and animals, but the energy as well. She sat motionless for hours trying to feel any Vis that might be hidden, disregarding her meal and the daily activity going on in the large chamber. Nothing happened for hours as she tried to understand Nephira's etchings.

Carmen didn't make any progress. Commotion in the grand chamber outside her cell came and went. Another meal was brought to her, and Terret even swam by to check on her. By this time Carmen, was lying on the sand, consumed in concentration and dejection, so Terret merely passed by. He did not view her as a threat, and she didn't move to confront him.

Carmen cried as she thought about Santiago. She would never see him again. Her child would be born in this cell and stolen from her if she didn't find a way to get herself out. Her heart ached.

That was the moment when she sensed it. Her heightened emotions allowed her to feel in a way that she hadn't hours before. It was small and barely recognizable, but it was there, nearly hidden in plain sight. Within the porous rock of the island, she found tiny stashes of stagnant energy. They were imperceptible if one didn't know what to look for. Now that she found it, she couldn't help but notice it everywhere. The island was practically buzzing with untapped power once she knew it was there. Vis was literally everywhere.

# Surface Tension

*Now what do I do?* Carmen wondered as time continued to pass without any further progress. This was her only option to save her child. She had to learn how to use this power, for herself and her daughter.

Carmen pondered all she knew about Vis, the history and the theory, and concluded it wasn't enough. All she knew was that Serras did everything with the Vis before there was a language, and then there was the curse that caused the creation of the Sirens. There was also the enchantment to protect Daris. After that… Carmen put her forehead in her hands and pulled at her hair… the Vis was gone. No one ever learned how it worked; it was just there. And now it wasn't.

Nephira's drawings seemed to indicate that Carmen should be able to pull the energy out and store it in her Ku. Carmen grumbled in frustration.

She sat on the floor of her cell, feeling the powerful energy in the rocks all around her. Carmen pressed her Ku up next to it, pressed against it, closed her eyes and tried to pull it out. Like plucking a petal off a flower.

Nothing.

For hours she tried to pull it out. At one point, she righted herself and pressed her hands against the rock wall and tried to physically absorb it with her hands. That's when she had an idea.

Resuming her position on the floor, Carmen closed her eyes. She focused on the closest energy source. Instead of trying to pull it with her Ku, she slid her Ku around the Vis and then slowly melded her Ku to the power. Instead of being able to take the Vis, the Vis took her. It absorbed her Ku in its power. Only then did Carmen feel the power it possessed fill her body.

The stash was so small she barely felt a difference in her Ku, but it was there, like a little glowing light, tucked away and waiting in her Ku to be used as Carmen saw fit— just as Nephira's drawings had indicated. A flutter in her belly told her that her daughter felt it too. *We're going home.*

Carmen turned to the bars that held her in the cave. She didn't know what to do, how to manipulate it, but there were only two Sentinels off in the distance, so now was her chance. Carmen focused on her Ku, put her hands out in front of her facing the bars, and then unleashed the energy in what she hoped was the right direction. Like removing a dam and letting the water burst forth.

Her body drained of the power she had just spent hours collecting, and nothing happened. Her KuVis was weak, and the power behind it was small. Carmen felt utter dejection. She was doomed.

*My family is finished.*

Carmen leaned forward and put her head on the bars and clasped them in either hand. She was about to break down and cry, give up on her quest for escape, when she noticed something in her right hand. She looked intently at the bar.

It was bent. It had worked, only Carmen didn't have enough Vis.

She gathered more. The process was tricky at first and then became simple with practice. Now that she knew how to collect it, the process moved along swiftly. Each cache was so small—nearly insignificant—that it wasn't until she had been pushing her Ku out to its limits and harvesting the tiny stashes for hours that she began to feel the shift in her strength. She had felt the Vis before like a light, but now it was starting to feel like the sun residing in her chest. She needed more Vis in her Ku than before, but it would work. With every little bit she gathered, it gave her the power to push her reach further, and soon she was gathering tiny Vis rations all over this and the surrounding islands.

To her consternation, the Sentinels felt the difference as well. They could feel her Ku growing stronger, like a buzzing energy inside of her body. She sensed their movement and their alarm. Finally, someone in the distance called for Terret to be brought in, and Carmen magnified her efforts.

She pushed her Ku out further than she had ever reached before, expanding to the surface and finding Vis stores in the ancient rocks and petrified roots in the earth. She absorbed it all into her and locked it away in the center of her Ku.

With her awareness reaching so far, she felt clearly and distinctly Terret's awareness of her efforts. The more Vis she tucked away in her Ku, the more agitated he became with her activities. He might not know how or what she was doing, but he could feel her Ku grow stronger and stronger as the minutes passed.

He began gathering a group of Sentinels together to stop her. Carmen redoubled her efforts. She didn't have enough yet. She wouldn't be able to do anything with the Vis against the small throng he was gathering. Finally, Terret called to his officers to arm themselves and made his way swiftly towards her.

When the Sentinels were mere feet from her chamber, weapons drawn, Carmen felt Sirens, about twelve of them, swimming ten miles in the distance. She knew Terret felt them as well because his reach could surely surpass hers by double or triple, but he was unconcerned. She had now become a bigger threat than them—only he didn't know just how much.

He did not know what she had just learned about the KuVis,thanks to Nephira's drawing, and Carmen was able to pull the hidden Vis from the Sirens themselves. They held such tremendous reserves within their very beings because of their curse. Carmen was able to fill up her Ku to the brink of exploding with power. She waited until Terret and his Sentinels were right in front of her cage. It was when they were right up to the bars that she released the energy she had been storing all night. She unleashed it without discretion, blasting everything in its path dozens of feet away from her.

# Chapter 18

## Carmen

Carmen could not believe the destruction she caused. Rocks, debris, Sentinels, and gore filled the water before her. She was perched inside the cell with everything behind her in perfect condition, but in front of her was a massacre. Sentinel bodies and their weapons littered the floor. The bars of her cage had been demolished and thrown out into the giant room before her. Carmen was shocked. Remorse began to creep into her countenance. *I did not mean for this to happen.*

But the feeling was quickly replaced. If this is what it took to save her child, so be it.

As she tread in place, eyes still scanning the room in shock, some of the Sentinels began to rouse. They saw her floating in the water unscathed. She sensed fear in their Kus.

After a moment, one of them shouted, "Get her."

All of the able-bodied Sentinels pulled themselves from the ground. Several of them looked a bit dazed, but they were uninjured. They made their way towards her. Carmen knew she couldn't outrun them with her decrepit tail, and she had expelled all of the Vis she had stored because of her inability to wield it properly. She looked around frantically.

Behind her, Carmen spotted the tiny hole in her cell, the one she had stuck her hand through when she felt air. The surface was very close, and the large chamber in front of her was wide open to the sky.

Kicking her pitiful tail, Carmen charged ahead, soaring towards the surface above. Just as she was breaking through to the top, she saw Terret out of the corner of her eye, lying on the ground, one of the bars of her cage piercing him through the chest.

Years later, Carmen looked down at her shriveled, pathetic excuse for legs without a drop of remorse. Although she developed a pair of Crural-looking legs—it was clear to her that Serras weren't meant to go through hegira as adults—she was never able to walk on them. Nor did actual feet form. At the end of her legs were just wisps of a would-be tail and skin. She was able to wear pants but never shoes. It could be easy for someone in her situation to feel sorry for herself: she was wheelchair-bound; her "people" had turned their backs on her; she could never return under water for fear of being imprisoned for being a traitor; and she had spent nearly two years in terrible agony while she lost her scales. But Carmen didn't ever feel sorry for herself or regret a single choice she had made along the way.

A loud bell rang overhead and the yard around her was filled with the delighted screams of children all running out of the school building.

# Surface Tension

"Mommy!" A dark haired girl in a red school uniform squealed and skipped over. "Where is daddy?" the child asked, confused by the change in routine.

"He's busy. I thought I'd walk home with you today."

"Ok!"

They ambled home slowly. Carmen listened to her happy five-year-old jabber on about all of the noteworthy things she did during the school day. When she seemed to be winding down about the important things and their conversation consisted mostly of stickers, Carmen changed her tone to one a little more serious and said, "Celia, I need to talk to you about something important. Can we put on our serious hats?"

She waited as the little girl got out the last of her wiggles, turned to face her mother, and then mimed putting on a hat—a gesture they had agreed meant it wasn't time for joking—while Carmen mimed putting on a hat, as well.

"Celia, you know that I love you very much, right?"

"Right!" Celia said as, if getting an answer correct.

"And you know that I won't be around forever. People just aren't made that way."

"Like Herman?"

"That's right, just like our frog, Herman." They spent a few minutes discussing the death of their pet frog, and Carmen tried to bolster her daughter for what she was going to say next.

"Just like Herman, it will be very sad when I am not around anymore, either. I want you to always remember how happy we are and how much we love each other."

"Yeah, Mommy, we're happy." The girl looked down at her plaid skirt and ran her fingers along the pleats. "You aren't going to be here very long, are you?"

Carmen didn't want to have such a tense conversation with her daughter at such a young age, but Carmen knew she was running out of time and, clearly, her daughter knew it too. They had to have this discussion before it was too late.

For the past few months she had been feeling her Ku begin to… wrap up. She was sensing a finished feeling to herself and knew that she was not long for this world. It wasn't an uncommon feeling for a Serra to know. After all, every meal they ate was sure to be made of an animal whose Ku had finished with its purpose. The first time Carmen felt it within herself, however, she was distraught that it was coming so soon.

The air on land was too thin, and she often struggled to draw sufficient breath. Her lungs felt like they were withering. They had become so weak that they eventually damaged her heart, which beat slower these days. Overall, the lack of salt water flowing through her system daily was taking its toll. Her body just wasn't made for such a harsh environment.

Carmen talked with her little girl, thinking she was too young to lose a parent, but at least she would have her father; that was more than Carmen had as a child.

"Your daddy is going to take very good care of you, though. He loves us so much." She tried to reassure the girl whose eyes were brimming with tears.

"But you take good care of me, too," Celia said as the tears finally broke and streamed down her face.

# Surface Tension

Celia placed her hand on her mother's heart. Carmen had taught her to connect her Ku and to feel the world around her. Doing this gave her a deeper understanding for the way of life and helped her to grasp such a tough, adult concept.

When they arrived home, Carmen gathered Celia on her lap and said, "Let's connect our Kus to finish this conversation. Ok?" Celia nodded and took a moment to do the task.

The two of them talked on the porch until the sun dipped so low in the sky that it threatened to leave them for the night. Celia was much more mature than Crurals her age, and Carmen knew it was because she felt the world for what it was.

"I have one more very important thing to tell you," Carmen told the girl who was curled up on her lap  Before she could, however, Santiago came out and enveloped both of his girls into a giant embrace. Carmen had held him in her Ku through the entire conversation so that he could hear all Carmen told their daughter without intruding on their privacy, but finally he just couldn't stand to hear any more.

"Come in my girls! Let's have dinner." And he picked Celia up and carried her into the house.

Carmen wheeled herself in, and they had a somber, but not depressing, dinner together. They avoided the topic that was on everyone's mind and steered the conversation clear of any talk of the future, choosing rather to relive memories they shared of the wonderful things they had experienced.

As Carmen tucked Celia into bed that night, her heart was heavy. She wanted to tell her daughter everything. She wanted her to know about the important role she could play to an entire world under the water, if Celia chose it. Carmen felt that the Heir should have the option to fight and die for the Serras and not be used as a pawn in their war. But also, it should be her choice, and she should not be tricked or coerced into it. Santiago could not do it because he had to raise Celia, but maybe one day Celia would be up for the task.

But that was all entirely too heavy for a child to bear, so she resigned to keep it simple. She would leave the information for Celia to find at a later time. For now, she merely said, "Celia, I want you to listen to what I'm about to say and believe every word of it, ok?"

"Shall I put on my serious hat?"

"Yes, this is very serious," Carmen said with a crinkled nose and a funny face. The two girls put on their serious hats, and Carmen continued. "I want you to believe in magic. Ok? I want you to believe that mermaids are real and that it's important to protect the world from bad guys."

"Mommy! You said we had to be serious."

"Oh, I'm being very serious. One day, you will have to make some big girl decisions, and when it's time for you to do that, I want you to remember to believe in magic. Remember that? Mermaids are real, and we must protect them from bad guys. Can you do that for me?"

Celia was skeptical but faithful as she shouted, "Yes!"

"Remember, there is a lot in this world to believe in that people will tell you isn't real. But trust your mommy when I say that they are."

Celia was confused but nodded nonetheless.

"This sounds like a lot of nonsense, doesn't it?"

# Surface Tension

"Yes," the little girl agreed wholeheartedly.

"It's ok. Let me tell you a little story."

"Ok!" Celia said, but excitedly now.

"One day, an evil man trapped mommy under water. Don't worry!" she added when Celia gave her a frightened look, "Mommy can breathe under water." She let the sentence hang and was rewarded by an astonished look from her daughter.

Carmen raised one eyebrow. "Mommy used to be a mermaid."

Celia looked at her skeptically but didn't say anything, so Carmen continued.

"He said I had to do what he wanted. He said that I was his prisoner and that he was going to steal you from me. Well, I didn't like that one bit! So do you know what I did?"

Celia shook her head frantically.

"I learned how to do magic!"

"Mommy?"

"Yes, my love?"

"We still have our serious hats on."

"I am still being very serious. Are you believing in magic and mermaids like I told you to?"

Celia looked sheepishly up at her mother and said with frustration in her voice, "I'm trying."

"You are doing a good job of it. It is important to question things you don't know. Right now, though, you can trust me."

"Ok, Mommy."

"I have a better idea," Carmen said taking her daughter's hand in hers. "Connect to my Ku."

Celia did as she was told.

"Do you feel it? I am telling you the truth."

"I do. I feel it."

Carmen smiled down at her trusting child and wished she could always stay so innocent. She squeezed Celia's hand before energetically finishing her story.

"I was trapped in prison, and I had to get away. I was going to have to learn magic. We call it Vis. Remember that word."

"Vis?" Celia repeated.

"Yes. It was my only option because I wanted to keep you safe! When the evil man came to get me, I used the Vis to blow the bars apart and broke free of my prison."

You did magic? I mean… Vis?"

"I did! But this made other evil men come to get me, so I swam straight upwards. They were much stronger swimmers than I was, and I knew I couldn't get away if I tried to swim, so I jumped out of the water."

"But, Mommy, you can't walk fast either," the smart child said, seeing Carmen's dilemma.

"But I knew how to scoot away quickly because I had done so many, many times. Would you believe that the evil men had never been on the ground before? They didn't know what to do!"

"You scooted on the ground like when we play?"

"I did."

Celia thought for a minute. "You are really fast when you do that. You always catch me."

"When I escaped, I called your daddy and he came to get me. Your daddy was always saving me back then. He just didn't know it. When we got home, I began to write everything down. Everything! This is important to remember,

Celia. I want you to know everything you can possibly know about magic and mermaids and protecting them from bad guys. Ok?"

Celia didn't answer. Her face was a mask of confusion.

Carmen laughed. "In a few years—let's say ten—I want you to read all of my journals."

"Your journals!" Celia became very excited. "I can read them?"

"Yes, you can read them."

Celia had seen Carmen writing in them almost nightly and always asked her what was in them. Her answer was always, "One day, you will know."

"I can't wait to read them," Celia said. She was just learning to read and had been mastering it quickly.

"I want you to read everything." Carmen stroked her daughter's hair and kissed her forehead. "And believe it all. Your mommy used to be a mermaid. We called ourselves Serras. I would never lie to you. Do you believe me?"

"Serras...." Little Celia tried out the word. "Of course I believe you, Mommy!"

"Ok, now go to sleep. You have done a very good job of being serious. Do you want to be silly for a minute?"

Celia threw off her imaginary hat, and the two girls got very silly, tickling each other and laughing until Celia started to rub her eyes.

It was only a couple weeks later that Carmen found she couldn't get out of bed. Her muscles had grown so weak that she could do little more than pull down her flower bedspread for Celia to climb inside. They sat silently for a while, knowing the end was near and feeling it saturate the room. Carmen stroked her daughter's hair while Celia placed her hand on her mother's heart, feeling it beating slowly. Neither of them wanted to lose this moment, this feeling.

Suddenly, Celia said with a catch in her voice, "Mommy, when I have a daughter, I'm going to name her Carmen."

At that moment, Santiago came in the room and crawled into bed on the other side of Carmen and wrapped his arms around both of his girls.

"No, Celia, you should name your baby Santiago. He is the reason for everything good that has ever happened to me. Before him, everything was meaningless. He changed my life. He *saved* my life," she said more to Santiago than her child.

Santiago and Celia were going to have a lot of challenges together without her… and a lot of good times. She was sad to miss it all.

"But Santiago is a boy's name," Celia said, "I only want to have a girl."

"If you have a girl, you can still name her Santiago. I think it sounds nice."

"Santiago is a boy's name. It would be stupid for a girl. You are silly, Mommy," she said with sincere incredulity.

And the three of them laughed and laughed at the absurdity of naming a girl Santiago.

# *Chapter 19*
## Santiago

Rogan encircled Santi in his arm, and they both sat in silent grief. She looked up at Tizz, who was sitting with her mother near Amed's head. The three of them had lost their father. Santi felt things were forever changed. She couldn't even bring herself to think about what Coral was feeling; it was too painful. Santi cried sobs that wracked her body as she thought about Amed. He had stood in as a father because he knew she needed it, and he did so happily, embracing Santi like his own daughter without hesitation.

Santi, Rogan, and Tizz were in a lot of trouble; even Sully was getting a lecture from Amed. Santi looked at her hands. She looked at Rogan's blue tail flicking gently back and forth, at Tizz's unruly blond hair. Looking at the gold band Sully wore on his arm was an excellent distraction as well—anything to avoid Amed's eyes. His disappointment in them was just about more than she could bear, and his lecture, calm and frustrated, was so different from her own mother's yelling tirades that always dissolved into Spanish. She preferred her mother's loud rants and quick punishments to Amed's Ku full of displeasure. She hated to let him down, and the four of them really didn't mean for their childish antics to get so out of hand.

"Do you realize," Amed said, piercing her with his words, "that you could have injured yourself, ruined the wildlife around you, and damaged the Serra relationship with the dolphins? We have cultivated it for hundreds of years, and they trust us like their own. You could have ruined that. Not to mention the dangers you put yourselves in by chasing sharks."

Amed seemed to be winding down, and she could feel the Kus of the other three kids lightening, but she felt worse and worse. She did not even remember whose idea it had been to wrangle some dolphins and make them chase the sharks, but it had seemed like a harmless thing at the time.

"The sharks were really small," Rogan said, trying not to smile.

It was probably his idea. He was always a little too adventurous when Sully was around. The boys continuously dared each other to do more and more extreme things until, inevitably, they were all in trouble.

Amed let Rogan's comment slide and excused the children to make amends with the dolphins and serve their punishment by helping the elderly Serras in the kinship hunt for their dinner. The other three children left the shelter to gather fish to feed to the dolphins, but Santi stayed behind, still looking at her hands.

"What is it, Santiago?" Amed said gently, coming up beside her.

"I…" She started to cry. At nine years old, it was hard for her to voice her feelings. "I'm really sorry we were bad."

"Oh, my little starfish."

Santi loved it when she was called "starfish." Rogan did it too, sometimes, though it was not as endearing coming from him as it was from Amed. "I never want to disappoint you."

"Listen to me right now. I love you as much as my other children, and, though I am disappointed in what you have done, I am not disappointed in you."

No one moved for several minutes as they all sat sharing in each other's grief. It didn't make sense that Amed could possibly be killed. He seemed too invincible. He was the strongest, most capable buck in the entire ocean. Even Zitja feared him. This didn't make sense. Santi had been living under water for a long time, but it still wasn't long enough to keep her from crying human tears or from being overwhelmed by the feeling of so many grieving hearts combined.

Slowly, others began to trickle away as they went back to their families or set to work to clean up the destruction. Finally, only Coral, Tizz, Rogan, and Santi were left around Amed's motionless form. Rogan touched Santi on the shoulder and motioned with his head for them to go. She didn't want to move, but Santi got up and followed him.

"She will want to be alone with him," he told her as he ushered her towards the Healer's shelter.

Santi drifted along beside him, overwhelmed with sensation. Amed was a father to her, more than anyone else had ever been, even more than her abuelo, whom she spent a lot of time with as a child. Amed had welcomed her lovingly to his family when she was young, and then again as an adult. He had wanted the best for her and had made it his duty to protect her while still pushing her to improve herself. She couldn't believe he was gone.

"What happened?" Santi asked, filled with anger and hurt. "I was only gone for a moment. How did things end so drastically?"

This made Rogan replace his grief with anger. "I did not see how it started because I was fighting, but when I freed myself, I saw you and your mom fleeing towards the shelter. Zitja was trying to pursue you, but my father was holding her back and fighting her off." He looked at her with what looked like hurt confusion as he said, "That is when the Sentinel reinforcements came. Hundreds of them." Rogan's eyes widened in further incredulity. "They handily outnumbered the Sirens. We were saved. It was about to be over. I think Zitja knew this. Her Sirens had completely retreated. They were fleeing for their lives as the Sentinels completely took over the kinship. Zitja stopped trying to pursue you so quickly." Rogan closed his eyes as he remembered, "He was not prepared for her change in tactic. He just..." Rogan opened his eyes and Santi felt the rip in his heart as painfully as in her own. "She killed him so quickly it did not even seem like it had happened. He was so close to her. Nearly holding her back from pursuing you. She just turned, and it was over."

"Oh, Rogan! I'm so sorry you had to see that."

"After that, she was so overwhelmed and outnumbered, the Sentinels drove her off. They are still in pursuit, I am sure."

Santi let out another sob. Amed died protecting her. Santi felt disgusting. She wanted to shed off her skin. To go back in time and do something differently. It hadn't even been twenty minutes. It was so recent, couldn't they turn back time just a bit?

Tilda was gentle and loving as she treated Santi's wounds. There was a remarkably stark contrast between the Healer's peaceful Ku and Rogan's frantic anger. He was swimming back and forth in front of the table she sat on, pacing a nervous wave in the water.

"Rogan..." she started, but didn't know what to say. What right did she have to try to calm him down? He was entitled to his anger. She was angry herself, but she was beginning to feel a little scared by his energy. There was a fierceness inside him, a dangerous madness, which she had never felt in any Serra.

When the Healer was finished, she gave Santi herbs for the pain. Rogan scooped her up and ushered her outside. He was eerily silent, and Santi could see his mind working and feel his Ku wrestling with something. Suddenly, he let go of her and turned her shoulders to face him. "I need you."

She nodded, "Yes of course. What can I do to help?" She would do anything for him. She put her grief aside to step up and be there for her Bondmate.

"We are going after Sully."

"Oh! Oh, Rogan." She was about to argue, to suggest an alternative, but she felt he needed support from her, and she nodded. Hopefully, she could talk him out of doing anything drastic.

"Do you have your sai?" he said as he adjusted his chest straps, looking at her holster.

"Yes," she said, almost regretting its presence. She wanted to help Rogan with his grief, but following after the Sirens was not a good idea. He picked her up and began hastily swimming away from the kinship, in the direction the Sirens had fled.

"What are we going to do, Rogan?"

"We're going to kill him."

"What about your father? Don't we need to stay and help your mom? What about his... funeral?" Santi wasn't sure what the burial practices were amongst the Serras. She had never been in the kinship for a death.

Rogan hesitated, trying to recall the meaning for the word. "My mother will be taken care of by the kinship and we will not have his *Haruvivo* until tomorrow. We will be back by that time."

She gave a curt nod. She didn't like the thought of pursuing Sully, but she was on his side. He did not like her decision to be a Sentinel, but had supported her; it was her turn to do the same for him.

They traveled down the coast as the sun was rising above. They were all seriousness, barely speaking. Rogan had said they were a few days from the waters the Sirens had been banished to but hoped they wouldn't have to go that far.

# Surface Tension

It was too dangerous for them there. When they caught up to the fleeing Siren's, they would try to summon Sully.

"Although the Sirens do not use their Kus, they still know when someone is touching theirs. I have to be quick and call to Sully without touching any of the Sirens. By doing this, they should not notice me, and I will be able to sneak around without their awareness." He paused and then added, "Hopefully," which made Santi's stomach tighten. She knew first-hand how treacherous it was to try touching Kus at random when she was looking for Amed and trying to avoid giving away her position to the Sirens.

They swam for a few more hours before they caught up to the Sentinels and Sirens. About a quarter of a mile in front of them, the battle raged on. Rogan and Santi continued swimming, drawing closer to the fighting.

"This is good," Rogan said. "I did not think the Sentinels would be able to draw them back into a fight. We will be able to keep our presence concealed in the commotion as I try to find Sully."

Santi's eyes went wide. "We're going to go into that? Rogan, this is not smart. We only just escaped this very thing earlier."

"No, we will stay a safe distance. If I can just see Sully, I will know where to direct my Ku, and I can keep our location hidden from the Sirens."

Santi felt relief wash over her that they weren't going into the battle. However, they were still swimming closer, and her nerves soon began to return as the distance between them and the fight dwindled. She hoped they would be stopping very soon.

When they were only twenty feet away and Santi was begging Rogan to not go any further, he stopped. He found them a secluded place to hide amongst some boulders and tall growing seaweed. Rogan was quiet as he watched the battle and looked for Sully.

"Rogan," Santi said with trepidation. She knew his mood was volatile, and she didn't want to sound unsupportive. "I am here for you in whatever way you need me, but I have to ask, is killing Sully what you really want to do?"

"Yes."

He didn't say any more, so she continued. "I will support you in whatever decision you make but..." She paused and Rogan continued to look at the commotion ahead of them, almost uninterested in what she was saying. "But would your father want this? Rogan, I don't think he would. It wasn't really his style to revenge kill other Serras."

Rogan said nothing, his heart hammering in his chest and his Ku sending out bursts of fury.

"Isn't there some sort of... Serra punishment system? Can he be put on trial? Be sent to... jail?" She didn't know the intricacies of the Serra justice system—that was not a lesson for Coral to teach. Rogan only continued to search for Sully, and Santi sat quietly.

She waited and watched Rogan for more than an hour. Neither of them talked as he concentrated on looking for Sully with his eyes and reaching out cautiously with his Ku.

Finally, Rogan pushed himself up with his arms suddenly and spoke, "Sully, come out of there and face me directly."

# Surface Tension

Santi's eyes went wide. It was going to happen. "Rogan, please. This is crazy. I know you're angry, but if you kill him like this, you will never be able to move on." Just then, Santi looked and saw Sully swimming swiftly in their direction. Rogan rose to meet him. "Your father would not want this!" Santi said.

Rogan finally looked at her. His expression was unreadable, but his Ku indicated that her words had finally gotten through. She felt a nearly imperceptible flash of hesitation.

But it was too late. Sully was there and Rogan swam to meet him. Santi pulled herself from behind the boulder but poised herself on top of it, ready to help, but knowing she should stay out of the mix at the moment.

"Sully!" Rogan roared as he swam headfirst towards his old friend. "Because of you, my father is dead."

Sully stopped swimming. He didn't know. Santi felt a moment of reluctance sweep through Sully that might have been regret. Then it was gone.

Rogan unsheathed the two short swords that were crossed on his back with the ease that comes from a move practiced a thousand times. Sully did the same with the machete tied to his thigh. Santi's mouth fell open. Thank Nephira he hadn't had that knife when he stabbed her mother. She held her hand to the sai at her hip, feet ready to kick off the rock if she needed to help—though she doubted very much she would be of any use if Sully got the upper hand. She watched, but the bucks weren't fighting, they were shouting, teeth bared, wild looks in their eyes.

"My family treated you like their own, and you have done nothing but cause us harm and death." Rogan got very close to Sully, challenging him to strike first. "What did we ever do to deserve this?"

"Your pious family turned your back on me after my mother died."

"We did no such thing." Rogan looked like he would strike his friend for the lie.

"Your family left me in Daris to deal with my mother's death alone. You treated me as an outcast. My mother was my last remaining family member, and then I was alone. During Daristor breaks, you did not invite me home with you."

"I did."

"You didn't, and you know it."

Santi felt Rogan's anger at Sully turn towards himself for just a heartbeat. "You pushed away from us. You did abhorrent things that my father told you were unforgiveable." Regret pushed through the anger. "That does not mean we did not love you. We were still there for you."

Suddenly, the remorse and regret were gone. Rogan pulled his right arm back and brought his fist—holding the handle of his sword—across Sully's face, punching him with the metal hilt. "And what you did to Santiago can never be forgiven."

"I wish I'd killed that little terrasite," Sully taking a swipe at Rogan, but they were too close to each other. Rogan blocked the hit with his forearm.

"Don't call her that!" Rogan shouted and turned in a tight circle, hitting Sully with his tail.

"She is a terrasite." Sully charged at Rogan. "They all are."

# Surface Tension

"You did not believe so at one time," Rogan accused and hit Sully again. This time, when the punch landed on Sully's face, Sully was ready and returned a hit into Rogan's gut.

"Every land-walker I've met only wanted something from me, and Serras would rather protect them than their fellow Serra."

"You thought those Crural women had something to do with your mother's death, but they didn't. You did horrible things to them. Could you not see through your grief? One of them died."

Santi was shocked. She did not know he had killed Crurals. Sully had truly been changed to the core. A wave of pity passed through her until Sully shouted at them., "I would kill every last Crural and Crural-loving Serra if I had the chance. And I'll start with you two."

Sully raised his machete in two hands and brought it down towards Rogan's head. Rogan was able to raise his blades in a cross to block it.

"You will not harm Santiago again as long as I live."

"Then I'll fix that right now." Sully was counting on Rogan's defense, and as soon as Rogan brought his swords above his head Sully swung his knife in an arch and brought it to Rogan's side.

Santi saw Sully's machete about to strike Rogan in the ribs, and she leapt from the rock. "No!" she shouted.

But the hit never landed.

Sully stopped right before he was about to strike the fatal blow that would have killed her Bondmate. Something was happening inside Sully that terrified him. He arched his back and let out a shriek that pierced Santi to the soul. "I will kill you all," he cursed them; anger and pain filled the water around them. Sully began to writhe around—much like someone who was under the influence of the Siren Song. He screamed wildly into the water, and Santi flinched. Sully's anguish was so strong she almost felt pain in her own body.

In an instant, Rogan sheathed his swords and shot an arm out towards Santi, grabbing her around the shoulders Slowly, they began backing away from the struggling Sully, awareness dawning on them. They knew what was happening, though neither of them had ever seen it firsthand. Above all, they needed to get away, to put distance between them and Sully before the transformation was complete.

Before their very eyes, Sully's skin began to grow paler and paler until it was translucent and his blue veins shown through. Starting at the tip of his tail and working its way up toward his torso, his tail and arm scales grew black, as if paint was being poured into his body and filling him up. He was still thrashing around and growling when Rogan grabbed Santi around the waist firmly and began to swim away.

Santi looked back over her shoulder as Rogan pulled her along. Sully's body twisted unnaturally, his screams filling the water and her Ku. For a moment—so quick she wouldn't have known what it was if she wasn't familiar with the object—Sully's gold armband caught the light. Santi remembered a young, copper-haired boy protecting her from the perils of the ocean and playing games with his friends. Santi turned back to help Rogan swim away, tears streaming at the loss of what once was. Sully was truly not the Serra she knew anymore.

Santi watched Coral fill the jellyfish with her thoughts. When she finished, it glowed bright blue and zoomed out of her hands. Santiago was always so intrigued by the transformation such a slow, almost lazy, creature went through as it changed into a bullet shooting through the water when it had a message to deliver.

Coral had been too devastated yesterday to send the news, but now she needed to inform Amed's aunts in the Tipua Clan of his passing. Santi asked if they would be able to wait for them to come for his Haruvivo.

"Sadly, no. Not even a cryptid could make it here from the Tipua by this evening. But I will see them soon, and we can mourn together." Celia had included in her message her plans to come stay with them.

"I still can't believe you aren't going to live here anymore," Santi mused as she sat on the floor of her shelter, stroking Amphitrite's head while Coral packed their belongings into woven baskets.

"You will remember, Santiago, that we lived in the Tipua for many years after the Sirens' attack on this kinship. It will feel like going home for me. Besides, with Amaratizz in Daristor, and you and Rogan going to Daris, I will be here all alone." She seemed to sigh in her Ku as she looked around the barren shelter.

It broke Santi's heart to think about saying goodbye to this shelter forever. "Will you keep the shelter?"

"No, I think I will give it up. Tizz is years away from needing her own shelter, and it is too painful for me to keep."

Santi nodded. It would be weird to have another family living here. The thought of Coral not being in this shelter made her stomach clench painfully. She restrained her tears; Coral didn't need Santi's grief to add to her own. Rogan and Santi had decided to give up the new shelter that was just made for them and move to Daris together. Rogan had another year of Sentinel training, and Santiago had to meet with Amed's successor, Krell, to continue the plans Amed had laid out for Zitja. They figured they would both need to be in the city for a while, and then they would decide where to settle down after that.

"I know," Santi sighed, "and I think you should be with your family. It will just be weird not to have ties to this kinship anymore."

"Once you visit me in the Tipua, it will feel like home to you."

"I'd like that," Santi decided. "I've never been to another clan before."

"Amed has a very large family who will welcome you with open Kus."

"You know," Rogan piped in, "I should think our kids will be from the Tipua Clan. Families do not make a home at Daris, and when we are ready for that time, it would be a good place to settle."

Santi thought for a moment and then asked, "They wouldn't be Nhori because you are?"

"No, Serras are considered part of the clan they are born in. That is why my mother and sister and I are Nhori but my dad is Tipua. Though it is a common occurrence for Serras to go back to the clan in which they were born for the birth of their pups. That way, a family will carry on its heritage."

"You wouldn't rather our children be Nhori, like you?"

"No..." He pondered. "I think I would like this better."

"I'd like that," Santi nodded. "I'd like our kids to be from your father's clan."

That evening, their kinship was bursting with mourners who had come from all over the ocean. Amed's position had reached his influence across all clans and kinships and introduced him to many Serras who both respected and adored him. Krell and Ocean mother Yazi had arrived to honor Amed's memory. Santi tried to be glad about meeting the Ocean Mother—an honor she was sure to feel when she had time to think about it later—but she was too distracted by grief to appreciate the moment.

Amed's body was wrapped in white cloth in the center of the kinship. It looked surreal to Santi, like maybe he wasn't actually in there. Grievers surrounded the body, filling up the square in the center of the kinship and spilling out amongst the shelters. Every nook was filled with a Serra, the space in the water above their heads stacked up so completely that the sun could not pierce through to light up the water. The darkness gave the memorial a somber effect that only added to the mood of sorrow.

Grendor led the ceremony and welcomed them all. He reminded everyone that they should reach out and connect to as many Kus as was in their ability—much like Santi remembered doing during the Sariahdiem ceremony when she was young. He waited for everyone to do so. Santi had so much practice at this she was sure she would be able to hold every Serra present in her heart, but she was pushed to her limit by how many were in attendance, and her ability fell short. Still, she opened up and allowed everyone in that she could. She became consumed by love for Amed and sorrow for his loss. He was well revered and loved. With so many in attendance grieving for him, Santi was left feeling consumed by the anguish. She felt a heaviness press upon her chest that made it hard to breathe. *Amed would have cherished feeling so much love throughout these people.*

Then Grendor started speaking of Amed's life.

"He was courageous even from the beginning. When he was only three, his mother was trapped by a rockslide that she was unable to outswim. He did not leave her side as he slowly and laboriously lifted each rock from her legs, some being so large it was near impossible for a boy of his size to heft.

"He had always taken extra care of her. Many assumed it was because she was a Crural and he regarded her as less capable than himself, but anyone who knew him knew the truth. He took so much care of her because of his outstanding love for her. He cherished her, and his protective drive led him through life long after she was gone.

"The Sentinel Opus was always his destiny, but you would never have known it by talking to him. The desire to be a Sentinel, to protect others and seek honesty, was his personal mission. He was affronted by injustice and always wanted what was best for everyone.

"I was with him the day he met Coral. Not many know this, but these two were Bound the moment they connected for the first time. This phenomenon does not happen but once every few centuries or so. It is believed that only the purest of hearts can be so aware of their connection upon the first meeting of their Bondmate."

Santi felt a distinct pang in Coral's heart that pierced her deeply. Often, Santi wondered how Serras felt a release without crying, but feeling Coral's Ku now made her understand. Coral didn't need the tears to express and ease her emotions; she was pouring her heartache out into the water through all the Kus around her. And everyone was with her; they understood, felt, and reciprocated the pain. Tears could never do such a thing.

"Such a pure soul is hard to find," Grendor continued, "and it is such an addition to our waters that his presence will not only be missed but will be felt. We lost a friend, but the ocean loses a spiritual force. It was truly a better place because of him."

When Grendor stopped speaking, everyone waited quietly and patiently until Coral was ready. When she was able to get her emotions under control, she entreated them all, "Please join me now to help Amed pass from this world into the next."

As she said this, she slowly unwrapped the white cloth from around his body. The care she took to remove the linen from his face, his torso, and finally his tail was so delicate, all mourners seemed to hold their breath so as to show her respect for the work she did.

Finally, when she had removed the last piece of fabric from his still brilliant blue tail, she placed her shaky hand lovingly on his chest, feeling his HaruKu for the last time.

Santi's eyes were puffy and swollen from the tears. She could barely see as Rogan and Tizz, along with Grendor and a few select Serras she didn't know, swam down to Amed. They each placed a hand under his body and slowly, with much respect and reverence, lifted him towards the surface.

As the group advanced with Amed's still form, the Serras above made way. They swam aside gently, and as they did so, the sun broke through the surface, illuminating Amed in an ethereal way.

When the procession had swum halfway to the surface, they stopped and sent Amed on his way alone. As he continued drifting towards the surface, Santi could feel the water trembling with an honest and sincere love for this man. He made his way slowly to the air above while the crowd made wishes and rained blessings upon his family. Rogan had informed Santi earlier what was to happen next, but she was completely amazed to see it unfold.

The closer Amed came to the surface, the more transparent and insubstantial he became. He seemed to be dissolving into the water, becoming less and less physical as he ascended, until his body broke the surface as nothing but effervesce and froth amongst the waves.

Amed was no longer an entity to be touched but a metaphysical presence to be felt. In that way, his body was no more for this world, but his spirit lived on in the water around them.

Santi stood on the bank of the little pond the next morning, clutching her mother tightly. "I'm glad you could be here for this," she whispered in her Ku. They were breathing air, but she didn't want to let go of Celia in her heart. "All of it."

"Me too, babee."

Santi couldn't seem to let go. Two days ago, she had been celebrating her Bonding surrounded by her mother, Coral, Amed, and Tizz; tomorrow she would be with none of these people. She would never see Amed again, and she didn't know when she would be with Celia again.

"Are you going to look for our family in the Najilian?" Santi asked. She pulled away and tried to regain her composure.

"Aye," Celia responded. "Coral said she will talk to Amed's aunts when she gets in the Tipua. They met jor abuela, and maybe they knew some of our family."

"So, then, you're still planning to come down? I'll see you soon?"

"Jes. Grendor said he'll help me to find them in the Najilian. I hope you can come, too."

"Mommi, if you are coming down, I'll be there."

Celia pulled her clothes out of their hiding spot and got dressed. The two women hugged again, and Santi watched her mom walk away.

The next morning, as they prepared to leave, Santi couldn't help but feel a weight of sadness on her shoulders. She and Rogan were going to Daris, and Tizz had already left to meet up with her Daristor group currently touring the NorMer Clan.

"Send me nuntiums all the time, Tizz," Santi had made her promise.

"Of course I will, Sister." Tizz had taken to calling Santi nothing but "sister" over the last few days, and a smile broke across her face every time she said it. Her Daristor group was scheduled to be back in Daris in a few months, and Santi was looking forward to seeing much more of her.

"Santi," Coral said, breaking her out of her thoughts. "I had completely forgotten about this." She held out a wooden box to Santi. "This was from Amed. It was a gift meant to encourage you."

Santi held the box in her hands. She didn't want to open it. Maybe if she kept it closed, never knowing what was inside, it would be like Amed was still there with her. Once she opened the box, she didn't have anything else from him to look forward to. There were no more lessons, no more talks, no more plans to be made by him. This box was the end of it.

"Open it, Santiago," Coral said, as if reading her mind.

Carefully, Santi removed the lid. When she saw what was inside, she dropped the top of the box, letting it sink to the floor of the shelter. Her chin quivered, and she blinked rapidly. She was glad she had opened the box.

Santi pulled out two brand new silver, sharp, matching sais. They were better than her old ones, but not unwieldy. She would easily get used to the weight.

The handles were wrapped in black leather tied by thin leather straps that crisscrossed down the length. The grips felt comfortable and secure in her hands. Santi held one out in front of her. The middle tine added another four inches to her reach. The two tines on either side made gentle 'S' curves that her old ones didn't. These could do a lot of damage.

Santi smiled and looked up at Coral. "Every time I use them, I will think of Amed."

She hugged Coral, and the two women sat quietly in shared grief. Knowing that Coral was headed to the Tipua in a few days, Santi struggled to contain her emotions the entire morning. With all of the terrible things that had been happening and their futures so uncertain, Santi didn't know when she would next see her. Holding on to Coral was like holding on to Amed.

Just then, Amphitrite swam up to Santi and nudged her in the small of her back. The turtle knew a journey was ahead, and she was anxious to get it underway. The animal loved swimming freely in the open water, and since they would be riding cryptids, Amphitrite would have a challenge on her hands to keep up, a challenge which Santi was sure the giant turtle was looking forward to.

They said their goodbyes to Coral and their friends around the kinship, stopping last to say goodbye to Wayne, who nodded his cowboy hat and hugged them goodbye. Finally, they set out for their awaiting cryptids. Santi was all tears.

"It just feels like everything is all over," Santi said, tears blurring her vision through the bright, pale water. "Nothing is the same as it was."

Rogan stopped and looked at her intently, taking her chin in his hand. "It would be a shame for things to always stay the same. Look at all the wonderful things that have happened, and think about what we have yet to come." Santi felt the heaviness in his Ku from the loss of his father. Rogan would always carry that loss with him, and she felt very selfish.

"You're right." She smiled. "We do have a lot to look forward to." They kissed passionately and let the tension and sadness dissolve around them. They used the kiss to bolster their spirits and give each other strength. When they broke apart, they were both able to smile.

"Shall we?" Rogan asked, and Santi nodded.

A few hours later, when they arrived at the border of the Nhori, Santi let out a squeal as she connected to her animal. "Nessy!" She bounded towards the animal and pet its neck vigorously. "Oh Rogan! You brought Nessy back."

He laughed at the name she had given the beast. "Well, I knew how fond you were of her." He helped her into her saddle and they both issued silent commands in their Kus for the animals to take them to the golden city. Santi was no less awestruck than she had been on their first trip. She stroked the neck of her Cryptid and marveled at its soft skin that was hard and flexible, yet rough and bumpy. It was greyish in color without being dull, much like its personality, Santi thought. Her Nessy seemed calm and docile yet there was a spirit within the animal that was full of life and adventure. Santi hoped this wasn't the last time she would get to ride her friend.

The creature swam at such a swift pace that were they to run into anything she would surely be dead on impact. It was impossible for her to do anything but hold on and stay tucked into the safe bubble created behind its neck. Luckily Nessy required no steering and maneuvered herself through the water with ease. At one point during the trip down to

# Surface Tension

Florida Santi had stuck her arm out to the side like she had many times in a speeding car to play "airplane" but it was too much for her and her arm was thrown behind her with such force that she had spent the first week of school nursing an injured shoulder. Santi knew better on this trip and opted just to enjoy the ride this time.

As their Cryptids swam further away from the Nhori and closer to their destination Santiago's heart lightened. She was excited for the next step in her journey with Rogan. She reached out her Ku and sent him her interpretation of an emotional hug; like a little burst of joy filled with tenderness.

It was hard to believe that just this morning she was full of sorrow about what was lost to her and what could never be again; now she was teeming with hope and excitement for what was to come. Santi would never forget Amed's love and influence on her. She was about to go to Daris for the first time—to receive real Sentinel training where she alone was the one who could defeat Zitja—it seemed the perfect way to honor his memory.

With all that was in store for her, she remembered something that Coral had told her during one of her lessons, something that Nephira had touted to her subjects so long ago. Santi smiled outwardly and looked forward to what was next on her journey as she thought of Nephira's wisdom, "We cannot live in regret."

*S.R. Atkinson*

# Acknowledgements

*A self-published book is anything but published by oneself. I have so many people to thank that it would be selfish-publishing of me to end this book without doing so.*

Top billing needs to go to my husband this time. I spent months at a time doing nothing but writing and grumbling. He was a champ through it all and picked up my slack. I am forever thankful to Dan for his patience and support. I'm happy to be on his team in life.

Next, my beta readers and their endless tolerance of my neurosis and perfectionism, they are the true heroes here: Celestie has been with me from the beginning and is only getting harder and harder on me. Kristine has a profound desire to make the characters real and loveable. Jessica makes sure I don't forget there should be lots of love and plenty of scenes with a turtle in them. Corrie is on a quest to eradicate anything cheesy or unrealistic. Erin has valuable ideas for building a rich underwater world. Marissa apologizes every time she doesn't like something but has great feedback for improvement. And Kristie, with her meticulous librarian ways, makes me see how terribly I'm explaining scenes.

As always, Tyler for his endless readings of each draft of every book I write. His scrupulous notes and whole-picture vision has transformed my small idea into an entire anthology. I am forever in his debt for his attention to the details of my mermaid world.

## S.R. Atkinson

Cassandra and Becky put the finishing touches on all my books to make then polished and presentable to the world. I could not call this story a book without them!

And lastly, endless thanks go to my family, friends, and the fans of Breathing Water. The outpouring of support and love through it all has been phenomenal and rendered me speechless on many occasions. My success is because of you.

I get to take pride in saying, "I wrote a book." But for all of these wonderful people, I hope they take pride in the role they played. For without them, this book is nothing.

*Surface Tension*

# About the Author

Born and raised in Utah, Savannah moved to New York in 2010 to pursue her dream of writing. *Surface Tension* is Savannah's second novel and book two in the *Siren Anthology*.

When not writing Savannah is often thinking about imaginary places, playing roller derby as Fancy Nasty, and eating more Cheetos than she should. Savannah lives in Hoboken, NJ with her endlessly patient husband, Dan, and their fat cat Poe.

_S.R. Atkinson_